I0760518

FREED BY HER DRAGONS

FATED MATE OF THE DRAGON CLANS, BOOK TWO

by

GINNA MORAN

ISBN 978-1-951314-56-9 (soft cover)
ISBN 978-1-951314-57-6 (hard cover)

Cover design by Silver Starlight Designs
Cover images copyright Depositphotos

For Inquiries Contact:
Sunny Palms Press
9663 Santa Monica Blvd Suite 1158
Beverly Hills, CA 90210, USA
www.sunnypalmspress.com
www.GinnaMoran.com

To my favorite heathen Heather Cortes,
You, my lovely, are a true firecracker, and I love having you in my life. XOXO!

Dead End

"YOU CAN'T JUST WALK AROUND here naked. It's against the Mortal World law." I stand in front of Kash with my hands on my hips. Flicking my gaze down his body, I drink in his chiseled body, following the line of his abs all the way down to the only soft thing—scratch that—damn.

I shrug out of my sweater and toss it at him. Kash remains stiff, crossing his arms over his chest, smirking instead of stone-faced like I try so desperately to be. My sweater hits his torso and falls down, catching on his raging erection like it's a coat rack. I knew I shouldn't have shown his body any attention, but it's still so incredibly difficult not to.

"And what is the Mortal Law going to do to me?" he asks, his smirk stretching into a cocky-bastard grin.

"Nothing, but the next trip we take, you better carry a bag of clothes if you plan to fly."

"And if I don't, kitten?" Kash flexes his hard body, bouncing my sweater to make it look as if it hovers in front of him like a magic trick.

"Then you're going to squeeze into what I bring, and I swear it'll be from my closet," I threaten, pressing my lips into a thin line. I can't smile, despite the image of him wearing one of my thongs flitting through my head. If I do, he'll test me from now on, and I'm not sure I can focus seeing his ass shake in some of my lace.

Chuckling, he finally breaks my gaze and wraps my sweater around his waist, the sleeves barely long enough to tie. I sigh and step forward, turning it around to cover up his junk. It doesn't exactly do much, but I can't back down. He might not consider the Mortal World a threat, but I don't want any trouble.

A shadow towers over me from behind, shading me

from the sun. "Be thankful it was only Kash, cookie. I couldn't give a fuck if anyone was brave enough to approach us." Maddox rests his warm hands on my shoulders. "Especially with the way you look at my brother now. If I were him, I'd have you bent over that bench."

I tip my head back and bonk him on the chest. "No need to give Granny Tucker in the house over there a show. She'll ask to spank you, and I'm not okay with that."

Rowan's laugh sounds through the air, and he smacks Maddox's ass hard enough to make him jump as he passes him. Hooking his hands under my arms, Maddox swings me toward Rowan, trying to knock him off his feet.

Lucky for Rowan, I will not be used as a weapon against him and stretch my arms back to clamp onto Maddox. Throwing my weight up, I flip fast enough to miss Rowan and squeeze Maddox's neck between my thighs. The move throws him off, and he lets go of me. I didn't expect to lock his head too close to my vagina either, but I clench him harder to keep from falling.

"Shit, grab her," Rowan says to Kash, circling to bear hug Maddox from behind. "We don't have time for him to get carried away, and it doesn't look like our mate plans to let the bastard go."

"Carried away? This asshole might poke my eye out," I say, my head hovering close to Maddox's bulging pants.

Kash locks his hands to my waist and tugs me from Maddox. "Got you, kitten." He twists me in his arms and smiles, holding me by my ass as I wrap my legs around him.

Maddox growls from behind us. "You think I'm the one who might get carried away? His naked-ass—"

Rowan smacks him on the back of the head, cutting off his argument. The two of them look ready to start throwing fire at each other in a fight for dominance, and I'm pretty damn sure I saw the familiar floral curtains flutter on Granny Tucker's front window.

Wiggling in Kash's arms, I wait for him to put me down and march the six feet it takes to get to Maddox now holding Rowan in a headlock. Positioning my legs, I try to look for an opening to get between them.

Kash meanders up beside me and drapes an arm over my shoulders. "You're going to need your dragon fire to break them apart." He points at Maddox's back. "Hit him right there, and it'll wind him."

"And burn his shirt," I mutter. "You're distracting enough."

Gently pinching my chin, he turns my head, so I meet his hazel eyes, sparkling with flecks of green and gold in the sun. "If you're not going to do it, then we might as well take a stroll down your memory lane and knock on McKayla's door."

If only the idea didn't make me as nervous as it does. Five years is a long time, and I don't think she tried ever looking for me. For someone who took the time to raise me—while strict and always reminding me of my mother's poor choices that put me in her care—she still managed to see that I got the best she could offer. And who knows. Maybe she wasn't as bitchy as I remember. I wasn't exactly easy. Hell, I didn't even tell her my plan. But now that I think about it, maybe that was how it was always supposed to be. If she had tried to stop me—I shake my head. There's no point in thinking about the what-ifs.

"What's it going to be? Summon your dragon fire and put my brothers in check before that nosy elderly mortal calls the human authority or race me to the door of McKayla's for the most awkward introduction of all time." Kash nuzzles his nose to mine. "Just think about it."

I groan. "These options are shitty. Can't you break them up and we sic Maddox on her? He's the expert in interrogation."

"Come on, kitten. You don't want to say, 'Hey, Auntie, I'm home, and I brought the mates you failed to tell me about. Oh, and your brother got me locked up at the Maximum Magical Penitentiary for life. Thanks for the warning?' I think it will go over just fine." Kash gathers my hand between his and caresses my palm. "Who knows? You might get emotional enough to summon a bit of dragon fire to intimidate her."

Kash rubs his palm to mine, igniting a flame between our fingers. The tingling sensation warms my skin, and I close my eyes, savoring his dragon's offering to mine. If only a huge fucking part of me wasn't chicken shit. The only luck I have is bad, and I'd probably set the whole neighborhood ablaze and set off the Magaelorum High Council's criminal detector spells or whatever shit they use to stop people from interfering or causing trouble in a world they don't want us to belong in.

"Just take a breath and command it to do as you want. Let your instincts take over. Your body will know what to do if you let it try." Kash grows the fire between our palms. "Now look at Maddox's back. Imagine the flame eating his shirt."

I groan. "Having you naked is bad enough."

"If he's naked, you can always tell him he has to stand guard with me," he teases. "Rowan will be less likely to piss off a witch."

Damn it. He's right. As much as I want Maddox to bang down my aunt's door and demand she tell us what the fuck is going on and threaten her into helping us—that's probably not the best approach.

I inhale a deep breath, curling my fingers around

Kash's flame, the tingling sensation giving me the feeling that the dragon fire is solid even though it dances and moves. Maddox shoves into Rowan, sweeping his foot out and knocking him down. He grabs his arms, trying to pin him, and I take advantage of the opening.

Glaring at the middle of his back, I imagine the fabric smoldering and revealing his taut, broad muscles. It's enough to get my dragon to take over, encouraging me to chuck it.

Bright flames spark across Maddox's back, surprising the hell out of him. He heaves a breath and crashes on top of Rowan. Kash pumps his fist and shakes me, a gorgeous smile crossing his face.

"Fuck yeah! Take that, assholes!" Kash says, blasting another ball of fire at Maddox, stopping him from retaliating. "Get your shit together. We have to move. You know we can't stay long."

Maddox growls and smashes his hands into the ground and catapults to his feet. "You better fucking run. If I catch you—"

Spinning, Kash bolts away, his tight ass on full display as he heads toward the end of the cul-de-sac where my aunt lives.

Fire explodes at my feet, startling me. "I meant you, cookie. You're in so much trouble."

I screech and charge after Kash, abandoning Maddox and Rowan on the sidewalk. Heat warms my back, and the scent of singed fabric permeates the air. Loud thuds of running footsteps kick my ass into gear, and I push myself to run as fast as I can.

"Get ready, cookie," Maddox says, his voice even like he's not even working up a sweat. "You're going to wish you tried harder in our training sessions."

Hands lock around my hair and yank me back. I smack into Maddox's firm chest. He restrains me from behind and lifts me off my feet. I expect him to throw me onto my back to dominate me, but the asshole shifts one of his hands and rubs his fingers across my ribs.

"Fuck! Stop!" I yell, thrashing like crazy. "Seriously. That tickles!"

"Make me," he mutters, continuing to stroll with me.

"Someone's going to call the cops!" My voice screeches through the air.

"I don't give a fuck. Make me stop." Moving his other hand, he kneads his fingers into my other side.

I scream and buck, his tickling worse than any other damn punishment. "Please! Fuck!"

"Make me," he repeats. "Make me, or I won't stop until you piss yourself."

I screech again, trying to break free. Tears cloud my

eyes, my body laughing and squirming despite this being utter torture. I hate being tickled, and I have the sudden urge to punch him in the balls.

"Come on, cookie. You don't want to show up at McKayla's covered in pis—" Maddox snaps his mouth shut and freezes. His fingers stop digging into me as he slows. Jerking my head back, I bang it into his chin, wincing through pain that doesn't even bother him.

Then he sets me on my feet.

"Are you fucking kidding?" Rowan asks, lacing his fingers behind his head.

My jaw slackens, my body chilling. I knew it was possible that Aunt McKayla could've moved away or something, but this?

"It was arson," a raspy, feminine voice says from behind us. "Happened a couple weeks ago. The couple living here had a fight and..."

I spin on my heels and meet Granny Tucker's milky gaze. The last five years didn't treat her well, her deeply wrinkled face covered in age spots. She hunches forward, resting her weight on a cane.

"And what?" Maddox asks, intruding on Granny Tucker's personal space, but she doesn't move or even notice.

The woman waves her hands. "Boom."

I hug my arms around me, my hope breaking and turning to ash to crumble among the debris of my childhood home.

"But don't worry, sweetie. None of us were ever meant to stay. The fates will get you where you need to go." Granny Tucker's eyes flicker with sparks of turquoise magic.

Ah, hell.

"Damn it," Kash says, scrubbing his face with his hands. Stomping forward, he gets into Granny Tucker's face. "McKayla, where the hell are you?" he shouts at the old woman. "Tell us!"

Granny Tucker blinks, widening her eyes. She screams.

Yelling in frustration, Kash grabs my hand and roars, blowing fire from his mouth at the already scorched rubble. He tosses me onto his back, not giving me a chance to brace as his dragon explodes from him, sending me clinging onto his scaly neck. Maddox and Rowan manage to keep up, jumping up with me, sandwiching me between them. Dozens of emotions crash through me in wave after wave. The intensity nearly knocks me out, and I squeeze my eyes shut and push everything away.

If only doing so didn't leave me empty.

Or hopeless.

Because without Aunt McKayla...shit.

What the hell do we do now?

Lycan Show

"YOU'RE LATE, RED," QUILLON SAYS, leaning against the doorframe to his house. "Now, I gotta be the damn bad guy again. I hate when you make me do shit like this. If you'd just obey the rules, I wouldn't be forced into making Kash stay that way."

Maddox and Rowan tense beside me, and guttural noises escape their throats. I don't even have a chance to process Quillon's demands as they charge him, gathering fire and preparing to attack.

Rose pops into view and holds her hands up, palms out. "Might I remind you of the consequences of trying to hurt Quillon? Whatever happens to him, hits Kash twice as hard."

Maddox towers over Rose, glowering over her head and at Quillon. "Now is not the fucking time for this bullshit, douchebag."

"Let me guess. Didn't find Auntie Witch?" A smirk crosses Quillon's face, his eyes reflecting green as his lycan form peeks through. "What a shame. Looks like I'm going to have to comfort my girl."

I stride to close the space and grab both Maddox and Rowan's arms. "This is pointless. You know the dickhead won't budge, and I'm just tired." Turning to glance at Kash, his looming dragon form watching us from a few dozen feet away. "Please free Kash, Quillon. That's the only way I'll ever feel better after today."

His jaw twitches in consideration. "No."

My brows pinch together in confusion. "What?"

He moves out of the doorway. "I said no. I think you underestimate me, Red, and I'm going to prove I can make your day better. Now go wait for me. Change into something nicer. You smell like smoke."

Anger bubbles through me, and I stomp past him and

into the house. Maddox and Rowan argue on the porch, and Quillon slams the door in their faces, acting like the coward he is. He even rushes behind me like he knows if he doesn't hurry, one of them will fling the door open and smolder his back.

"Hustle, Red," Quillon snaps, pushing my back.

I stiffen under his touch but don't say anything as he herds me into his room at the end of the hallway on the left. Rose laughs dancing behind us, finding way too much amusement in every situation that unfolds between us, and I roll my eyes at her as Quillon shuts the door and locks her out.

"You're no fun, Quillon," she says, scratching her finger to the door. "I don't understand why we can't all just share. Nova is so much fun."

"Find your own damn plaything," he snaps, turning away from the door. "She's mine."

I glare at him and back up to the corner of the room. Dirty clothes hang over a lumpy recliner, and I scoop them up and toss them in the hamper a few feet away. If I throw them on the floor, Quillon will just demand I pick them up. Touching them once is already too many times for me.

I plop down and cross my legs, never taking my gaze off him. I won't initiate conversation. I won't be more than I have to be to fulfill our agreement. One of these days, he'll give up. I'm too fucking stubborn to ever bow to him. It's bad enough Kash had to on my behalf.

"Shower and change into the outfit I hung on the back of the door," Quillon says, motioning toward the bathroom. "I'm bored out of my mind, horny as hell, and I got the pole in today. I want to watch you dance and break it in."

He has to be fucking kidding.

Hooking his fingers to the hem of his shirt, he tugs it over his head and rubs his hands across his hairy chest and down his stomach. He's trying to get under my skin, but I refuse to let him. His silent dare enrages me. I dig my fingernails into my palms, refusing to give him any sort of satisfaction of making me uncomfortable.

"Screw off, Quillon. You're the last man in the Mortal World I'd ever perform for." I lean back in the chair, continuing to glower.

The bastard unbuckles his belt, unzips his jeans, and tugs them down, revealing he goes commando. I thought now that he's out of the Maximum Magical Penitentiary and free from their restrictions, he might man-scape, but he hasn't. And fuck is he as hairy as a human as he is in his lycan form. The only thing different is his little dick tip peeking from his scraggly bush.

He shakes his hips, attempting to swing his flaccid cock, but it looks nothing like the helicopter move Rowan has done to make me laugh.

"Are you expecting me to fall on my knees or something? If you're going to try to hypnotize me, you should probably trim your pubes, so I can see your mini-pendulum swing." I smirk at my words, holding back my laughter.

He growls and strokes his hand along his shaft, trying to make it grow. "Fuck you. Go be a good girl and take the damn shower. If you don't, I'll keep Kash in his dragon form permanently."

My steely expression breaks. "You're sick, Quillon."

"What will it be, Red?" Quillon steps closer, and I finally avert my eyes to the floor, knots twisting through my body. "Put on that sexy little number waiting for you in the bathroom, with your hair up, maybe some lipstick...or your mate spends the rest of his life as a dragon."

I shudder and don't respond.

"All right, fine." Quillon turns toward the window and pulls the curtain. "You hear that, Kashy? Your mate's a real bitch. Selfish. You give up your freedom for her, and she won't even do a little dance to keep you as a man."

I flick my gaze to the window, angry tears bursting from my eyes. Kash bows to watch us through the window in his dragon form, his hazel eyes flickering with fire. Smoke pours from his nostrils, and he bares his teeth.

His fury plows into me, forcing the air from my lungs.

"Don't even consider it, kitten," Kash thinks to me, his mind open and heavy with his emotions. "I would rather remain in this form forever than ever have you do something like that for his ass."

I furiously blink my eyes, considering his words. I hate that as much as I want to agree with Kash, Quillon is right. It's one performance to free my mate for at least another day. I couldn't stand it knowing I could do this and chose not to.

"It's just dancing," I respond, chanting the words in my mind, saying them more for myself than for Kash.

"Nova, I'm serious." Kash growls again, the vibration quivering across the window pane.

"I am too," I say, opening my thoughts completely like he taught me. I want more than just him to hear my words. I want him to feel them deep in his being like he does our mate bond. "I know you want to protect me. I know you can feel how sick this makes me feel, and you think you're the reason for it, but you're not. Life has been fucking unfair and brutal, and I refuse to sit around and watch it be as ruthless to you. I don't give a fuck if this makes me uncomfortable. The idea of losing the ability to be held by you in your arms, one of my favorite places in the whole shitty universe, is far, far worse."

I get to my feet and force my gaze away from Kash to

where Quillon flops on his bed, watching me with his vile expression.

He can't hear my telepathic conversation with Kash—one I'm so thankful and still a bit surprised over every time one of my mate's voices sneaks into my mind—but Quillon knows what's going on. It's like he gets off on tormenting us. He really is a true criminal and undeserving of the freedom he gained with us.

"That's a good girl," Quillon quips, adjusting his pillows against his headboard. I nearly gag when he reaches into his nightstand for a bottle of lube.

"You're a sick fuck, you know." I swipe the stereo remote off the dresser and chuck it at him, missing his head by an inch. "Now, pick something good. I can't dance to most of the shit you like."

I stride to the bathroom and slam the door shut. Covering my face with my hands, I take a few deep breaths, calming my nerves. Fuck. What is wrong with me? This should be an easy decision. I should be able to slap on my show smile and act my way through the night. I've performed in front of an audience in skimpy outfits for years. I've been catcalled, objectified, and groped after shows with Galaxy Gold and the Sky Dancers. I've had money thrown in my face and fuckheads thinking that I'd be willing to give private shows because I survived and lived on other's generosity.

But this? Ugh. The time my mate needs me to suck it up and give in to a bastard in exchange for normalcy—I hesitate. I question everything. If I give him this sort of power over me now, what will he want next? A blow job? Then to fuck?

Swinging my arm, I punch the wall, sending pain radiating through my fist. My knuckles ache, my fingers turning red.

Music kicks on in Quillon's room, and I close my eyes, listening to the slow, seductive tune of something I've never heard before. Spinning around, I sway my body, losing myself to the song of my disparity, my anguish. The song I plan to murder Quillon to the second we manage to free him from the lycan curse, and in doing so, fulfilling Kash's debt.

I pull myself together and twirl toward the sink, using the counter to stretch and loosen my tense muscles. Instead of showering—because fuck that bullshit—I'm not preparing myself for him, I splash water on my face, tie my hair up into a high ponytail, and swipe a layer of messy lipstick across my mouth.

I force myself to smile in the small, rectangular mirror, stained with flecks of dried toothpaste from Quillon's purposefully slobby behavior.

"You are not dancing for Quillon," I say to myself. "You are dancing for your mate."

Spinning on the balls of my feet, I gawk at the skimpy lingerie and platform stilettos. The sheer fabric will leave nothing to the imagination, and it'll be as if I dance naked. Annoyance rushes through me, and I strip into my panties and bra and say fuck it, pulling the red lace and stringy combo over what I'm already wearing. If he says something, he'll get this damn heel to the face.

I strut to the door and fling it open. Ice trickles through my veins, stealing the warmth from my body. Quillon doesn't even react to my double layers like I expect, his eyes roving over me like he can undress me with his gaze. I stand frozen, clutching the doorframe. My body refuses to move. I've never had stage fright before, and it feels like if I try to take even a step, I'll die.

"Come on, Red," Quillon calls, snapping my attention from my thoughts. "Standing there like a whore after a walk of shame is killing my boner."

This fucker.

Kash's growl shakes the windowpane again, and I whip my attention to the open curtain. My chest tightens at his fiery intensity, his dragon form angry and smoldering with his need to burn the house down.

I nearly lose my nerve.

I almost lose my shit and start sobbing.

But one more look at Kash steels me against Quillon's attempt to control me like I'm his little plaything.

Forcing my mouth to smile, I put on my performance expression, choosing to dance with only Kash on my mind. The music shatters my nerves, reminding me that I'm a strong, fierce woman who survived in the Maximum Magical Penitentiary. I've experienced far worse than this, and if anything, this will only empower me to put Quillon in his damn place.

I sway my body, turning my gaze to Quillon, aroused and unashamedly jerking off on his bed. He's made a huge fucking mistake to think he could ever make me feel out-of-control and vulnerable, especially when he is the one truly exposed.

I mean, accidents happen, right?

He's going to regret his decisions to egg on my wild beast. My dragon is ready to roar.

Strolling forward, I gauge the amount of space I have, the room barely big enough to perform any floor routines. The height of the ceiling limits me as well, and I decide to stick to a few holds that will stretch my body and enable me to do the one thing I want: Surprise the cocky bastard.

Facing the metal pole, I lace my left hand around the cool metal and position my left foot at an angle before stretching my right leg up and over my head into the splits. I balance in place with my heel and grip the pole, stretching back.

Quillon releases a whistle. "Do it the other way. I want to see more."

I inhale a few breaths, trying to control my rage, and twirl around the pole. I'm not used to dancing in platforms, so I grab the pole in one hand and swing my back leg up in a standing split, and unbuckle my first shoe.

Quillon's eyes remain glued to my body, his hand picking up speed on his rub and tug monstrosity. I smirk, my mind whirling.

Curling my toes, I grip the unbuckled stiletto and sway my way to the floor. Quillon shifts up onto his knees for a better view. I take advantage of his position and closeness, climbing up the pole midway and smile. He returns my grin with lust-filled eyes like he believes I suddenly enjoy dancing for him.

So I kick out my leg, letting my heel fly off, smashing right into his face.

Roaring, Quillon loses control of his humanity, and his lycan beast bursts through his skin, sprouting long hair over his entire body. It happens so quickly, I miss the satisfaction of not only killing his teensy boner but making it disappear completely within the matted nest of gross wiry fur between his legs.

"You fucking bitch," Quillon howls, launching at me, his voice guttural and wet coming from his snout. His half-man, half-beast body tears at the comforter, shredding it with his talon-like claws.

Damn. I didn't think this through.

Swinging up, I curl myself around the top of the pole but can't get high enough out of his reach. Kash roars outside the house, screaming my name through my mind, warning me to watch out for his claws. The last thing I want is to get gouged by him. The pain I've gone through before...

I stiffen and drop down.

Quillon swipes out to grab me and misses, and I land on my knees. The feral smell of musk and something wilder blows over me. I don't move fast enough as Quillon snarls and pounces on me, trapping me to the floor with his hulking frame.

Leaning in, he snaps his teeth in my face, spraying me with his disgusting slobber. I cringe and twist my neck, trying to avoid getting it in my eyes.

"Get off of me," I command, fear and anger rolling through me. The house shudders with Kash's anxious stomping, unable to do anything against Quillon to save me.

"No. I'm fucking sick and tired of your bullshit. If you're going to be a bitch to me and treat me like I'm beneath you, then you're going to learn what it's like to be under me." Quillon snatches my wrists and pulls them over my head.

Heat bursts through my core, my whole body reacting to his threat. He doesn't have a cock at the moment, but I'll be damned if I'm going to lie here and find out what twisted plan swirls through his mind.

My arms glow as my dragon fire ignites in my veins, the sudden sensation feeling like I'm a balloon about to burst. Quillon snarls, his face morphing in shock. A screech bellows from his snout as the heat of my body singes some of his hair.

I break my hand free of his hold and sucker punch him in the throat and shove him off. Fire glows in my palm. I have my arm in warning, wishing I could get my body to release my power on command. I realize more than ever how frustrated and terrified I feel facing monsters out to get me.

"Stay away from me," I say, my voice deep with the rasp of my burning throat. "Don't ever touch me again."

"I guess you don't want to ever see Kash as a man again," Quillon snaps, glowering at me.

"Nova, please. Just get out of there. We'll figure something out." Kash roars again from outside the window, his desperate thoughts coursing through me. "This is torture, not being able to help you. Please."

I meet Kash's gaze, my eyes burning with unshed tears. "I don't care if he's a man or not," I say, unbuckling the other stiletto. "He's my mate, and I care for him regardless. So fuck off, douchebag. I'm done playing your games."

"You're going to regret it," Quillon warns.

I try to summon my dragon fire once more, but nothing happens. So I rush from the room, slamming the door. I won't stay with that asshole another moment. I'll sleep outside with Kash and in the safety of his shadow.

If only a hulking form didn't materialize in the door and block my way.

Maddox grabs me by the shoulders, stopping me in place. "Are you okay, cookie?" he asks, feeling like a brick wall against my palms. "Kash called me to come for you."

My bottom lip quivers, and I suck it between my teeth. "I'm fine. I was just going to see him."

Maddox slides his hand around to my lower back, holding me close, sensing that if he lets me go, I might run. "My brother doesn't think he can give you what you need in his current state. He asked that I be here for you instead."

I squeeze my eyes shut. I want to shove past Maddox and run to Kash anyway, but if he asked Maddox to be with me, he must need the moment more for himself.

"Rowan will be with him. Don't worry, kitten," Maddox adds, surprising me. "Now, come on. Let me feed you and give you what you need."

I shake my head. "The only thing I need right now is for you to teach me how to use my dragon fire. I want to be able to rely on myself. Kash was so worried about me—I couldn't stand it."

Maddox sharply nods his head. "Whatever you want."

"Really?" I ask, tilting my head. "This is a first."

He chuckles. "Well, I have to admit, I love the idea of wrestling with you and seeing you sweat. Punishing you when you fail to listen. Push your buttons..." Fire lights his eyes with the thoughts crossing his mind. "When do you want to start?"

I clench my fingers into fists, hearing the sound of the backdoor slamming as Quillon leaves. I meet Maddox's gaze. "Now."

Reward

"GET YOUR ASS MOVING, DELPHIA." Maddox's voice swirls through my mind. Even though it has been a couple weeks since learning he can do that outside of the Maximum Magical Penitentiary and their suppressant spells to contain its inmates, it still weirds me out a bit because he doesn't do it often. "You better pick up your pace. I'm not going to go easy on you for much longer."

Damn. If he's using my Drakovich name, I know he's

about to turn into a raging bastard if he believes I don't do as good as he thinks I should. I knew I couldn't expect him to stay tender and affectionate like he had been all night, working on different forms of meditation techniques to help me focus.

He'd never admit it, but the Mortal World freaks him out. And when Maddox is nervous, he acts like a tough asshole to cover it up. But I can feel his trepidation as if it's my own. This whole situation is probably only the frosting on his panic cake now that we have no idea what to do next. I don't even know where to begin to find my aunt, and her strange magical message through Granny Tucker? Utter bullshit.

"I hope you know you're making me hold back. I expected more fight from a hardened criminal. You tore a man in half yet you can't last for a round of cardio? It makes me question your mortal profession." Maddox shoots a burst of fire, hitting the ground at my feet.

"You're a lying asshole. This bond works two ways, remember? You're getting tired," I shout, swiping sweat from my eyes.

He growls in response, sending me a wave of determination to conceal his feelings.

Sometimes late at night, Maddox does let his guard down, and I can hear what's truly on his mind. It gives me a new appreciation of him, knowing his mental battles. He second guesses his ability to protect me and his brothers since he can't safely transform into his strongest form regularly like Kash can without any sort of magical shield to hide from humans and anyone from Magaelorum who might be after us. He's aiding a deadly fugitive after all.

"Focus on your damn self and move faster, cookie," Maddox calls, shouting from behind me. He does it to show he's closing the distance. "If I catch you, I will tackle you and have my way with you. I still have my restraints. Don't think I won't use them. You obviously need more motivation to control your dragon fire."

Damn. I both love and hate the sound of that. His brand of punishment shouldn't be so infuriatingly addictive. I shouldn't want to slow down just to discover what he plans to do to me with his restraints.

I crane my neck and peer behind me. Maddox's arms flex with his strides. Sweat glistens across his broad, bare chest, defining the ridges and peaks of his sexy, buff body. A wicked grin splits across his face and the cocky bastard winks.

I'm nearly certain he heard my thoughts wander to a place they shouldn't, but if he does, he doesn't comment. He either pretends he can't listen in on my thoughts whenever he pleases because I suck at keeping him and his brothers out, or he shuts me out of his head. Either way, only Rowan has ever admitted that they can hear me even when I'm not thinking directly to them. I can't decide which is better, though. Probably them pretending they can't.

"All right. You're making this too easy. I know you can move faster than this," Maddox says, closing the space even more. His long, muscular legs and tall frame give him an advantage over me. I hardly think this race is fair despite my head start.

"Well, if you'd stop making punishment sound so fun, I wouldn't want to lose to you, asshole," I call, huffing a breath, the exertion of speaking and running way harder than Maddox makes it seem.

"Unless I withhold something from you. I know how much you hate that." The soft thuds of Maddox's bare feet quickening in pace is enough to push me to get my act together. The fucker just had to go there. I wouldn't put it past him to work me up and leave me restrained to a bed while he sat and watched me squirmed.

"Sounds like someone might need a taste of their own assholeness," I mutter, gasping another breath.

"I'd love to see you try." He tosses another burst of fire at my feet, trying to either knock me down or haul ass. Which one? Who fucking knows.

A cramp clenches my side, trying to slow me down. It

takes everything in me to keep moving. We've been working out for hours in a constant game of chase, combat, and practicing control over my dragon fire. All I want to do now is prove to Maddox that everything he's been teaching me sticks.

At this point, I don't actually want to lose against Maddox and hear him gloat that I lost because I want his punishment. I would much prefer to beat his ass, so I can rub it in his face that I defeated a highly trained beast man. He outmatches me in skill and strength. It pisses me off that stamina is supposed to be my strong suit, yet he constantly looms right behind me. Damn him and his long legs.

"Brace yourself, cookie. I'm coming for you and your lazy, unmotivated self. You're about to find out what this grass feels like on your naked ass when I pin you down and claim you as my reward." Maddox's shadow appears next to me as he catches up. Fuck. "Or maybe we can find out if it's possible to get grass stains on those perky tits of yours. How does that sound?"

"Like fucking fun," I say, forcing my legs to haul ass faster to get ahead of him. "But it'll be your damn ass on the grass. You're mine."

Maddox races up beside me and grins, the strands of his long hair framing his face damp with sweat. He peeks at me in his peripheral vision as he swings out and slaps me on my ass hard enough that I might have his handprint of my butt cheek for days. "Go, cookie. Move. Don't slow down. I'll let you try a little longer."

Except I'm exhausted. I used to think training with Galaxy Gold and the Sky Dancers was difficult. It's nothing compared to the hardass former CO and leader of a dragon clan. And I know this is Maddox going easy on me. I've seen him in action. Hell, he and his brothers rough each other up for fun. These fireballs to my feet and stinging swats to my ass are his gentle side.

"You suck," I mutter.

"Just wait to find out exactly how hard," he responds, coming up next to me only to flick his tongue and waggle his brows.

There is no way I'm going to win unless he lets me.

Or I play dirty.

Grabbing the hem of my shirt, I yank it off and throw it in his face. The sudden distraction is enough to give me the split second I need to ram into his side. Maddox growls and tries snatching my leg as he stumbles to take me down with him, but I leap into the air, kicking my legs into the splits for a graceful landing. I don't stop to find out if Maddox recovers and rush toward the magnolia tree, blooming with giant white flowers.

My chest burns from exertion, and the edges of my vision darken, but I'll be damned if Maddox is going to beat me this time. It's going to feel so good putting this cocky bastard in his place. I'll show him that he might have skills and strengths, but I have my own talents. He'll see. He's going the fuck down.

"You haven't won yet, Delphia." His voice sneaks into my mind, giving away the fact that he could hear my thoughts. "You better figure out how to take me down, and soon. The bad guys never wait for you to be ready."

"Neither do you," I snap, thinking my response to save my breath.

And damn it.

Annoyance rushes through me. I bolt ahead, refusing to lose now. Maddox's thumping footsteps push me forward. I dash the remaining distance as fast as I can until I'm within jumping reach of a low branch. Vaulting from the ground, I launch into the air and hook my hands to the tree, swinging my body up. The branch shakes at my weight, but I manage to keep my balance long enough to see Maddox only feet away. I rock my body, kicking my legs, and throw myself toward a close branch and flip around, treating the tree like a prop to one of my many performances over the years with Galaxy Gold. I drop right on Maddox's shoulders and squeeze his head between my thighs, using my upper body strength to knock him back.

Latching his fingers to my hips, he forces me to fall with him. My knees hit the grass and I bow forward, pressing my palms to the ground. Maddox releases a deep, sexy-as-hell rumble from his throat, his voice vibrating against the apex of my thighs. Now this is one way to take the bastard down.

I straighten my back and sit back on his hard pecs. "Might as well reward me while you're there," I tease, squeezing my legs together to lock him in place. "How does it feel to submit to little me? Bested by an untrained, tired, *unmotivated* pain in your balls." I smile with my words, repeating some of what he's said before.

Maddox digs his fingers into my hips, arching his neck a bit to bury his face right where it counts. I screech and wiggle, trying to escape, but he hums loud enough to vibrate his voice across my body.

"Hold still, cookie. I'm going to melt your clothes off for your reward. I knew you had it in you." Maddox breathes a breath of smoke, his eyes lighting with dragon fire.

I laugh and throw myself sideways, breaking free of his grip. He might be teasing me about the reward, but I wouldn't put it past him to burn my panties right off of me anyway. He takes things literally and seriously, especially now that I've accepted that we're mates, even when he pisses me off.

"Don't you fucking dare, Maddox. This isn't Max. You can't just have me when and where you please. Someone could see us. Humans hike around here. We have neighbors." I try to crawl away from him, but he catapults to his feet and lunges for me. Hooking his arm under my waist, he lifts me up, dangling me under his arm until we're out from under the tree, and he can throw me up onto his broad shoulders.

"I think you underestimate my ability to care about any of that. You beat me, my sneaky, lucky champion, so I need to reward you. It's my duty." Here he goes. He's obviously serious, but at least he strides toward the house instead of arguing outside. "How else will you find the motivation to learn to take care of yourself? I know you prefer to just hide behind me and let me handle things, but—"

"I don't like to hide." I grab onto the porch cover and haul myself off his shoulders. Swinging back, I drop to the ground and land with perfect accuracy on my feet. "That's your ego talking."

He spins around, crossing his arms. "Are you telling me if someone from the High Council shows up, magic blazing, that you wouldn't run and take cover, expecting me to protect you?"

This fucker.

I glare daggers and place my hands on my hips. He's right and we both know it. I hate admitting it, but he knows how to summon his dragon fire effortlessly. I don't even know what button to push on my body to ignite it, and I'm too chicken to transform because of the magical collar Lazlo Infinity, the asshole responsible for getting me sentenced to life in prison, hooked on my neck.

The protective magic shields in place around the house aren't intended for huge bursts of magic like it takes to shift into a dragon. Kash can do so without much interference because he's bound to Quillon, and Quillon is tied to the damn house.

Maddox's face lights up with an irresistible smile. Fuck, I love when he does. Ruffling his fingers through his hair, he pushes the long tresses back. "I love being right, cookie."

"You also love being an asshole," I mutter, shifting on my feet, looking for an opening to dodge past him. "And because of that, I think I'll find one of your brothers for that reward. They don't get off on pushing my buttons."

"Maybe I'm just trying to light you up. Get your fire to spark like you asked me to." He chuckles at his comment, and I realize he's teasing me because he heard my damn thought about not knowing how to summon my dragon fire on cue. "Show you that you need a bit of a challenge to hone your skills."

"Or maybe I just need you to give me a damn instruction manual." Bolting forward, I slide between the small space between his body and the open door.

He misses grabbing me by an inch, and I squeal and run, putting space between us. Now that we're inside, I know he's going to go full-on beast-mate mode, and teasing him is so damn fun that I can never resist. If he wants to challenge me, he better be ready to accept a challenge of my own. I'm not going to just give him what he wants. He has a huge alpha-complex and loves getting his way. I'm determined to show him I will get my way too. Even if he is considered a leader of the Drekis, I'll climb his hot ass to be at his level if I have to.

Maddox play-growls from behind me, unable to resist another game of chase. His bare feet slap the tile floor, and I screech again, catching sight of him in the wall mirror at the end of the hallway. I can't get over how fucking fast he can be when he really wants me, and I brace for him to snatch me off my feet, drag me toward his room, and fuck me like the wild animal he keeps caged within him.

"Need some help, Doc Eyes?" Rowan peeks his head out from the first door on the right and stretches his hand out to me.

I leap to close the last few feet as fast as I can and let Rowan pull me into his arms. Clinging to him like a sloth, I tip my head back and laugh, watching Maddox materialize in the doorway from upside down. Fire lights his golden eyes, and he squares his shoulders and fists his hands, looking determined as fuck to steal me back from his brother.

"Take her to the bed and hold her still for me, will you? Our mate craves my reward but loves to tease me too much." Maddox licks his lips and kicks the door closed behind him.

My. Damn. Vagina.

The needy bitch wants me to give up on being a pain in Maddox's balls.

Hell, she even wants Rowan to join in.

"Don't you dare, Rowan," I say, locking my legs tighter around him. "He thinks I'll only learn to protect myself if he makes me cum. I need to prove his smug-ass wrong. I already am learning to protect myself. My reward should be him admitting as much."

Rowan spins out of Maddox's reach and throws a burst of his dragon fire in his direction, smoldering the fabric over his knee. I kind of wish he had aimed higher, because their fire doesn't hurt each other, and I'd like a window to Maddox's junk while he tells me I can take care of myself. It'll be like the cherry on top.

Rowan chuckles and aims again. Maddox twists on his feet, getting blasted right on the butt. He stumbles forward and catches himself on the wall. Smoke wafts from his athletic shorts before fading to show off his tight ass. He shakes it, taunting us.

I practically cackle, my voice erupting through the room. "Get him on his knees next."

"What do you think I'm trying to do, Delphia? Now take her to the bed brother." Maddox swings his arm out, throwing an orb of fire in our direction.

Rowan catches it and snuffs it out in his fingers. "I'll do so, but not for you. She hates when you use her given name. Maybe next time you'll think better of it. Now, I'll be rewarding her. But you can watch."

Oh. My. Fucking. Clitoris.

I screech as Rowan throws me on the bed, my body already zinging in anticipation. I've never met men so determined to satisfy my every need while yearning to just taste and play and enjoy my body while I savor theirs. And they're mine. I'm theirs.

Maddox crashes into Rowan, sending him off his feet. I scramble up and stand on the bed to peer at the two of them rolling on the floor. Clapping my hands, I laugh and jump, loving every second of their wrestling over me. I've never felt so wanted in my entire life. I can almost forget our shitty circumstances. I can almost pretend that we live and breathe and exist for each other. I had no idea how much I wanted it until the world finally hit a pause and didn't feel as if my life was doomed. But then, I'm constantly on edge, waiting for the universe to slam her finger on the play button and sit back, watching in satisfaction as my world explodes.

Because I'm paying for my mother's crimes.

For a fuckhead warlock's power trip.

"Nova..." Rowan's soft voice trickles into my mind, and I realize both he and Maddox have stopped wrestling and now sit on the floor, looking up at me. "We're going to fix everything. Our lives will be like this without all the bullshit."

"The High Council will reward us for our good deed. They'll void our work contract and overturn your convictions. We will be able to return to Magaelorum to our home in Star Fall Canyon." Maddox pushes to his feet and holds out his hand to Rowan to help him up. The two of them join me on the bed, where Maddox tugs me to sit between them. "We'll breed and bear powerful offspring. We'll—"

Snatching a pillow, I whack him in the head with it, cutting off his words. "We'll be requesting a damn post as gatekeepers to live in the Mortal World. I'll buy a chastity belt and lock you all out during my heat, and we'll get a dog." Because children? Moving to another realm, where they've falsely convicted me of a crime and never even gave me a chance? Fuck that.

Maddox mutters under his breath. "I don't like the sound of that."

"It doesn't have to be a dog. I like cats too," I tease, bumping my shoulder into his.

"What the fuck is a chastity belt, anyway?" Rowan asks, tilting his head. "If it is what I think it is, it sounds like torture."

I smirk. "I might give Kash the key. You two on the other hand...are way too excited. He understands I will not be having children with you after five minutes."

"You have been ours your whole life, cookie." Maddox laces his fingers through mine, tugging my hand to his chest. His heart thuds in even beats, the melody slowing my heartrate down until it falls in sync with his. "The fates don't care about time. Just that we've bonded in body, mind, heart, and soul."

I narrow my eyes at him in suspicion. "Who are you and what have you done with my hot-headed, stubborn as hell Maddox?"

Rowan barks a laugh from next to me, slipping his hand around my stomach to lean me back. Bending down, he smiles as he kisses me, just grazing his soft lips to mine without getting carried away. "I told you she'd never buy it, Maddy-poo. Your ass is permanently on the dickhead list she keeps."

I smack Rowan's chest, laughing aghast. "You were feeding him lines to say to me?"

He smiles and nods, stretching to kiss me more, peppering me with light caresses of his lips. "It's a work in progress."

I crane my neck to peek at Maddox. Sticking out my tongue, I tease him and then say, "It's ridiculous."

"And it's never going to fucking happen again. You obviously don't want me to romance you. You get enough of that from my brothers as they treat you with gentle protectiveness. But I know you want more than that. You enjoy danger. Some pain to remind you of the pleasure I promise." Maddox snatches my legs and lifts my hips, not giving my brain a chance to catch up to what he plans to do. "You want me to treat you like the wild woman you are."

I laugh and throw my body up, landing on his lap. Pushing him back, I straddle Maddox on the edge of the bed and clutch his face between my palms. I show him exactly how wild I can be, locking my lips to his, slipping my tongue into his mouth to taste the spicy cinnamon flavor of his kiss. His fingers dig into my sides, pushing me down until I feel his stiff bulge flexing between my legs.

I groan and kiss him deeper, grinding on him through our clothes. He's totally right about me. I don't need him to be romantic or sweet and gentle. What I need is to have someone who accepts every one of my flaws and calls me out with unfiltered honesty. I need him to test my strength and show me how powerful I can be.

"I'm ready for my reward," I murmur against his lips. Reaching out to Rowan, I grab the front of his shirt. "From both of you."

Kash roars, his dragon's call rumbling through the walls. I jerk up with wide eyes, trying to figure out what his calls mean.

Rowan swears under his breath. "Nova—"

The room quakes at the same time a boom startles me. A few of Rowan's books crash from the dresser and onto the floor. The lamps tremble, and I clutch onto the front of Maddox's shirt, feeling as if I might fall over.

The heat and lust flowing between us cools. My mind shoves away any and all thought of rewards and pleasure—of any sort of happy life—because we are incomplete without Kash.

Guilt ignites inside me, and I'm pissed off at myself that I forgot for even a second that he's trapped in his dragon form. Quillon's twisted behavior has my body in knots, my fury on the brink of exploding.

I rip away from Maddox and hop to my feet. Kash's powerful roar echoes through the room again, coming from outside the window. And something's different and utterly wrong. I know his call with every fiber of my being, and this one? It's nearly unrecognizable to my ears thought my soul knows it's him.

What the fuck? What the hell is Quillon doing? I know he's behind this. He's stupid enough to test me and seriously think he can get away with it, hiding behind his messed up bargain with my mate. Well, fuck that. I'm about to light his ass up and teach him that he doesn't have the power he thinks he does.

Rushing across the room, I bolt to the window and throw open the curtains.

Kash locks his dagger-length fangs into a small palm tree and rips it from the ground. Fire lights his dragon eyes, and smoke wafts him his nostrils. His pearlescent scales shimmer in the fading light of dusk, though the world remains warm in color because of his flames. Throwing the tree into the air, he whips his tail so fast that it splits the palm tree in two.

I spot Quillon standing a dozen feet away with his back facing me. He raises his hand and points at another tree. Kash shrieks, sounding as if being in his dragon-form is utter torture. A wave of ice blossoms in my chest, freezing my insides. But the emotion, the dread and defeat, doesn't belong to me.

In a form Kash usually feels the most powerful now has him feeling weak, useless, and like a true animal. I can't hear his thoughts, and I wonder if being in this form, under Quillon's control became too much and he cages his humanity tightly within him to bear this bullshit.

Kash stomps, spreading his wings wide, and stretches his long neck above the height of the house. His claws impale the grass like sharp stakes, ripping up grass and dirt. He breathes fire, burning a path through the grass until his flames consume another tree. Then he torches another and blackens the sidewalk with another wave of fire.

It's almost as if Quillon wants to burn the property, his sick-fuck mind not caring about the damage and only about enjoying his power and control over one of Magaelorum's strongest enforcers while he watches the world burn to ash.

"Kash!" I yell, banging my hand to the glass. I want—no need—to break Quillon's hold on him. I can't stand seeing him so destructive like this against his will. "What are you doing? Stop! Resist Quillon. You don't have to do this." Closing my eyes, I try to get into Kash's mind in his dragon form, but he shuts me out. Pushing into his thoughts is pointless like I hit my head to an impenetrable wall.

Quillon swivels and glances at me from over his shoulder. The douchebag smiles and winks, his eyes reflecting green in Kash's dragon fire.

With Quillon's one look, I realize it's not Kash locking me out. It's Quillon forcing him to. He not only wants to control his actions, he wants to control his thoughts. He purposely wants to separate him from his clan as a form of punishment.

"You despicable piece of shit!" I scream.

Rage ignites inside me, and I grab the lamp from the dresser and smash through the window. Neither Rowan nor Maddox can stop me as I risk cutting myself to escape the house and run to Kash.

My vision tints red with my fury. Delicious heat pours from my heart, spilling through my veins as it flows like lava right to my hands. The sensation feels indescribable—so powerful. I feel as if I can take on anyone in the universe and win.

Quillon widens his eyes in fear and holds up his hands. This is the first time he's ever given me satisfaction, and I want more. "My beast, stop her! Protect me!"

I can't stop fast enough before Kash shoves his big, cool snout into my stomach and knocks me off my feet. My breath gasps from my body, my fire sputtering out with a gust of his hot, cinnamony breath.

He pins me down.

Dragon Guard

"KASH, RELEASE HER!" MADDOX YELLS from somewhere behind me. Fire burns above me as Kash releases a warning growl. The ground quivers and rocks. Kash stomps around me without moving away, ignoring his brothers.

"If you hurt her, you will never forgive yourself," Rowan says, his voice deep with concern. "Please, brother. Don't lose yourself. You're a Dreki, not that asshole's pet. She is your mate and the one who truly controls your soul.

Let her in. Feel her. I know you want to protect Nova, but keeping her from your agony does no one good. It jeopardizes everything."

I suck in a shuddering breath at Rowan's words. Quillon isn't solely responsible for the wall Kash keeps between us. And it kills me to hear Rowan's speculation of Kash's reasons—or perhaps they're the truth. Kash thinks he's doing right by me by keeping me out. But I know he needs me. I don't want him to deal with this alone.

Holding my breath, I lie frozen in shock on my stomach. I turn my head and watch as Maddox and Rowan jump from the window and onto the lawn. Kash's claws penetrate the ground around my head, digging into the grass like long swords, stopping me from trying to push up. Heat warms my back with another breath of his fire. Trembles shake through my body, making my teeth chatter despite the heat. I don't mean to be afraid, but something about not being able to hear Kash's thoughts unnerves me. He lets his beast have complete hold of even his soul, worse than ever before under Quillon's control. This is the sick fuck's punishment for not following through last night. He's testing me by trying to keep me from a happy life with all my mates until I comply.

Kash releases a guttural noise and breathes a breath of my scent. If I didn't know any better, I'd think he was preparing to devour me alive.

Managing to roll over, I face upward and stare through Kash's claws and at his glowing eyes. Smoke billows from his nostrils, and he looks as if he's ready to torch me with his dragon fire. It won't hurt me, but it'll scald my soul, leaving me grieving for what I've done to him. What's worse? My heart aches, feeling as if Quillon is more important. I never thought I'd be jealous of the asshole lycan, yet here I am. I want nothing more than to break from Kash to attack the fuckhead.

"Kash, let me in. Don't let him consume you. He can't have this kind of control over us." I try to settle my racing thoughts. I can't think like this. If Kash even knew I considered it for a second, it would devastate him.

"Stay back, Drekis," Quillon says. His shadow falls over me, and he looks down, bracing his hands on Kash's foot. A leering smile splits his lips, hardening his features in a way that makes him look like a psychopath. Hell, he is a psycho. "If you get involved, I will make your brother put the bitch in her place like I should've done all along. This does not involve you. Kash is my guardian, and I will train him however I see fit. Now back off. We have too much shit to worry about. I don't need Nova acting as if she can do anything besides looking hot on her back beneath me."

Ah, hell. Fuck that.

My vision darkens as I somehow manage to summon my dragon fire from my heart again and into my hands. Quillon doesn't have time to react. I jerk my hands up and send a wave of orange flames through Kash's claws and at the lycan bastard.

Quillon screams, his voice rising to a pitch that I'm sure only certain animals could hear. I've never heard something so squealy and high escape a man with a deep voice like him before. It echoes through the air, long and loud, and utterly ridiculous to the point that I can't stop from laughing.

I cackle, the release of pressure from inside turning me giddy. I can't believe I managed this. I thought smacking my shoe in his face was good. Hearing his wailing agony? Fuck, maybe he's not the only psycho.

Quillon whacks his face with his hands and stumbles back, falling to the ground. The front of his shirt smolders and reveals his chest, the wiry texture of his body hair singeing and smoking. Rolling over, he puts out the flames and curls in on himself. Kash extracts his sharp claws from the grass and finally releases me from his makeshift cage.

"You are fucking dead, Nova. You psychotic cunt!" Quillon shouts, hiding his face beneath his hands. "I was going to give you another chance, but now I'm never allowing Kash to transform back into a man because of this. You can also forget our deal. I don't even fucking care about a cure for this curse. The High Council won't capture me again. I have everything I want right here. The witch who made me no longer holds power over me. I was trying to be nice because I thought I liked you, but you're no better than anyone else in Magaelorum."

Rowan rushes toward Quillon and kneels beside him. I expect him to check on his condition, but he surprises me by slamming his fist into the lycan's gut. "You can't punish them like that. I know what you asked our mate to do, and you're lucky to even be alive. That was never in the deal. It was her time and only her time. But you took things too far. You tried to manipulate her with this threat we damn well won't let you keep up. Now stop acting like you're the victim and accept that you're the one in the wrong. You fucked up and you know it. This wasn't either of their faults. You were aware that Nova is protective of us. You also knew that she was training with my brother right now and would see you doing this. She is barely learning to control her dragon fire. It was your mistake threatening her like you had. Now, get your ass up and go inside. Don't think you're a free man. Kash would rather turn himself in to the High Council to take you down than remain your guardian. The deal stands, got it? Maddox will take care of your burns if you get over your power trip, release Kash, and realize we're all on the same side."

Huffing a breath, Quillon groans and sits upright. I gawk at him and cover my mouth with my hand. Because shit. My dragon fire ate away his eyebrows, facial stubble, and the front half of his unruly hair, leaving him looking like a balding man. His blue eyes shine against his pink skin, sheening with the green reflection of his beast, and blisters pepper his cheeks. Even part of his chest hair disintegrated from the heat, now showing off his scrawny pecs.

"I don't need Maddox's help," Quillon snaps, dragging himself forward until he manages to find his strength to get to his feet. "I'll have Rose take care of me when she gets back. I will give Nova another chance and she can make up for this and earn Kash's freedom from his beast-mode later tonight. I have something easy for her to do for me."

"What do you mean when Rose gets back?" I ask, ignoring his comment about the supposed task. If it's anything like performing for him while he masturbates again, he's sorely mistaken that I'll even consider it. I'll just borrow Maddox's restraints and pin him down to pluck every damn hair from his body until he gives up his power trip. Kash would cheer me on, his tough, unwavering strength coming in handy.

"Where is the murdering royal highness?" Maddox asks, looming over Quillon.

I glare at Quillon when he groans instead of responding to either of our questions. "You know we can't trust her to go anywhere alone right now. She doesn't understand the social norms of the Mortal World. She will garner unwanted attention, especially because she refuses to even cover her damn wings."

"You can't tell a murderous fairy princess what to do, Red. If she gets into trouble, it's her own damn fault. We both agreed on that. And she knows how to handle herself. She would be gone before the mortal authorities or the High Council could ever find her." Quillon narrows his eyes at me, and he grimaces in pain scrunching his burned forehead. "Now, why don't you make yourself useful and cook me some dinner while another one of your mates serves me. You might be able to sweeten me up with some dessert."

Wow.

"Enough!" Maddox shouts, igniting dragon fire in his palms. "Let me heal you, and then you will take me to Rose. I will bring her back myself. Nova is right. The risk is too great. You might want to get caught, but I don't. I will not let you jeopardize our lives to stroke your damn ego, you cursed animal."

Quillon looks ready to test his luck to tackle Maddox, but Rowan slides between the two of them, holding his palms up. "Just tell us where she is, and Nova and I will retrieve her. We will be fast and undetected."

Curling his lips and flaring his nostrils, Quillon says, "Fine, damn it. But I swear, you two better be back within thirty minutes. If I have to come find you—"

"You'll what?" Maddox growls, gripping Quillon by his tattered shirt. "Your threats grow tired and meaningless." Turning to me, he adds, "Perhaps we will tip off the High Council to Rose's whereabouts and lock you in a closet since you've lost your power of manipulation with your decision to keep my brother in his dragon form."

I tug my hair loose from its ponytail. "Why don't we just do that now? Without Rose around, he—"

"I'll be fucking fine without her," Quillon snaps. "She doesn't do anything for me."

He's so full of shit, and we all know it. I open my mouth to argue and call him the dozens of swear words swirling through my mind. Rowan must hear them because he closes space to me and drapes his arm over my shoulders, hugging me to him. Inhaling a small breath, I settle my nerves and push the thoughts of murder from my mind.

"Everyone needs to calm down. We will get Rose and come back right away. You don't need to threaten us. It's pointless, and you're now only doing it to flex your faux authority," Rowan says, arching a brow, unaffected by anything Quillon tries. "And remember to watch your damn mouth from now on. You can't talk to Nova or any of us like that. Next time, it'll take you days to heal from what I'd have in store for you." Rowan turns to Maddox and purses his lips. "Don't kill him, okay? Listen for my call in case I need you." He says the words as if Rose might be stuck behind enemy lines or some shit.

"If you can't handle going to a mortal bar, you have a lot worse things to worry about, Dreki," Quillon says, chortling at his lame attempt to belittle my mate. "You'll find the place on Main Street at the end of the block."

Rowan turns me in his arms to look at me. His hazel eyes, the same color as Kash's, rove over my face, tracing their way across my lips and nose before searching my eyes. "I need you to take a few breaths with me. I know you don't realize it, but you're out of control, and I can feel your emotions on the verge of snapping. I'm afraid of what Rose might say or do to set you off on the way home. We can't go anywhere until I'm certain you won't torch a couple buildings by accident."

He's right. My feral dragon heart just wants to roar.

I do as Rowan asks and close my eyes, inhaling a few deep breaths as I listen to Maddox shove Quillon in the direction of the house. A hot breeze blows my hair forward, sending it clinging to Rowan's stubbly face. Kash's familiar presence lingers behind me, and I swivel on the balls of my feet.

A river of mixed emotions—sorrow, anger, disappointment, and something soft and gentle and stronger than everything else—floods through me. My heart skips a beat, going haywire like I've been starved because of the wall built between our souls, and I need so desperately to support and be here for Kash in the way I want and the way he needs.

Kash's hazel eyes shine in the sun setting in the distance. He lowers his body and huffs a breath of smoke. "I'm sorry, kitten. I couldn't control myself and hate that I scared you." The softness of his telepathic words caresses my mind, calming the wild emotions that Kash is stuck in his dragon form and instead as the man I've come to adore. "Please forgive me."

Stretching on my tippy-toes, I gently rest my palms against his cool snout, bringing his big head even lower to my level. I kiss the tip of his nose between his nostrils and try my best to hug his hulking body, refusing to deny him affection. Even in this form, he's my mate. I will not let him think it bothers me apart from knowing Quillon controls him. "What Quillon commands you to do is not your fault. If anything, I should apologize for my temper. I swear I won't allow him to force you to remain in this form, even if I have torture him to get him to do so."

Kash huffs a breath and my hair blows behind me. "If only. I'm bound to him. I'm just lucky your fire doesn't bother me any. My brother's punch to Quillon's gut on the other hand..." Whipping his long tail at Rowan, Kash knocks his brother's feet out from under him. "Pin him down or something next time."

I groan and rest my head against Kash's cool scales. "There will not be a next time. I will handle him when I get back. If he refuses to comply, then we'll figure it out, okay? You're mine."

Kash's eyes light with his dragon fire. "I know you will. But please, let Rowan handle things. I don't trust the fairy not to try to set you off on purpose. She survives on causing trouble and playing tricks. She was in Max for a reason."

I smirk. "Got it. Let the big, bad CO bring home the fairy princess."

Kash chuckles in my mind and expands his wings, taking flight only to land on the roof of the house. From his spot, he can probably watch us walk to Main Street, and I bet he will. Rowan grabs my hand, pulling me in close. I slide my arm around his broad back, nestling myself into his side, knowing how he wants me close as we leave the protective magical shield in place from the witch responsible for Quillon's lycan curse.

My skin buzzes with electricity at the end of the long

driveway, and I clench my jaw as I step onto the sidewalk like I'll somehow be electrocuted for leaving the premises. I don't know if it's because my dragon senses the shields similar to what the Maximum Magical Penitentiary uses to keep inmates at bay or what, but any sort of magic makes me anxious. I can feel it tugging at my core. The thought of witches and warlocks and the High Council doesn't help either. I wish I wasn't so messed up at just a little thought, but the dramatic change in my existence feels as if it left puckered scars on my soul.

Rowan hugs me tighter, trying to squeeze the nerves out of me. This is the first time we've gone out without his brothers. He doesn't have to say anything for me to know that my mind remains open to him, my still wild emotions from Quillon threatening Kash making it hard to put my guard up.

"You never have to with me, Nova," Rowan says, breaking the silence. I appreciate that he doesn't speak telepathically and chooses to let his words fill the air around us. He glances at the side of my face, waiting for me to acknowledge him with a nod. "What you went through, what you're still going through, it's a lot to handle. Even I struggle some days, and this shit—asshole covens and criminals—has been a normal part of my life for a long time. I can't imagine what all of this is like for you, and I won't pretend otherwise, but I want you to know I am here. Always."

I tip my chin up to meet his hazel eyes, the beautiful color sparkling with flecks of green and gold like the color of his scales. "I just...I wish things would've been different. I wish Aunt McKayla would have told me the truth instead of abandoning me to the fates. I'm so angry that she could've prepared me for all of this and didn't. I also wish I knew more about my mom and her life. My dad. Hell, I want to know what the fuck Rhett was doing, hunting me down, especially since we know it wasn't for you. Why me? Why our clan and our lives? I want answers, and I'm afraid I'll never get them."

"Don't be. We will get answers. Trust me," Rowan says, giving me a small shake.

I puff a breath through my mouth. Stating all of my questions out loud doesn't do anything to make me feel better. All it does is anger me even more. What terrible thing has my mom done that the Drekis beloved fates decided to screw up even my life? Is there anything I can really do to change it? Are we just keeping a few feet in front of the inevitable as the universe waits for us to trip?

Rowan groans in his throat and closes the space to my mouth, brushing his lips to mine. Hooking his arm around me, he doesn't give me a chance to resist and lifts me into his embrace. He kisses me deeper, strolling blindly along the sidewalk in the direction of the small town. Main Street is the only big road and way in and out of Violet Grove.

Drawing his big hand lower, Rowan squeezes my ass. "What do I need to do to help clear your mind?" he asks, sucking my bottom lip between his teeth.

I hum in my throat. "Fly me to the moon?"

He chuckles, the sound musical and easy-going. I want to listen to it over and over again. "While you sit on my face?" he teases, his eyes glowing with his inner desire.

"Not exactly what I had in mind. Can we even have sex as dragons?" My. Damn. Thoughts. Why am I even thinking about this? Maybe because Kash—or just my dragon wanting to explore new boundaries. Either way, now that the question is out there, I need to know.

"We can do it however we please. Hell, you could slather my back with lube and slide up and down the bumps of my spine until you cum if you wanted to." He wags his eyebrows, his eyes flickering at the thought. "Might be the best ride of your life."

I arch away with a loud-ass laugh. My cheeks burn at the visual bursting into my mind. "No fucking way."

His grin widens as he puts another image into my head. "Could be fun."

I pat his taut pecs through his shirt, whipping my head

back and forth, sending my hair sweeping across my lower back. "You'd ask me to pole dance, climbing and sliding up and down on your dragon cock after that, and I'm nearly certain if you blew a load in that form, you'd really send me to the moon." The ridiculous thought makes me laugh even harder, easing the heavy weight of anxiety squeezing my chest.

"There's only one real way to find out," Rowan teases, beaming a bright smile that lights up his entire face. His utter ridiculousness fills me with warmth and a strange need for a weird ass adventure I definitely need to get out of my mind.

"I'd prefer you hold onto it," he says, pulling my pelvis to his to show me exactly what these crazy thoughts do to him. "So let's hurry and drag the bratty princess home."

Rowan bolts forward, running down the sidewalk, kissing my throat to make me laugh some more. My eyes water from the shift in my emotions, and tears of laughter smear across my cheeks. I had nearly forgotten what it was like not to feel as if the world would smash me to pieces at any second. And Rowan's visual continues to play through my mind as he thinks it over and over again like if he does so enough, I might participate to prove my theory...hopefully wrong.

"Fucking fates, I'd hope so. I'll be honest. I've never

considered or even thought about it until you brought it up. I've never experienced...the deep-seated need to bone in my dragon form, and now I'm nearly certain when mating season comes—" He laughs and snuggles his face into my neck. "Thanks for this. I hope you think about it for the rest of the week, so it's all my brothers have to think about too." He kisses the smooth skin of my throat for just a second. "But be careful with Maddox. He will mistake your curiosity for need, and before you know it—"

"I'll never have to wonder again?" I tease, loving the sudden serious surprise of his reaction.

Damn. He loves the idea.

He wants to be the one to ensure I never have to wonder.

"Tame your beast, Rowan." My voice comes out breathy and whispery from the influence of his now raging desire. "We have other things to focus on."

He slows down and sighs, setting me on my feet. He pulls me back into his side with his arm around me like it's the safest place for me in the world. And maybe it is. In this moment, he feels safer than the magical shield protecting us from the High Council and the lunatic Lazlo Infinity ever could.

It's easy to forget the threats around us with his closeness.

A peel of laughter echoes through the air, drifting on the cool breeze. Rowan turns with me, keeping me close, to stare in the direction of the laughter. I've been so distracted by Rowan that I haven't even noticed how empty Main Street is apart from the creepy noise of unnatural excitement. I've never heard laughter anything like this high-pitched quick successions of hi-ha-he-ho.

What the actual hell? I don't believe what I'm seeing.

"Is this normal behavior for mortals?" Rowan asks, twirling his finger in the direction of a group of people dancing in a line from a building at the end of the block.

Leading the way, a man without a shirt and beer gut hanging over his belt waves his arms in the air. People follow his moves, dancing and singing a strange song I've never heard at the top of their lungs. It sounds more like a chant—and the chorus? Weird.

Sip the drink and eat the treat. We'll sing and dance until defeat.

"Uh, maybe? I think they're leaving a bar," I finally reply to Rowan, glancing at him, though his gaze remains locked on the crowd stumbling in the opposite direction. I had no idea so many people in Violet Grove would drink this excessively before dinner—leaving Main Street empty and eerie apart from the bar. My skin crawls as the crowd starts singing their song over. "It's a little early for what looks like a Last Call parade, but I don't know this town. I've only seen something like it in two places, both in big cities with drunk college kids."

"Fuck," Rowan mutters under his breath. He tilts his head and mouths the words to their song like doing so will help him figure out what's going on. "You're right. It's the bar Quillon says Rose is at, which means—"

"How much trouble can a fairy princess cause, anyway? It looks like the patrons are at least having a good time." I force a smile and fake bob my head to the sound of the cheers exploding from the group like I enjoy their weird-ass excitement. Even if it is unsettling, it's been so long since I've felt the energy of an excited crowd that I can't help savoring it. I never realized how much I lived for performing until I could no longer do it. And now, I probably never will unless it's for Quillon's gross ass.

"You just had to tempt the fates, didn't you?" Rowan says, releasing a rumble in his throat. He swipes his free hand over his face, palming his forehead. "You're lucky Maddox stayed home. I'm certain he'd have spanked you for that comment. We both know Rose is capable of complete destruction and utter chaos. What you hear is one of her enchantments."

I giggle and shake my head at his comment. He's right. Maddox would blame me for jinxing the situation. My red hair sweeps around me with the gesture and I twirl away from Rowan. "Then I will handle the fairy if you're too afraid."

He doesn't let more than a foot of space get between us as his hulking form once again looms beside me. Taking the lead, he strides forward in the direction of the bar, and I tease him by breaking away to make a flying leap down the sidewalk. I cartwheel out of his reach, and he cracks a smile, letting me tease him despite the worry in his eyes.

"I'm sure everything is fine," I say, hearing the upbeat music pulsing from the bar. Maybe willing the thought into the universe will calm the fates Rowan so strongly believes in. "I mean, they're just dancing and singing. Wouldn't people be screaming and running for their lives if something was wrong? I've been in the middle of a magical bar fight and..."

Fuck. Me.

The memory comes crashing back to me, stealing my breath. I've done a decent job keeping the fight that led to my murder convictions mostly from my mind until now. The sound of the bumping music from the bar no longer sounds energetic and upbeat. It sounds whiny and repetitive. Another group of people stumble from the bar, laughing and dancing, their cheers far from excited. It's sloppy, robotic, and eerie. Seeing the men and women up close rips the veil away, allowing me to see that they don't seem as drunk off their asses as I thought. And their chant? It's different than the first group's. They all slur so heavily that I have trouble understanding them. They almost sound like they're speaking another language—actually, I think they are.

"Shit," Rowan mutters, growling deep in his throat again. Muscles tighten and bulge on his arms as he stiffens. With his intense reaction, a few scales blossom over his skin, his dragon peeking through. "Rose must've enchanted everyone on this block, inviting them to dance with her before hypnotizing the whole damn bar. Offered drinks all around."

"I don't know why that's a problem," I say. By his flexing muscles, it obviously is, but I can't exactly figure it out without him telling me. My knowledge about fairies is pretty limited. I'm still learning about myself as a dragon. "I'm going to need a crash course, CO." I use his former title as a reminder that I wasn't born in his world.

"If a mortal accepts a gift from a fairy, it gives them power over them. Fae have their own magic, and Rose used hers. It's why she can negotiate contracts like the one between Kash and Quillon. It's also why Lazlo kidnapped her with you, because she intentionally bargained with you without your knowledge. We have to hurry." Rowan drags me with him, locking his fingers tightly around mine. Running the rest of the way to the bar, he only stops when we reach the closed door. "If she uses too much, she'll leave residue behind, which other fae can track. Quillon thinks she'd manage to get out of here before she does, but she's too curious. She loves controlling and dominating others. The Mortal World is the perfect playground for her games. Humans are extra malleable to fae influence."

"Damn it, Rose. I groan and shove open the door to the bar and halt in place. Goosebumps explode over my skin, tingling with nerves. Heaving a breath, I clutch my stomach, trying not to gag. This isn't a little prank or game. Rose is a full-blown psychotic fairy with an addiction to destruction. "Fuck. I'm going to kill—"

Rowan crashes into my back, nearly knocking me off my feet and onto the bloody floor. He snakes his arm around me, yanking me into his hard chest, and takes a step back toward the door. I gawk in horror, my mind begging me to scream and run, but my body refuses to cooperate. I thought seeing a man ripped in half was bad, but this? Oh. My. Fucking. Fates.

"Rose!" I screech, covering my mouth with my hand, afraid if I breathe too deeply that the gore strung across the floor could accidentally get sucked into my throat.

"I've always wanted to see what intestines looked like,"

Rose says, unfazed by the panic and disgust lacing my quaking call of her name. She doesn't turn in our direction and pokes the dead body with the toe of her shoe.

"So you gutted a human!" I can't control my voice, the words shrieking out again, ringing through the room. "What the actual fuck? I thought you might have been imprisoned because you found yourself in a bad situation with the prince you killed, but—you're...you're...I don't even know. Psycho doesn't cut it."

Fluttering her wings, Rose slowly twists in her spot, meeting my gaze. Blood soaks through her shirt, smears across her face, and sticks in her hair as if she might have rolled and tried to bathe herself in the blood of her victim. A wide smile splits her lips, and her pink eyes glow, turning brighter than the color of her hair. Her vine tattoos come alive and twist around her arms, swirling and moving like a serpent searching for prey. I've never been afraid of Rose—I mean, she looks so sweet and innocent—but damn. She looks ready to come after me next.

"You act as if he was innocent, dragon," she snaps, flapping her wings again.

"That still doesn't give you the right to do this!" I huff and swallow, my stomach twisting. "You're going to summon the damn High Council. You know we're supposed to stay hidden and out of sight until we find my aunt. You're going to ruin everything!"

"I'm making it better. A sacrifice to summon a warlock. I've grown tired of being imprisoned by your COs. I was supposed to have freedom in this world." Rose smiles wider. "So I've decided to get it myself."

Fear trickles through me at her words.

Rowan tries to turn me away from the bloody, oozing body, but my body remains stiff, my feet planted to the floor. The only way he could shield me from this brutal sight would be if he lifts me up, tossing me on his shoulder, and burns this place down with his dragon fire.

And shit. We might very well have to.

"You will thank me. I find dragons are best kept in control. We can't have you burning the world down before any of us have a chance to truly enjoy it," she adds, rubbing her hands together so quickly that they blur and sparkle with pink light.

Did she just hear my thoughts? Maybe my reaction speaks louder than my voice ever could.

Rose giggles and tosses her pink hair over her shoulder. "Now don't worry about this man. Mortals like him need to be gutted and splayed across the floor. His death will benefit all of us. You'll see."

I blink a few times, her words unsettling me.

Gathering fire in his hands, Rowan prepares to chuck

the massive flaming orb at Rose. Tension builds between us, and Rose slaps her glowing hands together, shooting blood spatter across the wall. I stare in shock as it flows and moves, creating a circle on the old wooden wall.

"Damn it!" Rowan shouts, throwing his dragon fire at Rose.

Musical laughter chimes from her mouth, and she claps her hands together again, bouncing and fluttering in her spot.

"It's time! I'm finally going to be free!" she says, cheering. "I will get my own court to rule right here, and your mates can serve me well."

A brilliant blue light flashes through the bar, stealing my vision. My heart crashes into my stomach. My mind spins as panic consumes me. I recognize what's happening and bump back into Rowan. He growls and snatches my hand, dragging me toward the door. My heart nearly bursts from my chest at the sight of a short figure materializing in the light.

Something comes over me, and I jerk away from Rowan instead of rushing away. My panic melts with the heat of my rage. Rose betrayed us. She fucking betrayed us by summoning the monster who caused all my problems. I can't focus on anything else apart from wanting to murder him like I did his brother. My dragon screeches within my soul, dying to tear the bastard to shreds before he can even materialize in the room completely.

"Nova! Focus. We have one shot, and then we run," Rowan shouts, the heat of his body engulfing mine to enhance my strength. He sees exactly what I see, and neither of us can run. We must take care of this. Lazlo's threat and need to destroy my life ends here.

Gathering my dragon fire in my hands, I summon the dark, dangerous wrath inside me that has been waiting to burst free. I yell as the fire shoots from me in a wave of molten power at the asshole using magic to portal into the bar.

But my fire fizzles out.

An icy sensation steals my breath, forcing my dragon to surrender. My throat tightens. The magical collar bursts with electric light around my neck, cutting off my dragon's roar. We weren't quick enough. Maybe I never stood a chance.

Lazlo Infinity comes into view, his white hair blowing behind him with power. Shouting a spell, he throws a magical chain in my direction. It clips to my collar, and he reels me away from Rowan faster than I can act.

All I can do is brace to be stolen away.

Leashed

"NOVA, FIGHT!" ROWAN SHOUTS, BLASTING a ball of dragon fire toward Lazlo. "Damn it, fight! Never surrender. You have it in you to resist."

A burst of Rowan's strength and determination shoves away the cold defeat flooding my mind. What was I even thinking? I can't just accept being kidnapped from my mates. We have too much to lose.

Locking my fingers around the magical chain, I yank it

as hard as I can, shocking myself. Pain explodes in my palms, and an uncontrollable screech rips from my mouth. I release the magical chain, unable to bear the agony it ignites in my soul. If I couldn't see that I'm still in one piece, I'd have thought a dozen hot knifes cut me into cubes, every part of my body radiating with surging jolts of stinging shockwaves.

"Sordona yveslicia tonar eht wob!" Lazlo flicks his hand, sending a burst of energy at the wall. Another portal of light explodes open when it hits, and the world around us shakes. "Do not fight me. We must go! You are mine, my pet."

"Go with him Nova," Rose urges, twirling her hands. "I'll take care of the Drekis. I promise."

Fuck that.

I grind my teeth, skidding my shoes on the floor, pulling back enough to give me a chance to fight. Fire crackles across my hand, my sheer will to survive kicking my instincts on. I swing my arm and throw it at Lazlo, watching the orb zoom with perfect accuracy at him. He shouts a spell, calling upon an electrical shield to protect him. My fire bounces off of it and smashes into Rose, setting her ablaze.

Another fireball crashes into Lazlo's shield. Rowan fights just as hard. He attacks the magic trying to separate us. The power trapping my mate falters, and Lazlo's focus on protecting himself proves stronger than keeping me from Rowan.

Rose screeches again, writhing and dropping to the floor.

Lazlo takes advantage of my body tightening at Rose's screams and hauls back the magical chain again, sending me falling face first on the dingy floor. I slide across the smooth surface, reaching out to find something to grab onto. Snatching the heavy base of a barstool, I drag it with me and swing it at Lazlo. The chair slams through the magical shield and into his chest, throwing him off. He releases the chain to catch himself before leaving himself open for another attack.

Rowan rushes toward me, blasting another ball of dragon fire from his palms at Lazlo, keeping him back long enough to grab onto me. Locking his fingers through my long, wild tresses, Rowan pulls me toward him. I gasp, but my breath refuses to come. The collar tightens around my throat, darkening my vision with pain unlike anything I've ever felt.

"Don't let him take me," I plead, sending my thoughts to Rowan telepathically. "Tell me what to do."

"Summon your fire again. Close your eyes and imagine it consuming you. I want you to transform." Rowan's thoughts remain even despite the blips of panic I feel trickling from his mind to mine.

Clenching my jaw, I squeeze my eyes shut and concentrate on unleashing my dragon from her cage. Heat warms my insides as my muscles spasm, but the collar around my neck tightens even more. All I manage to do is gather a small orb of orange and yellow flames. Lazlo's face contorts, his mouth widening into a wicked smile as his teeth elongate into fangs.

"Ezeerf kolraw!" The strange masculine voice booms through the room.

Lazlo hisses and jerks his attention away from me. The distraction gives me the moment I need to concentrate, and my instincts kick on, allowing me to siphon my dragon fire from the depths of my soul.

A wave of brilliant flames cascades over Lazlo, and he hollers and claps his hands. Blue sparks fly around him, blocking him with a wall of magic. The room quakes as the ceiling collapses. The overhead lights flicker and explode in a shower of glass. Bottles of alcohol crash to the floor, spilling their contents everywhere. Screams rip through the room, coming from somewhere next to me. The high-pitched beastly noise startles my very soul.

"We have to run! Brace yourself, Nova. We have to snap the chain," Rowan says, locking his hands under my arms to pull me back. "It's going to hurt like fucking hell."

It's now that I realize the flames weren't mine. They weren't Rowan's either. An ear-piercing screech steals my hearing as a black and gold scaled dragon crashes its enormous head through the wall—no, not the wall. It crashes through Lazlo's portal.

I stare in shock, unable to get my body to work, my mind disconnecting from the rest of me. The unfamiliar, yet stunning, dragon snaps its teeth, thrashing its long neck as it attempts to crash into the tiny bar. Lazlo shouts another spell, trying his best to keep the dragon away, his attention no longer on me.

"Hold still, Nova. This is going to hurt." Rowan kneels in front of me, hovering his hands over the chain tethered to my collar.

Gripping my shoulder in one hand and the chain in the other, he bellows, summoning intense fire. The shockwave of power whips through me, stealing my breath. The chain crackles and sizzles. Painful bursts of electricity snap across my skin and sink into me as the magic reacts to his strength and power.

Rowan roars, baring his teeth. "Fuck! Come on! Break!" Rippling muscles cut across his arms as he endures the same pain I do, trying to break through the magic.

Chaos shakes the room, sending my heart sliding into

my stomach. All I know is that we need to hurry and get out of here. The only good thing about Lazlo's arrival is that the dragon guards go after him first. Maybe now the High Council will see that it has been him all along. Maybe they will overturn my convictions. Maybe—

"Eaf eht og nuir vitisima!" Lazlo's sharp voice echoes through the room. A bolt of electricity lights the darkness, zooming in our direction.

Rowan growls and envelops me in his arms protectively, willing to risk his life to save me from Lazlo. It feels as if time slows, my body and mind bracing for the end.

"No!" A man with green, sizzling magic materializes in front of us, creating a shield to deflect Lazlo's power. Twisting on his feet, he snatches the chain connected to my collar and twists it between his hands. Fire explodes from the dragon guard, stopping Lazlo from attacking again.

I expect the High Council's enforcer to finish what Lazlo fails to accomplish. I cling onto Rowan as he gathers more dragon fire, his efforts slower, his exhaustion from fighting wearing him down.

"Please! No!" I plead, shocking myself in an attempt to break the magical chain again. "I'm innocent!"

The warlock ignores me and adjusts his other hand around the chain, getting a good grip on it. Rowan roars, his dragon peeking through his skin. Yanking me back, he tries to snatch me away to run for it.

"Kaerb won!" the warlock yells, his face alight with a neon glow that sharpens his features.

Rowan yanks me again, and the chain snaps in half, sending the two of us falling back. Whipping through the air, it tangles around the man and drags him away from us. Lazlo yanks the magic chain, sending the other warlock crashing into the strange dragon's snout. The huge beast flings the warlock forward. Lazlo can't move fast enough, and a blade materializes in the warlock's hand. He stabs Lazlo, surprising him. With a clap of his hands, the High Council enforcer sends sparks through the room. Two more figures materialize in the bar, arriving in a flash of his green light.

Lazlo yells another spell, sending chairs and tables flying their way. I nearly lose my shit at the sight of Rose's charred body crashing into the two figures. I don't get a chance to even see who the people are or what they look like as Rowan scoops me up in his arms and spins toward the door.

I cling onto him with my whole body, praying to the universe that I'm not suddenly dragged away and back into the madness. I pray that the street outside this old bar remains empty and not crowded with a dozen guards here to arrest me on behalf of the High Council. I pray just to survive everything threatening us in this moment.

Ramming his shoulder into the door, Rowan carries me outside. Cool, fresh air engulfs us, and I gasp in a deep breath, my body begging and craving to breathe something besides the smoke from dragon fire and warlock magic colliding.

"Maddox is coming," Rowan says, tightening his grip on me. "We're going to be ok—"

Bright green light ignites the world in front of us, stopping Rowan in his tracks. I instinctively summon my dragon fire, the effort easier by the second with my wild emotions. There is no fucking way I'm going down without the fight of my life. I can't—no, I won't—go back to the Maximum Magical Penitentiary. I won't. I don't deserve to be there. I would rather fight and die than return to that hellhole.

"Fates, is she feisty," a smooth, velvety rich voice says. Green electricity buzzes before me, shielding the two guys from the heat of my wrath. "You weren't kidding in your assessment."

"You know I never joke. I knew my mate would be a firecracker," the other man says, stepping through the force field of magical energy separating him from us. Messy black hair dances with sparking static over the guy's head, staying out of his face. Obsidian lashes shadow the man's jade green eyes, shining against his flawless sepia-toned skin. His angular jaw twitches with his smile, and the bastard winks at me.

I gape in surprise and confusion. Enforcers don't wink. They don't smile either, not when they're on a mission to take down a criminal.

Rowan growls again and sets me on my feet, nudging me behind him. Straightening his shoulders, he stands erect and on defense, shielding me from the men. With the building and the crackling power, running isn't exactly an option. We'll have to fight. "Fuck, they're not from the High Council."

"Then who are they?" I ask, squinting through the haze of magic at the man before us, the details of his shadowed body clearing as he steps closer and out of the magic fogging the air.

And holy fucking shit.

He's naked, tatted, and...is that a dick piercing? The silver jewelry glints in the light from the magic, making it look as if his cock winks at me. And by the size of dick, now growing to intimidating proportions under my scrutiny, I can tell he's definitely a dragon.

"My mate approves," the man says to the warlock. He grins at me, his straight, white teeth encouraging me to smile back like he dares me to resist. Swiveling his hips, he gives me a new view of his body and flexes his arms, showing off his chiseled muscles. "I can smell her delicious reaction."

His what? He what? Just...what?

"Get ready, Nova," Rowan whispers. "Don't let your guard down. They want to take you from us."

I stiffen and peer around, looking for a way to escape, feeling trapped as the warlock blocks the rest of the world out with his magic. Where is Maddox? Shouldn't he have heard Rowan's calls? Rowan said he was coming.

"The fates have aligned," the warlock says, sweeping his gaze over me, drawing my attention to him. "Everything is as it should be. All you need to do is say the words."

"What words?" I ask, forcing my voice to work. "Who the fuck are you? What do you want?" My soul screams, panic rushing through me. Maybe Maddox can't get here because the warlock shields us.

"Hurry, Theo. We must start now," the warlock says, ignoring my question. And Theo? I've never known anyone by that name before.

Craning his neck, Rowan meets my gaze. "Nova, run. Go now. I'll catch up." He scowls, summoning dragon fire into his palm. Releasing a roar, he prepares to blast it at the strange dragon and the warlock.

An explosion quakes the ground, and pieces of the roof fall around us. Rowan pushes me out of the way before something hits me. The earth shakes with an ear-piercing boom. Reaching out for Rowan, I try to grab onto him, but the asphalt cracks, splitting us apart.

"Nova, run!" Rowan repeats, bracing a light pole to steady himself. "Run and don't stop. Kash and Maddox are coming." Dragon fire billows from his hand, scorching against the magical barrier the warlock holds in place.

My legs refuse to move. It's like I'm trapped in some sort of force field. I know I should listen to Rowan. All my good reason screams at me to get my ass in gear and make a run for it. Why can't the rest of me listen? Why can't...damn it. My body does want to run but I physically can't. I'm trapped.

"Luos etam mailk eht Theo fo eht Darkonian Clan!" the warlock raises his hands toward the sky. "Luos etam mailk eht Delphia fo eht Litendrake Clan!"

Oh shit. I might not understand most of his spell, but I sure as shit recognize Darkonian and my birth-given name. Hearing the dragon clan name clicks my scattered thoughts together. This isn't some random dragon trying to catch me. It's the Darkonians Quillon said were searching for me.

The dick piercing man, Theo, steps through the second magic barrier separating me from Rowan. He strides in my direction like his sole purpose in life is to close the space to me as quickly as possible. My skin buzzes as static caresses my body and lifts my hair in a magical breeze. Silence blankets the world around me, cutting me and Theo off from the rest of the universe. He straightens his back and towers over me, looking down with a strange expression softening his features. Searching my eyes, he glides his tongue across his bottom lip and then smiles, his green eyes devouring me like I'm the best thing he's ever seen.

"Hello, my firecracker," he murmurs and glides his finger across my jaw. "Do you know who I am?"

I should be terrified.

I shouldn't like the way he looks at me so much.

Why can't I pull my gaze away from him? My throat dries, my mind whirling with a dozen thoughts.

I shake my head. "No," I whisper.

He tilts his head, leaning closer. "You don't have to be frightened. I'm your mate, Theo, from the Darkonian Clan and Prince of the Mountain Lands. I've been blessed by the stars and powers of Magaelorum to have the honor to claim you as mine. I've been waiting my entire life for this moment, Delphia. You are the most magnificent woman I've ever laid eyes on. My soul feels as if it finally has returned to my body." Extending his arm, he holds his hand out for me. "I'm sorry it took us so long to find you. Ambrose wanted to get things right and ensure you would be ready. The traitor heir—"

The door to the bar flies off its hinges, clattering in the street. It kicks the world around us back into action. Rowan's yells cut through the fog of my mind, and I whip my attention to him. He doesn't have time to react as another hulking naked man rushes outside, his body smoking from the heat of his body on this crisp night.

Wait, another man? The new guy looks identical to Theo, except his hair hangs to his shoulders, and he sports a full beard. I can't see the details of his tattoos, and he turns too quickly to get a look at his...damn it. Why do I always glance at naked guys' cocks?

His muscles ripple across his broad, glistening back tattooed with an intricate pattern that stops at his bubble-shaped ass. The asshole summons dragon fire and thrusts it at Rowan. Rowan flies off his feet and into the empty street. I suck in a breath, fear gripping me. A hot hand locks onto my wrist and hoists me from the ground.

"Let me help you, Delphia," Theo says, not even caring that his junk grazes my hip. "It's time to go home. Ambrose will see to it. He's the most powerful warlock I've had the pleasure to call my guard." The bastard warlock—Ambrose—has another thing coming to him if he thinks I'll just submit and go willingly. The Darkonians too.

Anger ignites inside me, stabbing at my dragon heart. It snaps me out of my strange haze, clouding my mind with curious attraction. I gather my senses and meet his eyes, capturing him with my own stare. He doesn't even see my next move coming.

"I'm not going with you. Now let me go!" I yell.

Swinging my arm, I slap the fucker in his bejeweled hard cock with enough force that he drops me. He shouts and clutches his junk, gathering fire in his other palm. I'm too slow to catch myself, hitting my ass on the hard concrete. I somersault backward and scramble to stand, holding my hands up protectively. Theo doesn't throw his fire at me, his face lining in confusion like fighting back against him was the last thing he expected.

"Clavosi notato nogard, Delphia!" Ambrose shouts, sending a bolt of green power at me.

It strikes me in the chest, knocking the air from my lungs. I stumble and hit my back to the wall of the smoldering building. My body tenses. Warmth builds in my core, traveling to the rest of me. I shudder at the sensation—all-consuming and strangely satisfying as it devours me in a cocoon of comforting heat. Pressing my back against the wall, I brace through another bout of trembles, my muscles spasming and aching.

The scales blooming on my arm tell me what's happening.

Oh. Fucking. Shit.

"Nova!" Rowan yells, fighting against Theo's twin, the two of them punching each other and fighting fire with fire. "Stop! Don't transform!"

But I can't help it. I've lost control of my beast and she thrashes wildly, yearning to break free.

Ambrose uses his magic against me, unleashing my dragon. The world shifts with my transformation, my body screaming in pain and relief. I crash into the building, smashing the smoldering wall under my heavy weight. I try to push on the ground to get up, but instead, I spread my wings and knock Ambrose and Theo's twin off their feet.

Everyone stops fighting and stares at me in awe.

A low whistle cuts through the air, the melodious sound snatching my attention away from my hysterical, foggy thoughts. The world surrounding Pierced Dick Man Theo shimmers with a golden light, turning him from intimidating to almost angelic. And gorgeous. Hot.

Why do I have the sudden urge to lick him?

I stretch my long neck, lowering down to his level. If sexy has a taste, I'm sure as hell about to find out. My dragon form is acting like a total out-of-control beast, confusing my human rational with these awkward desires.

"It's okay, Delphia. That's your soul wanting to learn everything about me, knowing that we've been cheated of a life of getting to know each other on every level. But don't worry. I'm here now. I got you. My brother and I will take care of you." His velvety voice hums through my mind, coaxing me closer.

An odd, purr-like sound escapes my snout, and I puff a breath of smoke through my nostrils. Tranquility pours through me under his intense light green gaze. Bowing forward, I bow my long neck and get at his eye level. My red and orange scales glimmer with a pearlescent sheen, reflecting to me from his glassy gaze.

"Allow me to introduce you to Tiernan." Theo motions at his twin with a smile. "May he approach? We both want to get a better look at our beautiful mate." We? I knew clans claimed females to share, but the idea of this other guy—Tiernan? No. Something's not right.

I whimper, wishing with everything that my body will let me transform back into my human form. "I—I don't want him to." My soft voice trickles through my mind.

Theo raises his palm to his brother. "She isn't ready."

"And she won't be until I complete their union," Ambrose says, raising his chin.

I growl at him, baring my fangs.

"Easy now, firecracker. He's right. You won't feel better until he does." Theo raises his hands and rests his warm palms under my chin, gently cradling my big head. "You won't feel as you should. Like me. Praise the fates. I've never felt so complete. Your clan will be thrilled that we've finally found you after all this time. Rhett stayed true to his word."

My heart stalls at the sound of Rhett's name. Theo's comment catches up to me as a dozen thoughts blast through my mind. I stand and swing my body around, whipping my tail across a building. If I don't fight my dragon's control over my humanity, I might lose myself completely. I could jeopardize the life I want with the Drekis—with my true mates.

Thunder booms overhead, startling me, and I stretch my wings out, my body craving to launch from the ground. I imagine jumping up and taking flight. I imagine it to be as easy as breathing, yet my dragon refuses to cooperate. I can't do it. The battle inside me grows too intense.

"Brother, watch out!" Tiernan hollers, summoning an orb of crackling, dancing flames.

Kash's familiar screech rings through the air above us, sending my heart into overdrive. Lifting my head, I catch sight of his magnificent dragon form, gold and green, glittering even without being drenched in sunlight. He swoops down, nosediving so fast that his form blurs. Slowing as he gets closer to the ground, Kash spreads his huge wings. Maddox drops from his claws and lands in a crouch only a few feet away.

"Get away from our mate, asshole," Maddox snaps, unsheathing a gleaming sword from a strap on his back. Where did he get the weapon? I wonder if he beat up Quillon for it. "Five seconds before you lose your head. Delphia is ours."

Theo releases a guttural sound from deep in his throat. Spinning on his feet, he summons a basketball-sized amount of dragon fire. He draws his hands back to chuck it, and I knock my snout into his back, sending him reeling.

"Don't touch him!" My dragon's roar echoes through the night, louder than the noise of Kash's booming wings as he circles above or the growls and popping flames as Maddox and Rowan prepare to go to battle against the Darkonians in my honor.

"Ambrose, do something!" Tiernan shouts at the warlock, waving his hand. He gathers his own power, unveiling black glittering scales across his arms. "Something is wrong. Delphia shouldn't protect that asshole. She should protect Theo. What did you do?"

"Nothing. They've bonded as they should've. I can see it in the linking of their souls," Ambrose says, gathering magical light in his palms. He throws it into the air, sending power raining on us, the sensation like a cool breath against my scales. "But I can also see she's bonded to the Drekis. The soul link shines just as brightly, if not more."

"What? Impossible! She belongs to our clan," Theo says, his voice rising in astonishment. He tries to dodge out of Maddox's way, but he can't move fast enough.

And then Kash blows a breath of fire from above, keeping him down. My heartstrings seemingly pull in too many directions. Dizziness blurs my vision, and I fall in my dragon form, hitting the magic shield the warlock creates. Fire explodes from my mouth, the shock of magic smoldering across my scales. Rowan punches Ambrose and rushes to me.

"Transform, Nova. You have to transform. We have to go," he says, rubbing his hands on my neck. "The High Council will show at any second."

I concentrate on his quiet pleas, savoring the sensation of his hands stroking my scales, trying to calm me down enough to focus. My humanity finally breaks free of my dragon, reeling her back in to cage her away. Shadows edge my vision, and I thunk on the concrete, curling in on myself. Tears blur my eyes as I heave a few breaths, my emotions whirring out of control.

A yell cuts through the air, dragging my focus from my quivering body to where Maddox punches Theo in the throat, stealing his breath. The man stumbles back, crashing to the ground. Lifting his sword, Maddox aims it, readying himself for the death blow.

"She is ours!" he yells, fire escaping his hands to light the sword aglow.

I clutch my chest, my heart ricocheting around my rib-cage. "Maddox, stop! Stop!" My voice screams through the air. "Don't kill him! Please!"

Maddox jerks his attention to me. "He'll try to take you from us, Delphia. I can't let that happen."

I shove my hands to the asphalt, scraping my palms. "Please, Maddox. I can't explain it, but if you kill him...I feel as if I'll die with him. I'm...he's...fuck, I think he's my mate too. I can feel it just like with you. And Rowan and Kash. So please. Don't do this."

Maddox stiffens at my words, slowly lowering his sword. "I don't understand. If—"

A bright blue light splits the sky open above us, cutting off his words. I jerk my attention to the portal, fear and shock consuming me. Fuck. Fuck. Fuck. I'd recognize the impending arrival from anywhere. They've found us. This is it.

Kash lands before me, shaking the ground. He prepares to fight in his dragon form. "Get her out of here, brothers. I'll hold them off."

"What? No. If you fight, I fight. I won't leave you," I say, jogging forward to touch his tail.

Green electricity erupts from beside me, cascading into

the sky like a brilliant firework. It pops and crackles, raining magic over us.

"Everyone, grab the dragon!" Ambrose yells. "Vot tu levia eht og shivomiotos!"

My stomach twists and turns, and I bow forward and clutch onto Kash. Green light blinds me, and the only reason I don't panic is because a collection of rich, soft voices trickles into my mind.

"Almost there, Delphia. Don't worry. We won't let anything happen to you. Just hang tight," Theo says, sending a wave of certainty with his words. I can't help but believe him. It's the strangest thing. With the Drekis, I questioned the possibility. I knew I felt a connection to them and our bond over the last few weeks has grown, but this sudden awareness of the intense connection with a man I've never met? What. The. Actual. Fuck. It's magic. Unreal.

The world slows and the light blinding me finally fades. I heave, my stomach clenching and threatening to expel my lunch. Tears burn in my vision, and I clutch onto Kash's back leg like my life depends on it.

A cool breeze plays with my hair, drawing the strands from my back. Quiet settles through the area around me, and I keep my eyes squeezed closed. I can feel the intense stares of everyone burning into my back, and I'm not sure how I'll peel myself away from Kash to face this confusing as hell situation.

"Ambrose, it's my turn to bond with my mate. Set our fates in motion." The gruff voice of Tiernan prods at my mind, sounding similar to Theo's yet hoarser, colder.

I jerk my head up and finally gather my bearings. "Hold the fuck on. If you so much as twitch your damn finger, I will transform into a dragon and bite it off."

"But Delphia. You must accept Tiernan, too." Theo strides around Kash's hulking dragon body only to have Maddox step in his way.

"She doesn't have to accept anyone," Maddox snaps, clenching his fingers into fists.

Two hot hands grab my shoulders as Rowan pulls me into his taut chest. He slips his big shirt over my head, covering my naked body. "You can reject him and the fates."

"Delphia, please. Don't. You're my mate. Let me prove my worth to you. I can protect you. Look how we saved you." Damn him. For being a giant, tatted, tough-looking man with a cock piercing, Theo sure sounds like he'd also be one helluva cuddler. He also sounds as if I'll break his heart at any second.

Rowan tightens his arms around me. "Nova—"

I scream and bow forward, agony crashing through me. Squeezing my eyes shut, I clutch my head, my brain pounding. I can't think, let alone make any sort of decisions in this moment. I can't do anything. Something's terribly wrong.

"Fuck! Someone is trying to summon her," Ambrose shouts. "Grab her. Don't let her go."

I screech again, feeling as if my insides are being ripped out.

Green light crackles as Ambrose summons power. "Where is your shield? Who's been protecting you?"

"No one," Maddox says, his words sharp. "We're not allied to any coven."

"What?" Ambrose asks.

I don't get the chance to hear anyone respond.

The world disappears.

The Darkonians

AM I DEAD?

I can't be dead, right? Death is supposed to be followed by rainbows and mansions, clouds of cotton candy and unicorns that shit glitter that cleans up itself. It shouldn't be like I feel now, alone and hot, sweaty and in the dark—fuck. Am I in hell? The pits at Max? Where are my mates? Where am I?

Ice water engulfs me, ripping me from the darkness. I

flail my arms, my whole body tensing in shock from the sudden change in my temperature. Someone hoists me up, and the world spins until my bare feet touch the soft grass. My knees give out on me, sending me to my stomach. I gasp and spit the cool water from my mouth. It tastes weird as hell, salty like the ocean but with a hint of something smoky.

A towel drops onto me, covering my body like a small blanket, and I shiver and roll to my back. Kash's big dragon head hovers a few feet above me. Stretching up my arms, I wait for him to lower his head, and I kiss him on his chin.

"Where are we? What happened?" I think the words instead of saying them out loud. My eyes blur, and I can't get a good look around to see if it's safe to speak without someone overhearing.

"We're at home," Kash responds, resting his head on the grass next to me. He huffs and shifts closer, engulfing me with his cinnamon scent and something else warm and delicious, like the summer sun heating his skin on a hot day. "You couldn't go inside because your dragon fire keeps scorching everything. But don't worry. You're safe. I'm not letting anything happen to you. None of those bastards will get within a foot of you without risking my wrath."

Protective is so sexy on him, even as a dragon. It makes my body crave to take on whatever form we have to as long as it means we can be together in the way we desire.

A smile stretches the corners of my mouth as I think of the excitement and adventure that could awaken my soul in this moment, bringing me the peace and satisfaction I need after the shitshow of the night.

I reach out and run the back of my knuckles across his golden green scales, my bond to him drawing me to touch him. "Can you transform?" This time, I say the words aloud, testing my voice. My throat aches a bit, feeling scratchy from yelling, but at least I can speak.

Kash puffs a breath of smoke from his nostrils. "That's up to Quillon. He's a scared little dickhead at the moment, sleeping in my shadow. The last thing he expected was us to arrive with the dragon clan he stiffed by agreeing to help us and without a murderous fairy princess to protect him."

My mind whirls with a dozen thoughts. Because fuck. The Darkonians slipped from my mind. So did Rose. I try not to think about her setting me up and how I couldn't control my anger and—I shove thoughts of her as hard as I can out of my mind and focus on the ones with us now. "Ah, hell. Where are they? Where are your brothers? How long has it been? What—"

Kash surprises me by licking my whole face, knocking me onto my back. "You have no idea how badly I want to kiss those quivering lips of yours to shut you up, so I can have a chance to answer."

Now that he mentions it, I desperately want that too.

"We have a bit of time to rectify that. The Darkonians and their warlock are currently scouting the area and adding extra shields to keep the High Council from finding us. Maddox is destroying everything he comes in contact with, needing to get out his aggression before he murders someone, and Rowan is keeping watch from the rooftop." Kash pushes his long nails into the grass, pushing up. "And like I said, Quillon is being his cowardly self in my shadow."

I spot Quillon sleeping in a ball in his lycan form on the other side of Kash's huge body. Anger rushes through me at just the sight of him, and I shift onto my hands and knees and crawl under Kash's belly to confront the bastard. There is something utterly satisfying about knowing he's terrified enough to have to sleep right next to his temporary guardian, but he's about to get a real fucking wakeup call.

A rumble of a breath escapes Quillon's hairy muzzle, his snores sounding like an old dog instead of the annoying beast he is. Fisting my hand, I punch him on his hip, startling him awake. He flails, exposing his groin to me, and I whack my open palm right where his cock should be under the mass of matted hair.

I feel absolutely nothing, not even a teensy nubbin lump. I knew with his transformation that I couldn't see his manhood, especially because he's smaller than my guys, but I still kind of expected something. Feeling for certain that his dick definitely vanishes somehow pleases me on a different level. Instead of scared shitless, he's scared dickless. No wonder he acts like such an asshole all the time. He has angry no-inch syndrome. No fun in the beast form he prefers.

Swinging my hand again, I whack him on his snout. "Hey, dickless. Wake up."

Quillon roars and flashes his fangs. His good senses must return to him real quick, because he stops short of raising his hand to hit me back. "What the actual fuck, Red? What do you want?"

I whack him on the top of his head next. "Release Kash. Now."

Quillon snaps at me but doesn't try to bite. "Give me a second to grow my dick back. Then we'll discuss what I want in return."

Fisting my hand, I prepare to punch him. "Oh-fucking-no. You better not be suggesting—"

With a shake of his big head, Quillon sheds his hair and morphs back into his human form. I growl and prepare to sock him in the nuts, but he's quick to grab my hand. Kash growls and shifts his big head to peer at us, blowing smoke from his nose. His eyes flash with fire, and I know he's fighting Quillon's control over him. I can feel his anxiety of not being able to hurt Quillon coursing through him.

"Cool your fire, Nova. I'm only transforming. You need to stop looking at me like a disgusting piece of shit." He jerks his arm, throwing my hand away from him hard enough to leave my shoulder aching from the gesture. "If I wanted your hand on my cock, it wouldn't be because I coerced you. I've learned my lesson with you. I'd prefer you to beg me for it. I want to see you kneeling before me, getting rug burn on your knees, while I fuck those pouty lips of yours."

I scowl and shove him, pushing to my feet. "You're a psycho."

He leers. "You think I'm the psycho? Look at the fuckers you've—"

Kash releases a deep, threatening rumble from his throat. Quillon clenches his jaw, hops to his feet, and has the audacity to smack Kash on his nose. The two of them stare at each other in silent conversation. Quillon's able to communicate telepathically with Kash because he vowed to serve him. Just watching them pisses me off. I nearly summon fire to burn Quillon's eyebrows off once again. This time, I'll take care of his hairy ass crack with a complimentary man-scaping from my dragon.

I don't get a chance to give him a courtesy hair removal because Kash transforms into his sexy man form. All my thoughts of revenge vanish, and I rush and hop into his arms, kissing him like Quillon isn't standing beside us, glaring.

"I'll give you two twenty damn minutes, understand? Consider it an advance for keeping the damn Darkonians away from me," Quillon says. I don't know what Kash said to change his mind, but I'm not going to question it. I'm not going to waste a single minute either.

"Hurry and carry me somewhere," I murmur through a kiss. Combing my fingers through Kash's dark hair, I play with the soft tresses and work my way down to his muscular shoulders. "He'll watch if we don't."

Kash moans his agreement and jogs toward the front of the house. He doesn't have a room here, the thought pissing me off more than ever. Quillon makes him sleep outside in his dragon form or on the floor at the end of his bed like a damn pet. I share a room with everyone, but I don't want to waste time going into one.

We don't make it farther than the half-bath just off the foyer. Kash kicks the door closed and blindly locks it. Setting me on the counter, he leans in and molds his lips to mine, slipping his tongue into my mouth to savor the taste of our kiss. I draw my hands around his sides, pulling his naked body closer. All I wear is Rowan's dirty, wet, charred shirt he gave me outside the bar.

Kash links his fingers to the front and rips the fabric right down the middle, exposing my body to him. He breaks from our kiss and leans down to suck my tight nipples into his mouth, sending an explosion of pleasure to each of my breasts. His big, warm palms rest on my legs, and he bends my knees, so my feet rest on the counter. Dropping to the floor in front of me, he holds my legs, keeping my body wide open for him as he draws his tongue along the seam of my body to my clit. I moan and arch back, not even caring if I bang my head on the mirror above the sink. Kash sucks and licks my body like he's starved for me, addicted, and just can't get enough.

I comb my desperate fingers through his hair, squirming and moving my hips under the quick strokes of his tongue. His passion fills me up with everything I've been missing since he bowed before Quillon. We haven't had a single moment of intimacy since arriving at this fuck-forsaken house, and I knew I missed our connection and bonding on the level our souls crave, but I had no idea how much I'd still ache, even in his arms.

My body buzzes with lust and a deep-seated need only Kash can quench. He hums under his breath in enjoyment, picking up the pace of his tongue while adding pressure with his finger by slipping it inside me, feeling exactly what he does to me. Tingles build between my legs, and I arch my back with my orgasm, the intensity rippling through me in a wave of spasms that practically paralyze me with pleasure, every muscle in my body tightening at once.

Getting back to his feet, Kash doesn't give me a moment to catch my breath and aligns his body with mine, his thick, intimidating cock throbbing and flexing with need to sink into me. Our wild instincts as dragons take control, and I gasp with the pressure of him pushing into me as my body adjusts to welcome him in. Every nerve-ending inside me explodes and sizzles with ecstasy. Kash repositions my legs into the splits, and my toes touch opposing walls on each side of the counter. I clench my body, using the walls to hold myself in place, my calves screaming in the good ache of my flexibility while my hips open for him completely.

He moans with his deep thrusts, swinging his body back and forth in a fast pace that leaves me panting and gasping each time he sinks into me. I bite my lip, trying to stifle my mouth, begging to scream out my pleasure. I'm so turned on, watching him bang the hell out of me in such a way I'm sure I'll walk funny after. But I don't care. Any ache caused by our passion is the best kind. I need it, crave it, yearn to feel it imprint in my memory to savor long after we're through. I want to get wet just thinking about this moment over and over again. How sexy Kash looks and how his eyes light with dragon fire. How his tattoos come to life and dance with his flexing muscles.

Releasing a sexy, throaty noise, Kash reaches down to my exposed clit and rubs his thumb over it while digging his fingers into the soft flesh of my thigh. A loud-ass moan escapes me, echoing through the small bathroom. Another round of intense explosions shoot through me, and I scream out in ecstasy and loosen my footing, the only thing stabilizing me in place. My head and shoulders slam into the mirror, cracking the glass. Kash leans forward and nestles his big hand to the back of my head to protect me through his last few deep, mind-blowing thrusts.

He grunts with his release, pulling me close until I wrap my body around his. He swivels and takes my spot with me straddling his lap. Snuggling close, he breathes in the scent of my hair, cuddling me in silence as we both catch our breaths.

"Fates, I missed you, kitten," Kash murmurs, brushing his lips to the sensitive skin beneath my ear. "Not being able to shift into the form you prefer has been torture, especially tonight."

I sigh against his shoulder, tilting my head slightly. "I want to kill him. Every second of every day he controls you makes me want to be the criminal the High Council accuses me of."

"It won't be like this forever. We'll get a cure for that asshole and drop him off in the middle of nowhere." Kash grazes his fingers to my jaw, getting me to ease away enough to kiss him again.

"But what if we can't? We don't even know what the hell is going on with..." My heart races as the Darkonians flit through my mind.

"We'll figure it out. I don't know who fucked up and promised them you, who can't possibly belong to them, as a mate, but I'm sure as shit not going to let them take you. I don't care if you bond—"

"Time's up, Dreki. I need your protection. The ass-holes just arrived." Quillon bangs on the door, interrupting our conversation. "If Red hasn't gotten you off by now, I'm going to have to reconsider my future plans with her. I need a woman who can make me blow a load with—"

The whole house shakes with several guttural growls, including one vibrating from deep in Kash's chest. Quillon groans and bangs harder on the door. Kash stands up and eases me off his still throbbing body and stomps to the door and flings it open. Locking his fingers to Quillon's shoulder, he drags him into the bathroom with us, slaps his palm over his eyes to block his view of me, and cages him against the wall. Fire smolders across the floor where Quillon was standing, leaving black scorch marks behind.

"Did he just protect that piece of shit lycan after what he said about our mate?" Theo's smooth voice laces with molten anger. I can't see him, but I can feel him. His unwarranted anger toward Kash's action gets under my skin.

Kash growls and presses his palm to Quillon's chest, smashing the breath from him, stopping him from speaking. "You have it wrong. I'm not protecting him. I'm protecting Nova and myself. He will learn that a mate's purpose isn't to pleasure him."

"A mate always comes first. In pleasure, in life, and in a clan," Tiernan says, his voice growing louder. His footsteps thud closer as he approaches the closed bathroom door. His legs block some of the light from the foyer, and he taps his finger to the wood. "As Prince of the Darkonian Territory and the Mountain Lands, I insist you punish the lycan accordingly. Delphia will not be disgraced or regarded in such a manner. Ambrose, kill the lycan and be done with him. I will not stand by and do nothing. She will know I am worthy unlike the forsaken one."

My eyes widen at his words, and I rush toward the bathroom door, seeing the glow of green magic. Flinging it open, I glower and raise my hands up, palms out, and guard the doorway protectively. I hate the fact that I'm doing so, because I want Quillon dead, but I'll fight these intruding, overbearing fuckers and their strange claims about me to protect Kash.

"Don't you fucking listen to his command, warlock," I snap, steeling myself under the sudden scrutiny. "If you even try to kill Quillon, I will bite your head off."

A low whistle cuts through the air, drawing my attention to Theo. My damn eyes. They automatically shoot my gaze down to the man's hardening cock, still winking at me with the sparkling jewelry. The metallic ring loops from his tip and disappears underneath, intriguing the hell out of me. If I wasn't half pissed and half scared out of my mind that the warlock won't listen, I might give in to my curiosity and creep closer for a better look.

Maddox tosses his big shirt at me, covering my face and blocking my view of Theo and his captivating nudity. I can't feel his emotions, but he obviously doesn't like the bold attention I give and can't seem to control. "No one is killing the bastard criminal. My brother bowed to him as his guardian to get access to the Mortal World. He will get what is coming to him in due time once his debt is paid."

"And now that his magical assistant is gone, he will be more complacent," Rowan adds, his voice remaining even despite the slight frown crossing his mouth at the reminder that I scorched her. I guess I am a real killer after all. My dragon thirsts for revenge and will get it however she wants.

If only I didn't feel the guilt of knowing what I've

done.

"Delphia will appreciate his sacrifice to be rid of the treacherous, untrustworthy, cursed mortal." Theo motions to Ambrose, a dark look flickering across his face. "Continue on. The lycan will pay for his crimes against our clan. I cannot bear to have him around."

Oh. Fucking. No.

Maddox swings his glowing fist, clocking Theo in the jaw and sending him skidding across the foyer and into the wall. Charging forward, Rowan tackles Tiernan and restrains him in a choke hold on the ground. My guys obviously outmatch these supposed twin princes in strength and skill. One of the perks of dealing with the vilest criminals of Magaelorum is kicking serious ass.

"Please move, Delphia," Ambrose says, gathering his green electric power in his hands. Our eyes meet for the first time, and I search his silvery depths. The brightness of his irises really pop against the umber creaminess of his skin, darker than the Darkonian's, softer looking too.

I thrash my head, sending my hair sweeping back and forth. "No. You'll have to fight me."

Ambrose smooths the short, tight curls of his bleached blond hair, nearly silver like his eyes. "The price of using magic against you isn't worth it. It is my duty as the Darkonians' guard to follow orders and keep you safe. Allowing the criminal, who prevented us from finding you and taking you from that vile prison to fulfill your duty as a Drakovich, needs to pay for his crimes. You must accept that CO Dreki should've never bartered with a Cursed One."

Is he fucking for real?

I don't wait to find out.

Throwing Maddox's shirt at Ambrose's face, I surprise him long enough to slam and lock the bathroom door. A bright flash of green light erupts in my vision, and I shove my back into Kash, sandwiching him to Quillon. Fire explodes in my palms, and I release a scary-ass growl from my throat. My skin shimmers with my red pearlescent scales, my dragon begging to break free to destroy this house.

"Stay back!" I shout, throwing my dragon fire at his feet. "I mean it, you fucking bastard. Don't test me."

The door flies off its hinges, and Maddox and Theo crash into the small bathroom together, throwing punches. I tense and hold my hands up protectively as Theo's body stumbles toward me as he falls back. Maddox snatches Theo's wrist and swings him at the wall, punching him in the gut. Kash reaches over his shoulder and attempts to grab me to get me to move. I hunch lower out of his reach. There is no fucking way I'm going to risk the bastard warlock getting an opening to hurt my mate.

"Control your possessive assholes before they burn the

whole place down," Quillon snaps from his spot, hidden like a coward behind the wall of muscle Kash creates that should be mine. "Come on, Red. Threaten to reject all of them if they don't chill out and leave me alone."

I really fucking hate that I know Quillon's idea will work. The smug fucker doesn't need that kind of satisfaction, but damn it. I can't bear the thought of something worse happening to Kash. His servitude to Quillon is bad enough.

Clenching my teeth, I get over my pride and chuck my dragon fire at the wall in front of Maddox and where Theo growls, pinned in place. "Enough! Theo, call your damn guard off. If he so much as messes up Kash's hair, I will reject you and any possible bond or whatever you've cursed me with."

"Do it already, Delphia. We can't humor even another second of his supposed claim. He's not your true mate. The fates—they've been tampered with." Maddox's broad chest rises and falls with his angry breaths. "It's impossible for your soul to bond to two different clans."

"Obviously not impossible," Quillon mutters from behind me. "But that's what your parents get for fighting and fucking up the fates."

Theo flares his nostrils, fire lighting his eyes. Maddox looks just as furious. The scar on his cheek glows with his dragon fire, and if I didn't know any better, I'd think he and Theo would team up to tear Quillon apart.

"Ambrose, I've heard enough!" Theo shouts, once again ignoring my threats. For acting all nice to my dragon, this guy is a real fucking dick. How dare he think he gets a right to decide who is punished on my behalf. "End him!"

Oh-fucking-no.

Hell no.

I prepare for the fight of my life. I brace for this asshole warlock to ruin everything. "Do it, and you won't make it out of here alive. Kash is mine."

Forced Bond

"DELPHIA, NO!" THEO LOCKS HIS hands to Ambrose's shoulders, yanking the warlock out of the line of my wrath.

Straightening his back, he blocks his guardian from me. And it's weird as hell. I thought Ambrose was the guy supposed to protect these muscle-man hot-heads and not the other way around. The warlock suddenly looks defenseless and weak in Theo's shadow.

But I can't disregard him. He's the biggest threat of all of them.

"Ambrose, I've changed my mind," Theo adds, staring down at his guard. "I'm not willing to risk my beautiful Delphia rejecting me, nor will I put her through the torment of a severed bond to her mate. I can feel her on every level. It's unlike anything I've ever experienced." This guy is going to give me whiplash worse than Maddox. At least with Maddox, he's an asshole even when he's nice. I don't think I can handle Theo's unpredictability.

"I want him out of here or I can't guarantee I won't kill his magical ass," I mutter, clenching my fingers into my palms.

"Please, firecracker. Don't misplace your anger. Ambrose does what he's told. If you feel the need to punish someone, I'll accept the consequences of your wrath. I'm tough and willing to prove it." Theo's serious face lightens with a twinge of a smile. It's like he wants my punishment and dares me to do my worst.

It intrigues me and pisses me off, like he disregards my capabilities.

"That's...not necessary," I say, unable to shift my gaze away.

I remain firm in my spot, studying Theo. His biceps bulge with his hardy muscles, and I drink in the sight of him still standing naked before me like this is the most normal thing in the world. His cock awakens under my scrutiny once again, and I finally snap out of my pervy inspection and flick my gaze to peek at Maddox. I expect fire to spew from his glowering face. I expect him to get between Theo and me. But he stays in his spot, not intervening as I memorize every inch of Theo's body. None of my mates do, remaining even-tempered and without the jealousy I expect with their protective attitudes.

"Would you like to touch me, Delphia? It is customary for mates to explore each other's bodies after a binding ceremony. I would be enchanted if you allowed me the honor." The thrill of his words sends desire rushing between my legs. All I can think about is getting close and personal with his cock bling.

What a sneaky, greedy bitch my vagina is. I'm more than fulfilled and taken care of by my mates. I shouldn't want to know what fucking Theo is like.

I blink my eyes and shake my head, shifting my gaze once more to Maddox, knowing he would be the one to react first.

He doesn't. His jaw doesn't even twitch and none of his veins bulge like he's keeping himself in check.

Honestly, it's really fucking weird.

Quillon groans from behind me, stopping my silent interrogation of what Maddox might be thinking and locking away from me. "All right. If we're all cool here, I'd like to head to my damn room before you all start boning Red and not letting me participate."

Oh. My. Fuck. This asshole.

"And when you're done, Red, meet me in my quarters. You still need to earn Kash's time. I had a few things in mind to make up for the shit you pulled with me before. Try not to exhaust yourself and remember to stretch." Quillon slides out from behind Kash, acting like his life wasn't just on the line. "Wear something skimpy. Your choice this time. I like my entertainment in lace."

Maddox snatches Quillon before Theo tries anything, hanging him a foot off the floor by his neck. Releasing a loud roar, Maddox shouts in Quillon's face, freaking the bastard out enough that he shifts into a lycan. "Nova will not be visiting your room tonight or ever again. Your power over her is over. Do you understand?"

"She will if she wants more time with your brother. Of course, now that she's expanding her dragon-sized cock collection…" Quillon lets his words trail off and glances at Kash. "Get outside. Remember where you stand with Red and if she'll choose to work for your freedom unlike last time. I'd be worried. It seems the competition around here grows fierce."

Maddox shakes Quillon until he returns to his human form and his voice stops sounding like a creepy, wet, guttural slur of words. "This is not, and will never be, a fucking competition. You will not try to get into Delphia's head and make her question our bonds to her. If you do—"

Kash comes up behind Maddox and touches his shoulders, getting him to drop Quillon. "Brother, it's okay. Nova knows I'd never doubt her bond to me. She also knows I don't expect her to work for even a minute of my freedom. I trust you will take care of her as you should."

I open and close my mouth, my brows puckering. I hate this. I hate everything about this. He can't even fight for his freedom. "Kash—"

"No need to say anything, kitten." Kash picks up Quillon off the floor, now silent and smart enough not to speak.

The bathroom turns awfully claustrophobic with everyone's emotions running hot and feral. I spot Rowan in the foyer with Tiernan. Neither of them speak or react or even try to intervene.

Kash shoves Quillon toward the door and away from the others. Turning back to me, he holds his arms open and waits for me to step into his embrace. He kisses me softly, just caressing his lips to mine. "I meant what I said. I don't want you working for my freedom, okay? Whatever that asshole has in mind isn't worth it."

But it is worth it to me. I can't stand the thought of Kash transforming into his dragon so soon. I haven't even had a chance to process any of this, and I need him to stay.

"We'll ensure she is taken care of, brother," Maddox says, speaking up.

He gives me a look like I better not fucking protest, but damn it. How am I supposed to just sit back and not do anything? I doubt Quillon would ask me to fuck him, at least, not with my mates on the verge of burning this hell-hole down.

I get my shit together, so no one sees how badly it gets under my skin. Straightening my shoulders and ignoring the fact that I stand here as naked as most of them do, I summon as much authority as I can. "I'm going to walk him out."

Maddox tries to grab my hand, automatically wanting to test my resolve. "Cookie, that's not—"

I jerk away and glower, crossing my arms. I don't mean to react as I do, but I'm still so angry over the situation, over the uncertainty. I hate not knowing what's truly going on with my life and what happens next. At least if I walk Kash out, I can try to process. I can take advantage of not burning under everyone's need to make clear that my soul pulls in every which way and no one's willing to let go of their share.

"I'm walking him out," I repeat, tightening my mouth and hiding my lips. "You will give me a moment."

Fire flashes in Maddox's eyes, and Rowan sweeps his gaze over me, his brows furrowing like he hates the idea of me even being a couple feet away from him. I shake my head in warning, both Maddox and Rowan's intense need to follow us nearly pushing me to agree. But I just need a breath of fresh air, untainted by the angry smoke of dragons. My body still yearns for more time with Kash as I feel deprived of his company and affection. How that affects his brothers? I have no idea. If they're jealous that I'm overprotective of Kash, they don't show it. I can feel everyone's gazes on my back, though. A dozen questions linger unsaid in the air.

If only I had the answers. I don't even know what the hell is going on or what questions I should ask and try to solve first.

Kash rests his warm hand to the small of my back, guiding me the short distance to the driveway. Rowan hovers near the door, watching us, and I pull Kash toward the shadows of the house and out of everyone's view before they all start crowding the foyer.

Kash touches my cheek, swiping the hair from my face. "Nova, I know this situation isn't ideal, but we'll get through it."

"It's weird as hell. Maddox isn't actively trying to pummel the Darkonians. I don't like it. It's not like him," I whisper, standing on my tippy toes. "Do you think the warlock spelled him or something?" I don't know why the thought crosses my mind now, but I can't help it. I mean, the warlock had cast some spell, awakening something in me that shouldn't be possible. He basically rewrote the stars to align my fate with someone not intended for me. I just want some answers.

"You should talk to him yourself, kitten. We haven't had time to discuss anything, but I trust my brother with our lives. I hope you do, too." He kisses my forehead and tries to ease away.

I grip him tighter and crash my mouth to him, my soul screaming to make him hold on a minute more. Fire lights his hazel eyes, and his gilded scales ripple across his skin. He struggles to remain in this form already.

"I do," I whisper. "I just...fight a little longer for me?"

He sighs. "I'll fight forever."

I kiss him once more. "I will too."

Kash eases away from me, his dragon waiting to burst free. I hug myself, watching him transform before me, turning into the magnificent creature that makes my heart sing. Bending down, Kash lowers his head to my eye level, and I kiss his snout. He flaps his wings, nearly knocking me off my feet. Warm arms catch me from behind, and I swivel and meet Maddox's golden gaze.

"Come on, cookie. Kash will be fine. He can better protect us like this anyway while Ambrose gets things ready. We can't stay here. It's no longer safe now that the High Council felt your magical residue." Maddox links our fingers together.

I smack him in the chest with my free hand. "You're out of your damn mind if you think I'd ever go with the Darkonians, Maddox. Who are you and what have you done with my sexy, asshole mate, who would never agree to accept aid from a clan intent on claiming me."

He raises an eyebrow, with fire flashing in his eyes. If I didn't know any better, I'd think he'd spank me for calling him out. "If you think I'm even remotely okay with this, you're wrong. I am only doing as you have requested and refraining from killing them and starting a war."

It's my turn to grimace. "You're doing this for me? Because of the bond?"

"I can't tell if you're being serious or not with you blocking me out." Maddox tilts his head and searches my eyes.

"I'm blocking you out?" I question, my nose scrunching.

He surprises me by smirking and leaning closer, his

cinnamon breath warming the skin below my ear. "As you should right now. I don't want the Darkonians to use that against us if you unintentionally spill your thoughts and any secrets we want to keep. My sole intent is to only accept their help to keep you safe. I don't want to bond with them."

My eyes widen as realization sinks in. "And what about me?"

"Fuck no. I'd be lying if I told you otherwise, but I also know that it is what it is. You're mine, Delphia. You're a Dreki and our intended. I don't give a lycan's ass that these fuckers were misinformed by the fates, but it doesn't mean we can't use this to our benefit. Perhaps you can get them to do something about Kash's deal. The warlock can help us with a cure."

"So you're not okay with them coming in here and trying to stake their claim on me." It's not a question. I can feel it in my bones. "Yet you're okay with me working them to get what we need."

He shrugs. "That's up to you, cookie. I won't stop you either way. Just be prepared for a constant reminder of who your true mates are."

I lean away from him and tilt my head back to meet his fiery gaze. "I had no idea you had a criminal streak in you, Maddox. Look at you turning into a lawbreaker. Asking me to coerce the Darkonians. Tease a warlock."

He smirks. "Don't think that will stop me from wanting to punish your naughty ass for tonight. Your constant curiosity over these assholes drives me wild. Makes me want to try harder to keep your attention on me. When I see you checking out the royal cocks..." He growls and tightens his hold on me. "I want to pin you down and fuck you until you only look at them and think of me."

Heat floods my face at his remark. "Or maybe you should bedazzle your dick instead."

"They've only done so because they want you to be easily persuaded by cock." He chuckles at his own comment, his voice light and musical, so different than what I'm used to. It's like he knows what I need in this moment and gives it to me. "I don't need any help with that. Plus, you're already a huge pain in my cock half the time. There is no need to add to it."

"I should kiss it right now and make it feel better, huh?" I tease, reaching between us to playfully stroke my hand over his hardening erection.

"Don't test me, cookie. You're hard enough to resist as it is, especially smelling the excitement my brother aroused in you." He reaches around to my ass and swats me.

I stroke his cock faster, loving seeing the flames light his eyes with his desire. "But messing with you is my favorite pastime."

He spins me around so quickly that I don't have a chance to brace myself as he spanks my ass, reminding me that I'm still naked and exposed. "And punishing you for being a bad girl is mine."

Maddox tries to swat me again, and I run toward the house, my heart feeling lighter now that I know Maddox isn't just going to comply with the Darkonians, even in this weird situation. And maybe he's right. We can use them to help Kash. They can also get the High Council to overturn my conviction.

"You better hurry, cookie. You teased my dragon too much. If I catch you, I will bend you over and have my way, and right now, we have other things to worry about. Don't be the cause of my weakness," Maddox says, running even faster.

"You can only blame yourself," I call over my shoulder.

I dash away from him, pushing my legs to run me as fast as I can. Rowan waits in the foyer and throws a fireball at Maddox, sending him crashing into a decorative table. He growls and shoves it, getting back to his feet just as I reach the door to his room, fully intent on teasing him for the rest of the night to distract myself from everything else.

A yell sounds over my giggling laughter, and I freeze in my tracks and spin toward Rowan. "Where are the Royal

Dicks?" I ask, fear clenching my chest.

"They followed you out," Rowan says, glancing at Maddox.

Another yell rips through the air, stealing my breath. It's Quillon.

I scream and run toward his room, my mind spinning in panic. The floor shakes, and a glass shatters from the living room as something breaks. I don't even have to look to know that Kash fell off the roof in his dragon form.

"Nova, wait!" Maddox and Rowan yell in unison. "Let us go first," Maddox adds.

But I can't stop.

Yanking the door open, I stand in shock, horror, and disbelief.

Blood stains the floor, streaming around the room in a magical current.

I can't do anything as Ambrose stabs Quillon through his heart.

Clan Battles

"NO!" I SCREAM, GATHERING DRAGON fire between my palms. "Stop!"

A hulking body crashes into me, knocking me off my feet. My fire smolders across the tiles and scorches the wall. I gasp, my breath escaping me from the force of the crushing weight on top of me. Hot fingers lace around the back of my neck, pinning me down. Bucking my body, I try to break free of the hold of...Tiernan. Theo continues to restrain Quillon as his deep ruby blood gushes from his lycan body.

"Delphia, calm down. He gave us his permission to use his connection to Magaelorum to create a portal home," Tiernan says, his smoky, sweet breath caressing my skin. It reminds me of roasting marshmallows, like burning sugar, and something else. "We've offered him the power he couldn't refuse."

"Liar! Get off me, you fuckhead! He's killing him!" I try to jerk my head back to head-butt him, but he's too strong. It feels like my self-defense training from when I was younger and the intense combat skills Maddox has been teaching me the last few weeks are worthless.

Tiernan shifts his weight, easing his hand from my neck only to shift it lower between my shoulder blades. "Ambrose is not, so calm down. He knows what he's doing."

"Release her, now!" Maddox's husky voice erupts through the room, his hulking frame seething in the doorway. "She said to get off, and you will respect my mate."

Tiernan digs his arm under my breasts and rolls with me, using me as a shield like the fucking asshole I should've known he'd be. Maddox looms over us, fire crawling up his arm while the scar on his cheek glows red. I grind my teeth, hating the feeling of Tiernan's hard body beneath me. With him, I still have my good senses. My soul doesn't scream to protect him, not like it had done with Theo.

I do the one thing I know will loosen his hold on me. I arch my hips up, curling into a half backbend and slam my ass down as hard as I can on the fucker's junk. I expect him to yowl in pain and throw me off. But he doesn't release me. He only groans and breathes in a breath of my hair.

And then his body retaliates by hardening against my ass crack, and I clench, stiffening. "You did not just get a boner from my body slamming your cock," I say, trying with everything in me not to move. If I move, I'll feel more.

Maddox roars, spewing smoke as his dragon partially breaks free. Grabbing onto my ankles, he jerks me away from Tiernan, hanging me upside down. My red hair cascades toward the floor, and my world blurs as Maddox spins.

"Fist your hand, cookie. This fucker needs to be put in his place," Maddox says.

I automatically do as he commands, my brain turning into mush. My body submits to his alpha nature. The world blurs even more, dizziness stealing my senses. My fists clock into the side of Tiernan's head and knock him off his feet and into the dresser.

Green light buzzes through the air, cutting off Maddox's roars of anger, his calls for punishment for the man who doesn't have my soul in a forced mate bond, born of magic and the damn asshole warlock.

"Grab Delphia and let's get the fuck out of here," Tiernan says, his voice echoing through the room. "We don't need the Drekis. They'll just get in the way. She should be our only concern."

It's now that my mind finally catches up with me. I realize Maddox has gone silent only because he's frozen, and I'm stuck upside down as he still clutches my feet. Ambrose used his power to stop my mate. And now...what the fuck. Did Tiernan just tell someone to grab me?

Two hot hands lock around my calves and pry my ankles from Maddox's frozen grip. I scream out and flail, trying to get enough momentum to flip out of Theo's hold and back on my feet. He nearly loses his grasp on me, but instead of dropping me, he catches me in his arms. Our eyes meet, and I stare into his green eyes, and my heart races, my whole body buzzing at his closeness.

"You don't have to be afraid, firecracker," he murmurs, rubbing his lips together. He loosens his arms only to wrap me in a different sort of embrace—not one born from control but of affection. "We're going to get you home and get this all figured out."

"Home." The word comes out so softly that I'm not even sure I say it out loud.

"Mmmhmm. You won't have to worry about any of this bullshit. You're royalty, Delphia. It pains me to know how you've been living with a Cursed One."

I tighten my mouth. "This is far fucking better than Max. Now, put me down and have your guard release my mate from his magic."

Tiernan moves into my peripheral vision, his unnerving likeness to Theo stabbing at my soul. I want to yell at him to get his imposter ass away from me, but Theo raises his palm and stops his twin in his tracks.

"Space, brother. She's upset with you," Theo says, rubbing his hand along my back. "You don't want to push her away."

"I don't give a shit. She's my mate too. How can I even try to bond if you won't even let me within a foot of her? I must make her see reason. You are already attached to her, and it'll cause us problems. You know what we were supposed to do. Get our princess and leave the Drekis. That's how this is to work. We can't take her home and surprise our clan with the fact that our intended has been claimed by others." Tiernan's voice lowers with his annoyance.

"I can take care of that," Ambrose says, his suggestion snapping me out of my haze of curiosity. "We can even finish the lycan off and use him as a sacrifice, so the cost doesn't fall onto you."

Oh. Fucking. Shit.

Taking a deep breath, I scream, startling all of them. Fire escapes my mouth, my dragon bursting free right in the bedroom. I slam through the ceiling, my enormous body filling the house. Panic whips through me, my anger giving my dragon control. Because there is no way I'm going to allow these assholes to think they can turn against my mates. It's like they only cooperated to gain enough of our trust to betray us. And I'm pissed. I'll eat the fucking warlock alive.

I thrash back and forth, sending debris raining around me. The hole widens enough to give me a view of the electric green light surrounding Ambrose. His wide eyes shine with fear, his shock so strong that I can smell the scent of his panic—like rainwater splattering on hot asphalt—and it ignites something wild in me.

Jerking my head down, I open my mouth, releasing a roar loud enough to startle Ambrose. His magic falters, and I prepare to bite his damn head off.

"Nova, don't!" Kash's voice booms through my mind. The realization that Tiernan wasn't lying explodes relief through me.

I don't get to enjoy it long.

Pain bursts on the back of my neck as Kash's huge fangs pinch me hard enough to yank me up and out of the roof. It caves in under the force of the wind from Kash's flapping wings, and I can't stop myself from releasing another screech, shooting more fire toward the warlock in my last-ditch effort to ensure he can't use magic against me.

The ground shakes under my weight as Kash flips me onto my back. He uses his clawed feet to pin my wings at my sides and bows down, stretching his neck to get in my face. Fire reflects in his eyes, and smoke billows from his nose. He doesn't speak to me telepathically and just remains silent, pleading with his entire soul for me to calm down. I feel it deep inside me, penetrating my anger to fill me with his love and tranquility, his level-headed reason.

"Hey, kitten," Kash finally says, his voice stroking my inner beast like a dragon tamer.

I puff another breath of smoke through my nostrils. "Those bastards lied to us. They have no desire to work with you as my mates. They were going to murder Quillon as a sacrifice." I feel like I'm tattling, but I don't know what else to do. I want Kash to get as riled up as Maddox and Rowan do. I want him to tear the rest of the roof off and gobble up the warlock before murdering the Darkonians. I want—

He snuggles his snout into my neck. "We're not killers, Nova. We have to think things through. If—"

I wiggle and cut him off, knowing how untrue his

words are about at least me. "But I am—"

A whistle shrieks through the air, cutting off my argument. Shadows move in my peripheral vision, but I can sense it's Rowan. Quillon too. He somehow managed to get to the lycan. I know it's Quillon because I sense Kash's soul swelling with anger. Stretching up, Kash launches into the air a dozen feet, sending a gust of his intoxicating scent over me.

Kash lands a couple yards away. The ground trembles under his weight, and the ear-shattering sound of the house collapsing bangs through the air. I dig my talons into the grass, pushing up. My heart feels as if it flees from my body. Maddox is still inside. He was frozen under Ambrose's magic, and he could very well die as the house implodes onto him.

"Maddox!" I yell, my voice echoing over the cacophonous noise. "Kash, get Maddox. Save him!"

"I'll get him, Nova," Rowan says, dusting off debris. "Ambrose is busy protecting his incantation and the Darkonians that he's safe by default. It's how I got to Quillon. But don't worry. I'll get him. Just transform and watch our backs. This could've broken a protection spell." Rowan rushes toward the burning house, the flames eating away at everything, sending billowing smoke into the night.

I close my eyes, trying to will my transformation into a

human to happen, but my dragon heart wants nothing more than to remain in control and ready to burn the world down. I had no idea I'd feel so strong and unstoppable like I do now. The power of my huge frame, of my easy access to my dragon fire, the ability to fly and feel as free as I had as a sky dancer—it's intoxicating. How can I just suppress who I am when my clan needs me?

"Red, hurry the fuck up," Quillon calls, clapping his hands from below me.

I jerk my attention to him and growl. I can't believe how he stands there, still covered in blood, but alive and still his douchebag self.

"I will not carry the damn blame if the High Council shows up and captures you. You're making it way too fucking easy for them," he adds, risking his hand by smacking it against my snout.

Nudging my nose into his gut, I knock Quillon onto his ass. He covers his face with his arms, cowering away like he expects me to blast him with my dragon fire. And damn it, is the thought tempting. He's lucky I can't snag him by his head to toss him into the destruction of his house.

"Come on, Red. Be a good fucking girl already. Transform and I'll let Kash free for the night. Just hurry your scaly ass up. If something happens to you, these assholes with devour me. The only thing keeping me alive now is that you don't want Kash to die, but if you die, I'm pretty fucking certain the bastard would sacrifice himself for revenge." Quillon peers over his shoulder and hooks his fingers to his bloody shirt, tugging it off. "I'll even give you my damn shirt."

A flash of green light brightens the night, startling me. I flap my wings and let my beast control me to attempt to launch into the air. Despite my instincts and deep-seated nature, my ability to take flight falters, and all I do is smack the ground instead of flying into the sky.

"Nova, transform, now!" Quillon yells.

Hair bursts from his skin with his transformation into a lycan. I try everything I can to get my body to comply, but nothing works.

"Ralloc eht nogard. Emat reh tseab!" Ambrose shouts, materializing in front of me. Green electricity crackles in his hands as he casts some sort of spell.

My body prickles, a strange heat spilling from my chest to flow through the rest of me. I open my mouth to spew fire, but nothing happens. My throat tightens as sizzling pain ignites around my neck.

Quillon roars, drops on all fours, and charges Ambrose. Flicking his hand without even looking, the warlock shoots a ball of energy at Quillon, sending him to his stomach. The world quakes, and I jerk my attention to Kash. His large form crashes into the house, sending a wave of smoke, dust, and debris into the air. With Quillon spelled, Kash can't do anything either.

"Ralloc eht nogard. Emat reh tseab!" Ambrose shouts again, sending a bolt of green lightning toward me.

I tense and try to open my mouth to breathe fire again, but the same pain radiates from my throat. It's useless. Ambrose uses his magic against me, and I can't even fight back. No wonder witches and warlocks control the High Council. No wonder they're in charge of Magaelorum. And now, I'm starting to doubt Ambrose even serves these supposed dragon princes. It might all be a façade.

Jerking his hands at me, Ambrose sends another bolt of electric magic at me. "Ralloc eht nogard. Emat reh tseab!"

My muscles freeze and shudder, and the edges of my vision darken. Pushing through the pain, I get my shit together and flail backward. If I can't incinerate this fucker with dragon fire, I'll crush him under my weight.

Light blinds me, and one second I'm fighting to put space between me and Ambrose, and in the next, I open my eyes, staring at the world from the ground. Did I pass out? What the hell happened?

A shock of power startles me, drawing my attention from the smoldering rubble of the house. Ambrose stands a few feet away in my line of sight, coiling a glowing chain made of his magic around his arm.

And fuck. It's like the one Lazlo used to snap a magical leash to the collar he spelled around my neck, one that leaves me open to be controlled.

"Calm down, princess," Ambrose says, shuffling closer. "Don't fight. It'll only hurt worse if you do."

I release a strange, low, guttural noise from my throat in response. My soul aches unlike anything I've ever felt. I had no idea that such a thing was possible, but it feels as if my very essence has turned tangible and Ambrose prods it with a sharp poker.

"That's good. Just settle down." Stroking his hand along my snout, he caresses my scales with his cool fingers. "I'll get you to the palace soon enough. We won't have to worry so much in the Mountain Lands. We'll also fix what the fates messed up. It's unfair for your intendeds to have to deal with something that should've been avoided. You never belonged to the Drekis, princess."

Oh, no.

Oh-fucking-no.

Panic seizes my heart at his words.

An explosion sounds from the house, and a huge wave of fire erupts into the air. Ambrose spins to see what's going on, and an enormous dragon launches from the flames. The onyx beast blows a breath of blue fire from its mouth with its screech. In the moonlight, each facet of its scales glitters with magical silver light. My heart and soul ignite at the sight.

Seeing this breathtaking dragon gives me the will to fight.

Swinging my long neck, I prepare to attack Ambrose. I prepare to kill him while his attention lies elsewhere.

Spinning on his feet, Ambrose catches me in the act. "Ralloc eht nogard. Emat reh tseab!" he shouts.

I lose myself to the electric agony of his magic.

Dangerous Magic

THE DEAFENING SOUND OF MY own screams rings in my ears. I writhe and twist on the ground, trying to escape my skin. The fire coursing through me burns hotter than anything I've ever felt. It's not the soothing, inviting warmth I experience with my dragon fire. It feels as if the devil invades my essence, torturing me from the inside out.

"Ambrosc! I ordcr you to stop!" Brilliant bluc firc cascades through the sky above me like a river of blue flames floods the world. Theo's massive dragon form expands its wings, blocking my view of anything but him.

The pain inside me fades, exchanging the devil's fire for the soft iciness of fresh snow after a winter storm. I gasp, my heart throbbing in erratic beats, my head swimming with shadows. Theo shakes the world as he lands beside me, towering over my placated body. I feel tiny as I curl my knees to my chest, the tightness of my throat refusing to release me completely.

It's now that I realize I'm no longer a dragon.

"Delphia, I'm so sorry," Theo says, his thoughts swirling through my mind. "I did not command him to do that. He will be appropriately punished."

His gigantic dragon head lowers to the ground beside me, and I meet his green eyes like they're made of precious stones. He nudges his snout into me, trying to roll me over onto my back for a better look.

I flinch and shriek, an intense fear rising in me. But it's not from him. My soul warns me of danger and panic consumes me. I can barely lift my head, let alone fight the incoming threat. Theo pays no attention to the world outside us, worsening my trepidation. What kind of mate stands idly by instead of doing everything he can to protect the one who supposedly holds a piece of his soul? Not my mate. Theo merely threw his soul at me and expects me to keep it.

He's insane to think I'll just lower my standards. The Drekis have raised the bar immensely for me.

I cringe and tense, waiting for a monster to attack Theo, but nothing happens to him. A figure emerges from behind Theo's massive body, the electric green light stealing my breath as Ambrose holds power in his palms. I jerk my hands up protectively, grabbing at my throat. The collar tightens, the magic leash turning visible.

"Protect me! Be the mate you claim you want to be!" My thoughts crash from me loud enough that Theo finally reacts and roars, the power of his breath making Ambrose stumble and catch himself on Theo's leg.

"Calm down, Theo. I'm not a threat. I just need her still to unleash her properly," Ambrose says, his deep voice filling me with dread. Just his closeness sickens me, and I heave as my stomach muscles ache. "She's fought so fiercely that the magic entangles around her. She's hurting."

"You're lying! Do not come any closer. If you can't do it from there, you'll have far worse things to worry about. I will not let you capture my mate." Theo's voice hums through my head as he speaks telepathically. Ambrose must be able to hear him too, because the warlock stops in his tracks. "What you did was so far out of line. How dare you think you can control the woman who holds my soul. I should take your head, you bastard."

"Do it, Theo." My voice comes out as a whisper, the raspiness of it begging me to find water to drink. "I want him dead."

Theo huffs a breath of smoke through his nostrils, but he doesn't respond to me. Stretching his massive wings, he blocks my view of Ambrose as his scales flicker with a metallic sheen, like the onyx glitters with streaks of platinum along their ridges. He transforms into a man, his hulking frame continuing to block my view of the warlock.

Theo kneels in the grass next to me, his naked body so close that I can feel the heat of his soothing dragon fire emanating from his skin. My mind goes to war against my body and soul, trying to get myself under control. A whimper escapes my mouth and the desire for him to lift me into his arms overtakes my rationale.

How can I hate him and want him at the same time? This fucking magic. This fucking bond. Why can't I just reject him and hope things return to normal? Who am I kidding? I'll never have the normalcy found in thinking I'm human in the Mortal World again.

And Maddox is right. If I reject him, how will we get the help we need? We've hit a dead end with my aunt, but the Darkonians know more about my family than I know.

Like he senses my deep-seated need, Theo slides an arm under me, half lifting me from the grass. His touch shocks my skin, tugging me from my wandering thoughts. My dragon must sense that Theo will protect me and allows me to lower my guard just a bit.

"I yearn to give you everything you could ever desire, Delphia, but the death of my guard is not one of them I could follow through with," Theo says, caressing his fingers along my cheek. "He is part of our clan, and despite his despicable actions, I can't justify killing him. But he will pay. I swear it to you."

"It's not enough! Look what you've caused! You've ruined everything. How can I trust you? You refuse to accept that the fates have chosen my rightful mates." I flinch and roll away, not allowing him to touch me anymore. Just the thought digs under my skin. "I want you, your brother, and that fuckhead warlock to leave me alone. Get out of here."

Theo frowns at my words, his face twisting in astonishment. His surprise infuriates me. He can't possibly be this dense, can he? "But Delphia—"

I raise my hand up, cutting him off. I guess he can be. "You betrayed me, Theo. You acted as if you would help me and my mates, but look at what you've done. You act nice up until you realize you can't have your way. I would rather get captured by the High Council and finish off my life in prison than ever, and I mean ever, agree to go with you."

Theo's expression morphs into a series of lines that

pucker his expression. A strange wave of pain swells through my chest, and I realize my words trigger a physical ache inside him. Inside me too. It hurts my very essence to think about returning to the Maximum Magical Penitentiary, but I don't know what else to do. I cannot—no, I will not risk Ambrose or the Darkonians using their power against us. This bond between Theo and I isn't real. It was forced upon me.

I hate that I have to keep telling myself that.

I hate in this moment, feeling his fear and remorse and something warm, strange, indescribable, makes me question everything. Our bond feels real.

But the circumstances? How can he think this will ever work? I can't even trust him to help us. He's proved he's only here for himself.

Kicking my leg at him, I knock him back. "Now go. I will not ask you again."

"Please, Delphia. Don't consider such a life. You're better than that." Theo crawls closer to me, not allowing much space to get between us. "Think about the Drekis. Do you know what will happen to them if you turn yourselves in?"

I push myself up on my elbow, my eyes wandering to the flaming debris of what's left of the house. If I didn't feel the presence of my mates, I might panic and rush to them, but something inside me keeps me in place.

And then I hear Maddox's whisper. "Reject him, Nova. I was wrong. We don't need them."

I spot pieces of the debris shifting. Maddox throws a beam away as he escapes the wreckage with Rowan beside him. Their faces line with rage unlike anything I've ever seen. Their muscles ripple and flex, their bodies preparing to go to war for me.

And this is how I know they're my true mates. They will protect me always. Always. I will never have to question our bond, our wants and desires for our future as a clan, or whether or not they will betray me. Because they won't. Betraying me is betraying themselves. They would rather fall together than risk even a moment apart.

"Stay back, Drekis," Ambrose calls, his voice once again sending my soul shuddering in fear. He steps in their pathway and challenges them with his magic. "This is between the princess and her mate. You will not interfere."

"Stand down, warlock. I don't want to hurt you." Rowan gathers dragon fire, his body prickling with his dragon readying to burst free. "He is not her mate—"

Ambrose claps his hand, freezing the world around us once again. My heart thrashes against my ribcage, threatening to break through to throw itself in my mates' direction. I tense, my body trembling, the edges of my vision turning red with the heat of my dragon fire coursing through my veins.

This warlock is far too powerful. His bravado and nonchalance over being able to control something as crazy as time itself creeps me the hell out. He's no better than Lazlo. The High Council either. Anyone who just stops the world without even a second thought is a complete psycho—he's worse than a psycho. He might have a god-complex and we're his creatures to play with.

I don't understand any of this, and my mind screams that I should do something, anything, because this isn't right. How can my world keep going and continuing on without my mates? It's unnatural. I will not allow my life to pass theirs by.

"Stop!" I yell, pushing through the pain tightening my throat. Rage heats my skin, and the grass shrivels under my touch. "Release them! This isn't right. You can't do this to us. I won't stand by while you do, you fucking asshole."

Ambrose bares his teeth, his face morphing with hard lines as he reveals the true monster he keeps hiding just beneath his skin. "What are you going to do about it exactly? They will only get in the way, and I need to fix the chaos I've caused. So shut up, calm down, and let me do my job. I will unfreeze them when I'm ready and not until I unleash you, princess. I can't do so while protecting myself." Ambrose ignores a warning growl from me and stomps forward.

Energy glows in his hands, sending static through the air. I tense, my whole body tightening, but I can't run. It feels as if I smack into a brick wall.

"Sorry, Delphia. Our guard is right, and it has already taken too long." Theo shoves me forward hard enough to send me to my knees. I hadn't even seen him move from his spot. For a second, I thought he was Tiernan. He manhandles me like I expect Tiernan to. "My brother grows angrier by the second because we waste time instead of helping him and returning home."

"Then fucking get him," I snap. "He'll probably blame all of this on me instead of you. Your fucking twisted attitude is enough." If I can convince them to do something else, I might make it the couple feet to my mates. Magic isn't foolproof, which Lazlo proved to me. I can break the spell. We can get away.

Ambrose shifts closer, setting me on edge. "Hold her still, Theo. Let's be done with this already." He acts as if he can't even see or hear me any longer, focusing on his magic.

Surprising me, Theo obeys his command and snatches my wrist too quickly for me to fight him off. He pulls me into his arms and onto his lap, our naked bodies pressing together with no space between us. I swear I can feel the hardness of his dick jewel on the back of my leg. If Ambrose wasn't rushing my way with his glowing magic, I'd think more about it.

With a whisper of a spell, he touches my neck, ignoring my thrashing body. Theo murmurs my name in my ear, attempting to settle me down while he restrains me until Ambrose straightens his back.

My chest heaves, my body, mind, and soul wanting nothing more than to charge Ambrose and punch him in his face. I want him to experience the pain he put me through. I want him to realize that magic doesn't make him invincible, and I can sure as hell make him pay for his wrongdoings.

"You have my permission, firecracker. Seek your revenge," Theo says, pressing his chin into my bare shoulder.

He loosens his hold on my waist and slides me off his lap. Curling his body, he kicks his legs out, propelling to his feet. Ambrose raises his hands in surrender, but Theo struts toward the warlock and grabs him by the front of his shirt. Theo lifts him off his feet and tosses Ambrose on the ground next to me. Our eyes meet, and I flare my nostrils in anger and swing my fist, sucker punching him in the throat.

He doesn't fight back, and fury swells inside me, my dragon now free from his magic. I growl and punch him in his gut next, wanting him to know what it feels like to be helpless.

The world unfreezes as I break his spell, and Ambrose

heaves, unable to suck air into his lungs. Rowan and Maddox charge in our direction, but Kash roars, his huge dragon head reaching over them to grab Ambrose with his teeth. Not only was the spell on Maddox and Rowan broken, so was the one on Quillon, which released Kash.

Swinging his neck, Kash throws Ambrose, sending him tumbling through the air two dozen feet until he rolls across the lawn. "You cannot kill him, brothers," he says, telling Maddox and Rowan the same thing he told me. "It is not our way."

"We can't trust him not to take Delphia from us!" Maddox yells, smacking Kash on his hindquarters with a glowing fist. "We will do what is necessary to protect the only thing that is important to us in the whole damn universe."

"Please, Drekis. We can work this out. My guard made a careless mistake," Theo says, getting in the path between my guys and Ambrose. "I've made a mistake too. I want to start over and prove that I agree with you about Delphia. She is most important, and while it's hard to accept, I know we must work something out between our clans. Fighting will only hurt her in the end."

"You will hurt her." Rowan stomps ahead, his determination and protectiveness warming my essence. "You *have* hurt her. An alliance between us isn't an option unless you can give us certain assurances, which I don't think you can."

"And what about Tiernan? Will he agree with you?" Maddox asks, standing tall, his longer hair blowing behind him. "Do you think he will accept his mistakes? I sure the hell don't. It's fucking bad enough you rewrote the fates to bond with a woman who doesn't belong to you."

"But she does." Theo brings his hand to his chest. "I felt it even before my guard ensured it. I've been waiting my life for her."

"Impossible," Rowan snaps, squaring his shoulders. "She's ours. She's always been ours. The fates brought her to us. If you were her mate, Rhett would've completed his task to bring her home. But the fates ensured he would fail. Instead, she found herself in an impossible situation that dropped her right in front of us."

"As a criminal." Theo twists his mouth, his green eyes sparkling with fire. "What kind of life is that for her? You can't seriously think your bond is worth a lifetime of imprisonment."

All right. I've had enough of them discussing me like I'm not here, like I don't have a say in where I belong in the world. The one thing I know is that I'm not a damn criminal, I feel a connection unlike anything I knew possible to men who will fight for me, and I will decide what happens now.

"But maybe I do," I snap, trembling with my emotions. "It's a damn shitty one, but a life I will choose over your warlock coming in on your behalf and trying to sever the bond I have toward my mates. I'm willing to risk facing the High Council and returning to Max again to ensure Ambrose can't mess with me anymore."

Theo sighs and fusses with his hair, pulling on the strands in frustration. "Delphia, what did I tell you? The Drekis will not go without punishment. They are wanted just like you—"

"They will be fine if I tell the High Council that I forced them with Lazlo Infinity's help. They won't be able to deny it with this fucking magical collar." I cross my arms over my chest. "I will tell them how he used Rose to open a portal and how Quillon was the one to guide us through. They'll have to listen. The Drekis will be heroes. They can be the ones to turn me in."

I have no idea if such a plan would work, or if my mates would even go for it, but I need the Darkonians to back the hell off. I need Theo to know that he and his brother can't just come blasting into my life.

Theo's eyes widen with my words, my threat obviously plausible enough to him that he looks ready to drop to his knees and grovel before me.

Like he can hear my thought, he kneels in the grass and

crawls closer, risking growls from the Drekis to take my hands into his. I flick my gaze in their direction and shake my head, getting them to refrain from attacking. Ambrose stands waiting where Kash threw him like he expects Theo to give him a command. As for Tiernan, I have no idea what keeps him from intervening. Quillon hides like a coward near the house, and I wonder if he'll try to make an escape before anyone else notices him.

"Delphia, I'm begging you. Please forgive me for this mess. This wasn't how I imagined meeting my intended would be, and I regret my actions. I know you're angry. I know you don't trust me or my brother, but I want to fix it. Allow me to do better for you. I just want you to give me the chance." Theo brings my hands to his chin and snuggles his cheek against them. His black hair hangs on his forehead, some of the strands veiling his jade eyes.

Maddox swings his head, sending his hair whipping in his disagreement. "We can't trust them. The second you agree and we enter their lands, they can turn against us."

He's right about that. I know he's right, but the part of me that has bonded with Theo feels the Darkonian prince is being earnest.

"What if I have Ambrose ensure your safety?" Theo asks, getting to his feet. He keeps one of my hands in his, and I gently tug myself away.

I don't care if I look paranoid or ridiculous, but I run past him and jump into Rowan's open arms. His bulging muscles engulf me, steadying my crazy heartbeat with the feeling of safety that comes from his closeness.

"I will put you under Darkonian protection. All that I ask is that you agree to come with us. You know Delphia does not belong in that vile prison. We will keep her safe until her name is cleared. We can work together," Theo says, stopping just out of arm's reach. "Isn't that right, Ambrose?"

"I will need your brother's agreement," Ambrose responds instead of going along with Theo.

"Then get him already." Theo's lips twitch with his words. "And brace yourself. He's pissed we haven't helped him."

"Can't you just leave him?" I ask, the words escaping my mouth before my brain has a chance to catch up. But damn it. It's what I want. I want nothing to do with Tiernan, especially after the shit he pulled.

Theo smirks. "Another minute wouldn't hurt anyone—"

A strange static shocks me, the air suddenly quivering. Rowan growls from deep in his chest, his dragon threatening to burst through his skin. Raising his hand, Maddox points toward the sky, and I clutch Rowan more fiercely.

Light illuminates the horizon over the trees in a familiar glow. It's a portal.

"The High Council," Ambrose mutters. "The shield here fissures. They'll be able to pinpoint the magical residue soon enough. We have to go."

Muttering a spell under his breath, Ambrose sends the wreckage of the house blasting away. I spot Tiernan propping up part of the ceiling to keep it from smashing him. He drops the rubble and gathers dragon fire in his palms.

"You fucking bastards!" Tiernan yells, blasting fire at Theo's feet. "How dare you just abandon me in that fucking mess."

Ambrose flings his hands out, igniting a shield in front of him, stopping Tiernan's dragon fire from hitting him next. "We didn't abandon you. We had other things to worry about besides your shortcomings."

Whoa shit.

"The High Council is on the move, and I need your agreement to accept the Drekis under the Darkonian protection," Ambrose says, flicking his own magic at Tiernan.

Tiernan scowls. "Darkonians have never allied with the Dreki Clan. They've—"

"Do it for Delphia. It is the only way, brother," Theo says, risking stepping closer.

"Why? She won't even give me a chance. Why should I

give in to her demands?" Tiernan turns his attention to me, his eyes glaring daggers that feel as if they stab right into my being. "Those fuckers will reap all the benefits of our power, and what will we get?"

"Delphia's time," Theo says, straightening his back, remaining calm yet commanding. "You can prove to her that you're a worthy mate."

"I want to ensure it. I won't agree to any of this otherwise." Tiernan tightens his jaw. "I want time with her—guaranteed and without interference."

It takes everything in me not to react. What the hell is up with these demands? He can't expect—

Static shocks me, cutting off my thought. I drag my attention back to the sky, growing lighter and brighter by the second.

"They're coming," Ambrose says, rubbing his hands together. "Give me your command, Tiernan. You know I can't do anything otherwise. It must come from both of you."

"No," Tiernan says, fisting his hands. "The High Council can have them. There is always visitations."

What the actual fuck.

"Tiernan!" Theo shouts.

My hair floats on a magic current, my body screaming to run, to transform, to do anything I can to get away.

Dread steals my breath like my dragon senses my impending doom. It was easy to threaten accepting a life at the Maximum Magical Penitentiary, but now that I face that fate...fuck.

"I'll do it," I say, digging my fingers into Rowan's shoulders like I can absorb his strength to face the Darkonian shithead. "I'll give you a chance. Both of you. But you have to accept that the Drekis come with me. We're a packaged deal."

Theo and Tiernan stare at each other in silence.

"The lycan has to come too," I add, frowning with my words. "The only way to get rid of him is finding a cure."

A loud pop echoes through the air.

Ambrose gathers power. "Give me the command. We have minutes."

Tiernan slowly nods his head. "I accept the Dreki alliance."

Raising his hands, Ambrose extends them toward the sky. "Good, now grab the lycan. We will use him to portal. Everyone else, transform."

Magaelorum

FROM OUTSIDE THE PRISON WALLS of the Maximum Magical Penitentiary, Magaelorum is unlike anything I could ever imagine. The infinite, crystalline indigo sky meets a vibrant emerald horizon of lush trees. I still can't get over the fact that this place of wonder is in another realm apart from the Mortal World. The breathtaking view captures my attention, refusing to let me go. Huge dragons glide through the sky and disappear over the red-rocked mountains of the Darkonian Clan's territory.

"Would you like a tour of our kingdom, Delphia? I can feel your desire to explore." Theo's sultry voice sounds from behind me, but I don't shift my gaze from the beautiful scenic expanse I view from the balcony of the guest bedroom—my bedroom. Yellowish-pink clouds decorate the horizon with the glowing sun, brighter than usual without the mucky smog of the Mortal World.

"I don't know," I murmur, touching the guardrail. "This view is quite the sight already. I'm not done enjoying it."

The thumps of his bare feet draw closer from the metal door, three times the size that I am in my human form. If I transformed into a dragon, I wouldn't even hit the ceiling. I could sleep in that form if I so choose. Hell, the double king-sized bed might even fit me, though I suspect it's intended for something I haven't thought about...until right now.

"I could teach you the customs that you have been denied learning by being kidnapped and taken to the Mortal World," he thinks to me, his presence vying for my attention. "Such as it being customary for males to wait for an invitation from their mate before joining her in her living quarters. In here, you can invite anyone you please, even at the same time. You will notice upon accepting an invitation to our rooms that our sleeping arrangements aren't as accommodating for more than you. It eases any territorialism within a clan, but now I see it's especially important with the current circumstances."

I try to remain expressionless, my thoughts about screwing more than one of my mates at a time in the big-ass bed proven right. My body reacts to the image swirling through my mind. Heat builds between my legs and I squeeze them together, silently begging the universe that Theo doesn't notice. "And what if I invite the Drekis to stay with me around the clock?"

"That's your prerogative during your free time, though I hope you will consider what I have to offer you, firecracker." The warmth of his breath tickles the hair over my ear. I hadn't realized how close he was standing to me. "I've noticed your curiosity toward my body."

I shiver at his closeness and swivel on my feet to face him. "How can I not be? You have a bejeweled cock. I've never seen one in real life."

"It's a gift to you," he says, the corner of his lips curling up into a smirk. "Do you like it?"

I suck my bottom lip between my teeth and glance down, despite knowing he's wearing pants. But I can't help it. My damn eyes want to double check to be sure. "In the Mortal World, if a man chooses to give a woman jewelry, she's usually the one to wear it."

"I can arrange such a gift for you if you'd like." His eyes wander down my body like he's imagining bedazzling my labia with matching jewelry to his, and I automatically clench my vagina.

"Uh, no thanks. That seems like an awfully big commitment for a man I just met." I step away from Theo and shift my gaze back to the scenic expanse of emerald trees stretching out for miles. "Now, if you were serious about showing me around, I'd like you to take me to my mates. I need to make sure your asshole warlock hasn't done something that will get himself murdered by me." I can feel they're okay, but I would still prefer to keep my eyes on them at all times.

"You don't trust me to keep my word," he says, cutting me off, stopping me from heading to the door. It's not a question but a statement. We both know it's the truth, yet he wants my confirmation.

"How can I?" I ask, crossing my arms over my chest. "And even if you do, your evil twin might not. He's pretty annoyed I won't allow him to bond our souls."

"I was rather lucky to go first, wasn't I, Delphia?" It completely goes over his head that what he's done to me was utter and complete bullshit, and he's lucky I need his power at the moment.

I purse my lips. "It's Nova. My name is Nova now. I legally changed it in the Mortal World." I don't know why I bother correcting him instead of calling his ass out. Maybe because anything else I could say will just bounce right back out of his head. It's not like I'm not used to Maddox slipping up and calling me Delphia too.

"I don't like it. It doesn't suit you." This guy. Is he joking? Theo remains tight-mouthed, yet calm, like it's cool if he offends me by voicing his dissatisfaction about something personal to me, something that is part of my identity.

I furrow my brows. "If you're trying to impress me with your charm, you're failing miserably. Now, please. Take me to my mates."

Theo frowns, his obvious disappointment washing over me. Slowly nodding his head, he extends his arm out for me to take. "Whatever will make you more comfortable while we arrange things around the palace until things settle. We've had to excuse our servants and guests to ensure word doesn't get out about our arrival until we're ready."

"Ready for what exactly?" I ask, allowing Theo to lead me from the balcony towards the massive door. The room itself reminds me of the cave Maddox chose to live in at Max, but this room is far more luxurious. The polished stone floors sparkle with rainbow light from the various types of unfamiliar jewels embedded in the rock walls.

"To guarantee the High Council doesn't act against us." He crosses his free arm to rest his hand over mine. "Things are complicated."

Turning my gaze away from the ornate fixtures, lit with magic, I get captured in his stare. "But you said—"

"Don't worry, Del...Nova. We know you're innocent, and we will prove it. If the High Council doesn't agree to our terms, they will have a war on their hands." Theo stops at the closed door. "No one will take you from us. You belong to the Darkonian Clan."

"Don't go trying to stake your claim on me yet, Theo," I say, straightening my shoulders and stretching my neck, attempting to appear taller. I wish there was a damn step or something to climb on, so I could be at his eye level instead of feeling as if he looks down at me. "I want to be honest with you. This bond your warlock forced upon my soul doesn't give you an automatic relationship or whatever with me. I agreed to come here because I felt this would be the best option for my mates and me, considering the circumstances. Don't assume anything else, okay? I don't want you expecting more than I want to give."

Theo's eyes flash with fire, his face remaining sharp yet handsome. "Your honesty gives me hope, especially because I know how you thought you could use the Drekis to your advantage, and look where that led."

I wonder how he knows. Maybe Quillon. I guess it doesn't matter. "It might've been like that at first, but—"

"No one blames you, and I don't judge you for doing things you felt you had to do in that vile prison." Reaching out, he caresses his fingers along my jaw. "You remained in control where many others would have succumbed to their circumstances. Cunning and smart. Brave."

"I'm far from brave," I say, my voice softening under the intensity of his gaze. "If I were brave, I'd have followed through with my threat to return to Max."

"I happen to disagree. Coming here, agreeing to share your time with a clan you don't think you belong to and also putting the Drekis above yourself by making such sacrifices—you're braver than some of the toughest dragons I know. You act like a clan leader should."

I'd usually laugh and brush off such a compliment, but I can feel that Theo believes his words completely and isn't saying them in an attempt to win me over. A part of me knows I should steel myself against him. The Drekis are my true mates, and I've accepted them as mine and me as theirs. But this thing with Theo? I don't even know what it is. I hate that he put me in this position, igniting a bond between us that might not have occurred otherwise, but then again...fate did the same with my bond to the Drekis.

It's in this moment that I realize how much I miss the

Mortal World and its familiarity. I miss how I could date and get to know someone or just fuck them and move on without any strings attached. It was all my choice and my decision. But in this world, in my new life, fuck. I don't even know. It feels right and wondrous and impossibly easy to connect with strangers—the instant connection nearly unbelievable yet undeniable—that it makes me question every mortal relationship I've ever had. Because nothing compares to having this intense bonding of souls connecting me to another being, or the perfect reflection of my soul mirroring in another—in several others. But what this mean for all of us? I wish I knew.

"I wish I could read the stars as well, Nova," Theo says quietly, the low velvety sound of his voice making my soul hum.

I inhale a small breath, realizing I projected my thoughts to him. I've opened up my mind when I know I should stay guarded.

"I'm glad you didn't." His voice whispers into my mind, filling me with an unfamiliar, inviting emotion that warms my insides. "You must understand how difficult this is on me."

He thinks this is difficult on *him*? What the actual fuck.

And like that, the warmth disappears and icy anger

swells through my body, pushing him out.

Breaking my eyes away from his, I yank the heavy door open and rush into the grand hallway of the Darkonian Palace. I need to put distance between me and Theo. He confuses the hell out of me, and I suddenly so desperately want to be with the Drekis.

"Nova, wait," Theo calls from behind me, his thudding footsteps picking up pace as he decides to chase me. "Please. I didn't mean to anger you."

"Well, you did. Now please, this is my free time and you're trying to take it for yourself. I just want to see my mates," I call out over my shoulder.

"Nova, please. Let's just talk for another moment. I want to apologize," he says, his voice growing louder as he catches up to me.

Something feels wrong. I'm not the only one feeling desperate, but I don't think Theo's reason is the same as mine.

"After I see my mates." I close my eyes, opening my mind, trying to get a better sense as to where Maddox, Kash, and Rowan might be. I know they're here. I can feel them, but something doesn't sit right with me.

"Nova, stop. Just stop for a second," Theo repeats.

My body buzzes with static, the hairs on my arm standing on end. Fuck. I can't see Ambrose, but I can sense his magic. He's doing something to my guys. I know it. "N—"

Theo tackles me from behind, engulfing me in his arms. Spinning midair, he flips to take the brunt of our fall onto his back. We skid across the gleaming stone floor with me on top of him, pinned to his chest. All I can do is brace myself as the bejeweled ceiling speeds by, the force of our collision dragging us several dozen feet.

Releasing one arm from my body, Theo grabs onto a metal beam, sending our bodies spinning over the ledge of an open balcony. I screech at the quick movement and how I fly away from him and hang over another expansive room a hundred feet below. My arm screams as he catches me by my wrist, and my mind kicks into action, using the strength of his hold to swing myself. Like we're the closing act for Galaxy Gold's aerial acrobatics show, Theo swings his muscular arm, throwing me up into the air and back onto solid ground. I land on my feet and automatically raise my arms up with a damn smile crossing my face. I forgot how thrilling it was to fly through the air in my human form, unsure of whether or not I'd make the perfect landing.

Theo climbs up the narrow beam, using his bare feet to walk along the side, his arm muscles bulging as he carries his weight. He doesn't hop back onto the landing and instead continues up a few feet. He catches my gaze, knowing I now watch him, and readies his body to do a shoulder mount.

My mouth falls open in surprise. Theo slowly stretches out his legs and torso, holding himself in an aerial shoulder mount plank. I'm in complete awe, devouring how his muscles flex and bulge, his strength admirable and sexy. I wonder what else he can do and where he learned such tricks. I can nearly imagine myself performing with him in front of an audience, balancing on his ripped abs.

The bastard grins, showing off his straight teeth before playfully sticking out his tongue at me, showing off a glittery barbell.

If a whisper of a swear word from Rowan didn't sneak into my mind, I might've continued to watch Theo's obvious attempt to impress and distract me. And then I feel a blip of pain coming from Maddox next.

I tense, my heart sinking into my stomach. I was right about something being wrong. Theo was trying to distract me, but why? I need to find out.

Seeing the change in my expression, Theo releases a small growl and slides down the sturdy beam. I spin and dash away, not even giving him a chance to reach the floor. I have no idea where I'm going, but my feet carry me along at a pace fast enough to stay ahead of Theo.

"Nova, damn it!" he shouts from behind me. "Stop! The Drekis asked me to keep you away until they're done."

Done? Done with what?

I don't stop to ask, letting my instincts and need to find my mates lead me to the grand black metal staircase, spiraling to what I think is the ground level. It's hard to tell with the way the palace seems to be set up for our human and dragon forms.

A loud whistle rips through the air from behind me as Theo unleashes some sort of warning. I expect a dozen men to come charging at me from the shadows. I expect to get tackled and dragged to a dungeon to be held prisoner just like I was in Max. But what I don't expect is for a wave of dragon fire to explode a dozen feet in front on me. My human rationale betrays me, my body freezing in panic like it'll burn me alive, and I halt in my tracks. A silhouette blocks out the soft light emanating from above as a black dragon roars above me. Tilting my head back, I catch sight of Tiernan transforming into his human form midair. He freefalls from thirty feet above and lands on his feet amid his flames.

"You called, brother," Tiernan says, stretching his naked body in front of me. "Need some help taming our mate?"

And damn my eyes. They devour every damn tatted and pierced inch of him, wanting to imprint his muscular body into my mind.

"She looks a bit wild. In need of some attention to get

her settled down," he adds.

I shock the hell out of him by flinging out my hands, shooting an unexpected burst of dragon fire at him, knocking him onto his naked ass.

Theo swears from behind me, but I ignore him and run in the direction my body wants me to go. He releases another whistle, and Tiernan growls, trying to knock me off my feet again with his fire. My hair blows in front of me, veiling across my face. My heart races to beat my legs, trying to escape me to reach the Drekis first.

"Maddox?" I call, my voice sounding like a gasp. "Rowan? Kash?"

Silence greets me, but I can feel them. A blip of their pain sneaks through me, igniting fear in my heart. Shit.

"Nova, stop!" Theo yells from behind me.

Tiernan releases a guttural noise from his throat. "Just blast her. You're being too gentle. She's tough."

Fuck. Fuck. Fuck.

Grinding my teeth, I brace for the explosion of dragon fire to consume me. I have a feeling if Theo doesn't do it, Tiernan will. He doesn't share the same bond that I have with his brother. He won't feel my hatred like Theo would, and it makes this more complicated. If he can't empathize with me, he has nothing to lose in trying to put me in my supposed place.

I reach the spiral stairs and wonder if I should just risk running down them or test my ability and transform into a dragon...definitely not transform. Knowing my luck, I'd falter and crash to the floor. I'll have a better chance at just hustling my ass.

Swinging my leg over the railing, I test my luck and begin to slide. Tiernan dives from the landing beside me, transforming into a dragon. He lands gracefully near the bottom of the stairs, blocking my path.

I do the only thing I can think of.

Jerking my weight to the side, I throw myself off the railing and do my best to flip in the air. I can't get enough force to prepare to land on my feet and end up landing on my shoulders. I see stars, the air heaving from my lungs. But it doesn't stop me from getting to my feet and bolting away. Neither does Tiernan.

His massive dragon form only makes it harder for him to move as I dodge right under his belly and toward a gleaming corridor.

The fucker blows another hot breath of fire at me, not caring that he scorches a decorative table and the back of my clothes in the process. And fucking hell. Cool air drifts across my ass cheeks, giving Tiernan a peek at my naked skin.

Theo whistles once more, and a door on the right side

of the corridor flies open.

I summon dragon fire in my hands, the action now instinctual with the stress of the situation. Ambrose gathers his electric green magic in his palms. Tensing, I expect him to blast me, shocking me off my feet. Anger lines his brows, and he draws a circle in the air—not a circle, but a chain. Shit. He's going to leash me again.

My mind screams to stop, to turn and run, to do anything I can to escape this asshole warlock. But my heart and soul holler to suck it up and be brave for the Drekis. I've survived a short time in Max. I've faced a scarier warlock. I'm a damn dragon, and this guy is a snack. I can't let him intimidate me. I can't.

A roar sounds from behind me, and Ambrose flinches and ducks, scrambling out of the way. Fear ignites inside me at the threatening call of an angry beast, but I push through it and race into Ambrose's room. Surprising me, he flicks magic at the door, slamming it shut on Theo and Tiernan. I jerk my attention to the expansive room and cover my mouth with my hand.

I scream.

And then I scream again, tears welling in my eyes.

Blood stains the floor and spatters across the wall.

"Graulot momensi trevistitato!" Ambrose shouts.

Heat laces around my neck, stealing my mobility. All I

can do is stare through my teary vision and silently scream at the three hulking forms on the floor.

This warlock is dead.

If only a part of me wasn't dead too.

A Life of Lies

"IF YOU CALM DOWN, I will release you from the spell." Ambrose strolls closer to me, his presence igniting panic into my very essence. "You weren't supposed to see this. The Drekis never wanted you to view them this way, nor did they think you'd agree with getting the Darkonian mark."

The Darkonian mark? What the hell?

I dart my gaze away from Ambrose and to my mates on

the floor. Each of them lies unmoving on their stomachs without their shirts. Expansive winged dragon tattoos cover their broad backs with an intricate design glowing red within the new, unfamiliar tattoos.

"The spell leaving them immobile will wear off within the hour," Ambrose adds. "The act of such an alliance comes at a price, and the pain that comes with it is said to be the worst imaginable."

I try to open and close my mouth, to push any noise free, but Ambrose continues locking me in his spell. I can't even hear Theo and Tiernan in the hallway. They probably have no clue that they're being used and manipulated by a warlock they trust as their guard.

"Erf eth og," Ambrose whispers, waving his hand over my body.

The imaginary restraints release me, and I drop to my knees before falling to my stomach. My mind spins with dizziness, and I remain on the floor, trying to will my body to get itself together.

A cool hand touches my bare back, my skin exposed from where Tiernan burned the fabric. "I'm sorry I did that. I just—you're wild and pissed off over things I'm commanded to do by your mates, and I don't want to face your wrath. With it comes the protectiveness of fierce dragons, so don't blame me for guarding myself."

Turning my head, I rest my cheek to the floor. "You leashed me again." It's all I can manage to say.

"With good reason. I'd never use it to force you into doing anything, and I won't apologize for controlling your unpredictable side. You've been put at a disadvantage by the traitor Litendrake heir and your mother for taking you into a world you were never intended to grow up in. I'm actually rather surprised your mother ever left you and allowed you out of her sight." Ambrose's words dig deeply into me, opening an ache inside me unlike anything I've felt for my mom since I was a child.

I lick my dry lips. "My parents died in prison when I was young...at least, that's what Aunt McKayla told me. She raised me human with a man named Darius, who never said more than a few words and was constantly in and out. McKayla didn't tell me she was a witch or that I was a dragon." Calling a woman I now know isn't related to me my aunt still feels strange. My whole life in the Mortal World and before finding Galaxy Gold almost feels like a dream. "But I don't know what to think anymore." Because the Darkonians mentioned my dad as if he were alive.

Ambrose kneels beside me. "I don't understand. I knew that Delilah dealt with Dark Ones to hide you, but McKayla? McKayla Lioht? That doesn't make sense. She was an outstanding witch and worked with the High Council."

"You have the wrong woman in mind then. Her coven deemed her a traitor when she helped my mom leave Magaelorum." I shiver at hearing Rhett's coven's name, knowing that McKayla was his coven sister and they worked together at the Maximum Magical Penitentiary. "And after that, she went by another name: McKayla Fyre. The Drekis and I were trying to locate her in the Mortal World, thinking she could help us like she had with my mother, but we hit a dead end. That was right before you showed up."

I know better than to spill our plans or anything about my life to someone who can use it against me, but a part of me hopes that maybe Ambrose isn't as bad as I think or at least that maybe he can help us too.

Ambrose falls silent beside me, and I prop up on my elbow to look at him. Green sparks in his silvery eyes, his dark skin making the color of his irises pop. Rubbing his hand over his platinum bleached blond curls, Ambrose loses himself in his thoughts.

"I need to take you somewhere, but I know neither the Drekis nor the Darkonians will allow it." He says the words like he's contemplating with himself and not asking me if I will agree to such a thing.

"Where?" I ask, pushing upright.

He sighs. "Fuck it." Locking his hand to my wrist, he

yanks me onto his lap. "Yoque bavito lotuessa!"

Bright light blinds me.

The world disappears.

Heat swells on the tops of my hands, and I cringe and fling my arms out, trying to cool them off. Goosebumps prickle over my body. Blinking my eyes, I try to push the light away. Ambrose's cool hand remains around my wrist, his grip the only thing stopping me from falling into darkness.

"Take a breath, princess. Nice and slow." With Ambrose's words, my body goes out of whack, my mind struggling to orient itself to the sudden shift in the world. "I need you to stay calm. The shield is fragile here."

"Here?" My voice comes out as a whisper as my vision clears.

Oh. My. Fuck.

This can't be real. I'm not back in the Maximum Magical Penitentiary. Ambrose wouldn't betray five brutally beautiful, protective dragons, would he?

An alarm rings through the air, startling me, and I step closer to Ambrose like this fuckhead would protect me. Why did he bring me here? What are his plans? Shit. Shit. Shit.

Dread pours over me as inmates march from the building in single-file lines and into the prison yard. Electric magic hums along the high walls, lighting the dark yard. This isn't the time of day for the shifters and fae, so I squint and peer around, hoping to catch sight of who is out here.

"No one can see us. I wouldn't risk bringing you to Max if I couldn't protect you. I know you don't trust me, but you should know that I wouldn't risk endangering the mate of my familiars. It's why I act as the Darkonian princes' guard." Ambrose adjusts his hand, sliding our fingers together.

I'm too afraid to tug myself free. I have no idea how his shield works, and I don't want to test my luck. "Oh, uh—"

"But none of that matters at the moment. We have someone we must see, who isn't allowed visitors." He cuts off my question before I have a chance to ask him what he means by calling the Darkonians his familiars. From what I know of witches, based on my limited Mortal World knowledge, is that a familiar is an animal who serves a witch or something. But the Darkonians don't do that. "We have to hurry. I anticipate we have only a couple minutes before their security spell picks up on our magical residue. People usually try to escape and not infiltrate this hellhole."

"Unless they're Lazlo Infinity," I mutter under my breath.

Ambrose lifts an eyebrow but doesn't comment, choosing to tug me along with him and deeper into the prison yard. I tense, squeezing his hand tighter, the memory of my short stay here feeling more like a nightmare. Dozens of figures move and meander around the dry grass and dirt field yard, mingling together in small clusters.

We stroll past a woman with long, dark hair twisted into a braid, and she smiles and twitches her fingers in our direction. I inhale a sharp breath, my fear getting the best of me, but Ambrose doesn't even glance in her direction. A man steps right in our path, causing Ambrose to halt and pull me into his arms. I bite my lip to stop myself from screaming out in surprise. Because the man doesn't look at us. His eyes focus on the beautiful woman. With a smile, he flashes his capped fangs and closes the space to her, kissing her softly.

Ambrose groans under his breath and drags me around them, not letting me gawk at what I think are a witch and a vampire sharing a passionate prison yard moment for long.

"Make sure you touch no one," Ambrose says, keeping his voice low, "and help me keep a lookout. Witches don't have their magic here, but they can still sense it. It'll draw their attention."

"Maybe you should just take me back to the palace, Ambrose." Because I really fucking don't want to be here.

"I need you, though. I doubt anyone from the Tenebris Coven will speak to me. They must hear it from you." Ambrose picks up his pace and practically jogs with me toward the back of the prison yard where I know we'll find the pits.

I should have terrible memories of being thrown into a deep, dark dirt hole, but all I can think about is my time getting banged by Maddox because he didn't want to take me to see where he lived within the prison. And fuck, does my body set itself off now.

Ambrose clears his throat and flicks his attention to me, but I keep my eyes on the grate-covered isolation pits. Groans, swears, and even someone singing trickles through the air. A CO stands near the towering wall with his arms crossed over his broad chest. He looks familiar, maybe one of the few guards I've interacted with besides the Drekis. I don't get long to think about it because Ambrose stops at the opening to a pit at the end of a long row.

"Nepo alliveta Tenebris sanctu vas," Ambrose murmurs under his breath. "Tasha Tenebris, we've come from the Mountain Lands to speak with you. It's about McKayla Li-oht."

A figure saunters into view, tipping her head back to peer up at us. "I have nothing to say that I haven't already said. Leave me in peace, Dragon Tamer. I know who you are and your allies. You will not get anything more from me. Losing my coven and magic was enough." The woman's eyes flicker with a soft blip of purple magic that fades as quickly as I see it. "Do not come again. I will not help you."

"Tasha, wait. I'm not seeking your help. All I want to know is who accused your High Priestess of her crimes against Magaelorum and High Priestess Lioht. The records have always been sealed."

"Was it McKenzie?" I ask, my mouth speaking before my brain has a chance to realize that it's me now talking. From my short time with my aunt's twin, I can't help but wonder. "She called my Aunt McKayla a traitor. She seemed like the type. She wouldn't even help me after it was her coven brother responsible for—"

Ambrose slaps his hand over my mouth, shutting me up. "Too much, princess."

"Let the dragon speak, warlock," Tasha says, returning to her spot beneath the grate. "I want to know her connection toward the coven who now claims the Tenebris power."

"McKayla raised me in the Mortal World after my parents died," I say, meeting the witch's gaze.

She scowls. "Impossible. She's why my coven burned."

I reach up and touch my chest, my thrumming heart attempting to escape my ribcage. "What? Aunt McKayla wasn't the sweetest, but I can't imagine her hurting anyone. She raised me as family when I had no one."

"A dragon clan would never allow one of their females

to be possessed by a witch." Anger lights Tasha's eyes.

"No one knew. I didn't even know. I barely found out a few weeks ago that my aunt had been lying to me all my life." I suddenly feel so desperate for her to believe me. "She spelled me to suppress my dragon. It was Rhett Lioht who broke the protection spell."

"Did you say Rhett Lioht broke the spell? He knew about you and what his prior High Priestess had done?" Tasha's voice rings louder through the air, and I squeeze Ambrose's hand at her anger. She might no longer have her magic, but it still feels as if she can summon it. And she's pissed. "When was this?"

"Just a few weeks ago," Ambrose says, answering for me. "He died in the process. Delphia was falsely convicted for his murder, which is why I need to know who your accusers were. Was it the Liohts? Are they acting against the High Council? If Rhett knew about Delphia, he had to have known that McKayla was alive."

Wait, what? I frown and flick my gaze to his. "What do you mean?"

Tasha growls, dragging my attention to her. She grips the strands of her chestnut brown hair, yanking at them. Another blip of residual power lights her gaze as if she might still carry some sort of magic despite knowing that the High Council gave it to the Lioht Coven.

"Are you implying that my coven not only perished due to false accusations, but they were also burned by dragon fire for a crime that was never committed?" Tipping her head back, Tasha releases a high-pitched scream, the grief and anger in her voice penetrating my soul, sending pain through me.

My bottom lip quivers, and I wobble on my feet. Sliding his arm around my waist, Ambrose hugs me to him. He chants something under his breath, sending a wave of warmth through me, pushing away the all-consuming icy grief of a witch who seems in a worse position than I was. Tears blur my vision, and I can't blink them away fast enough before they spill onto my cheeks.

"Tasha," Ambrose says softly, the witch's name a breath on his lips. "Please tell me the name of your accusers. I need to know it. We can help each other."

Tasha drops to her knees, her wild mess of brunette hair cascading over her face to veil her expression. Her shoulders shake with her silent sobs, and I've never so badly wanted to hug someone in my life.

"It was your allies," she whispers, dropping to the dirt completely. "The Litendrake Clan testified against us. They accused my High Priestess of treachery and murder. They said we spelled them and went after the gatekeepers to access the Mortal World."

Ambrose stiffens next to me. "Are you sure?"

Throwing her hands up, she says, "Of course I'm fucking sure."

Pursing his lips, he glances at me, a dozen thoughts flickering through his gaze. "We must go, but we will come back. Thank you."

"Wait, don't leave," Tasha says.

Scooping me into his arms, Ambrose surprises me with his embrace. I raise my hands to slap his shoulders, to get him to put me back down to speak more with Tasha, but the world erupts with light.

My hair flies around my face, floating with the static from his magic. My heart feels as if it slides into my stomach as the world spins. I hug Ambrose tighter, burying my face into his neck, breathing in his herby scent.

"I'm sorry, Delphia," he murmurs, stroking his hand along the length of my back.

The bright light fades from my eyes, but my mind and body feel as if they remain separated, and I can't get my shit together to focus. It takes another minute of silence before I can even lift my face from the crook of his shoulder.

"I know I shouldn't expect you to do anything for me, but I must ask that you keep our visit to the Maximum Magical Penitentiary a secret," Ambrose adds, the pleading tone of his voice dragging my attention from the scent of his skin, getting my body to finally react to meet his gaze. His silver eyes dart back and forth as they search mine, trying to determine the chance of me agreeing to such a thing. "I'm afraid things aren't as clear as I thought."

I finally process his words. Swinging my hand, I slap Ambrose across the face hard enough that he drops me. My ass hits the polished stone floor, sending a burst of pain through me. My hands slip through something liquid, and I realize we're in the same room he transported me from.

"Stay away from me, Ambrose," I snap, anger lacing my words. Scrambling to crawl to my mates, I put distance between me and Ambrose to touch my hand to Maddox's chest first. I exhale in relief, the sensation of Maddox's steady heartbeat thrumming against my palm. "I will not keep secrets from my mates."

Two hands lock under me, and Ambrose drags me away from Maddox. Chanting something under his breath, he sends me flying toward the wall. I tense and grind my teeth, expecting to crash, but I stop short before colliding into it. My bare back, still peeking through the scorched fabric of my clothes, grazes the cool rock walls.

I hover a few inches in the air, and Ambrose closes the space to meet me at eye level. His Adam's apple bobs in his throat, his silver eyes sparking with his green power. I can't move or speak or even look away from him as he restrains me with his magic. Fury swells inside my heart. The second he lets me go, he'll regret ever using his power against me.

"Delphia, I know it's wrong of me to put you in this position, but you must understand. The Litendrakes...that's your father's clan. Alliances are fragile, and I worry what the information will do." He stands ultra-close with only a few inches between us. His cool breath caresses my mouth, the sensation like a whisper of a kiss. And now I can't stop looking at his lips. "Will you please just give me some time to sort through some things?"

Whispering near my lips, he chants a spell, releasing his magic hold on me. Instead of dropping me to the floor, he catches me in his arms. I wrap my legs around his waist to steady myself, the new closeness of our bodies sending a wave of something strange between us. Something warm and electric. Something all-consuming that ignites my body with tingles and the urge to discover what his lips taste like.

Shit.

"Please," he murmurs, his embrace no longer infuriating me. "Just a day or two. It's all I need."

"Only if you tell me why you're doing this. Why is it so important? You said the Darkonians were your familiars. Shouldn't you trust them?" I ask, digging my fingers into Ambrose's chest. "And about my supposed father's clan...that can't be right. My dad died."

"Franco Litendrake is very much alive. Who do you think arranged things with Rhett Lioht for us? It was the traitor Litendrake heir, Finnegan, who ran away with your mother. You were supposed to be found and brought directly home. It was only after we learned of the attack on Rhett and your conviction that the Darkonians would let me take things into my own hands. You are very precious to them, you know." Ambrose licks his lips. "Which makes you precious to me, princess."

Why the hell do I like the sound of that?

How can I go from hating Ambrose's guts to wanting to do as he asks?

"Fine," I say, exhaling a small breath. "But I have some conditions."

His mouth tightens, but he doesn't respond, waiting for me to speak.

"I will tell the Drekis and ensure they tell no one," I say, studying Ambrose for a reaction.

"You must allow me to ensure it with magic." Ambrose shifts me in his arms. "I can do it right now while they rest."

"Only if you agree to my other conditions." Because I will get what I want. I've had enough taken from me and decided for me. I will not allow him to think he can manipulate me on matters I don't care about. "I want you to cure Quillon of his lycan curse, so Kash can be freed."

"That will take time," he says. "It's a huge cost on my life to agree to something like that."

I narrow my eyes. "Then no deal."

He sighs. "I didn't say no. I just want you to know the consequences on my life."

I shrug. "I don't give a fuck. I'm already paying the price for a ton of other people's fuck ups, so you can join my pity party."

Slowly, he bobs his head. "I suppose you're right, princess. Now, is there anything else?"

A dozen thoughts cross my mind, but nothing seems as important as freeing Kash and being able to confide in my true mates. "You'll tell me anything I have questions to. No secrets."

"Done. No secrets." Ambrose sets me on my feet, the sudden absence of his body sending ice over me. "Now, I need you to hold your mates' hands for the spell. I'll be quick, but it will hurt you."

Fucking great. Just what I need.

Puffing a breath of air through my lips, I follow Ambrose to Maddox's side first. Ambrose reaches and grabs onto Rowan, tugging his unmoving body close enough that I can take each of their hands.

"We'll do Kash last, since he's bound to the lycan," Ambrose says, kneeling at Maddox and Rowan's heads.

He summons a black bag from nowhere and pulls out two matching, glittering athames. I stiffen at the sight of the bejeweled daggers, fear clenching my chest. I squeeze my mates' hands, trying to remain calm. They might be angry that I agreed to this. Maddox might lose his shit that I didn't demand I speak with him first. But I don't know what else to do in this moment. I want answers, and I want my mates safe. If Ambrose can help with either of those things, the looming argument will be worth it.

"I'm going to freeze you in place, so you don't move," Ambrose says, not waiting for me to respond as he chants his spell.

My heartbeat pounds in my head, my whole body pleading for me to change my mind. My soul wants nothing to do with Ambrose's magic. All it wants is for my mates to wake up. I've never wanted something more desperately.

"Brace yourself, princess," Ambrose says, aiming the athames at the tops of my hands. "Eht Drekis vot og elliativita timlin nadia vu."

Stabbing the daggers through my hands and into my mates', Ambrose ignites green power in his palms, sending it through the hilts of the athames and into my body. Searing pain blasts through me, but I can't scream. I can't do anything.

A holler erupts from the hallway, Theo's familiar voice

cutting through the air.

Ambrose doesn't have a chance to react before Theo's huge black dragon form crashes into the room. Snapping his fangs, Theo nips the front of Ambrose's shirt and yanks him off his feet. The warlock doesn't fight or resist, allowing Theo to drag him.

"Theo, wait," I call, my voice quivering in pain.

Theo jerks his attention to me and roars, spewing fire. Flames consume us all.

True Mates

A DEEP, GUTTURAL GROWL RIPS me from darkness. Something warm slaps my ass, sending a stinging sensation across my skin. I snap my eyes open and stare at the balcony doorway. The low moon hangs in a purple sky abovc a dark green forest.

"Give her one more little spank, Maddox," Rowan says, his voice humming in my ear. "Our mate needs to know she's in trouble."

"I mean, what the hell is she doing showing off that sweet, tight ass of hers." Kash rubs his palm over my ass cheek.

I remain still, a smirk playing on my mouth as I savor the comforting presence of my mates surrounding me.

"It's so kissable." Rowan's lips brush my other ass cheek.

"Watch out, brothers. She needs her punishment. She's asking for it. Waiting," Maddox says, bending low enough to whisper in my ear. His cinnamon breath wafts over me, and I can nearly taste his kiss. "Isn't that right, cookie?"

A whimper of desire escapes my mouth, and I clutch the blankets between my fingers and tease him by wiggling my ass. Rowan and Kash both groan their enjoyment. Heat builds between my legs, my desire consuming me. Their closeness is all I can think about. I need it, crave it, and want nothing more than to lose myself to our passion.

"Tell me I'm right, and I'll give you what you want." Maddox's hand travels the length of my spine all the way until he slips a finger between my legs, discovering what his closeness does to my body.

"What if I want more than you, Maddox?" My question comes out breathlessly. "I'm so starved for all of your affection. I just want to be close."

Silence greets me, and I wonder if what I asked

might've been too much. We've never really talked about something like this, but knowing the three of them are caging me in on this monstrous bed, all eager for my attention...I want to give it to them.

Turning over, I prop up on my elbows and meet Maddox's gaze first before turning to his brothers. Rowan's hazel eyes sparkle in the soft lighting from above, and his molten dragon fire courses through the brandings on his arms. Reaching out, Kash wiggles his fingers, coaxing me to give him my hands. Our palms touch, and his warm fingers enclose around mine and he hauls me to him.

I laugh, landing on top of him, straddling his waist. "You have no idea how happy I am to see you like you are right now."

"How happy? Show me, kitten. I want whatever you want. It's been a long couple days," he murmurs, arching up to kiss me.

The bed shifts beside us, and Maddox twists my long hair in his hand, lifting it off my neck. Drawing his tongue up my throat and to my ear, he sucks my lobe into his mouth, his other hand cupping my breast to give it a squeeze. "We're as starved as you for affection," Maddox says, guiding my head away from Kash so he can kiss me next. "We're your mates, okay? We can all be together how you desire."

Rowan caresses his hand over my thigh, teasing me. "If that's what you want. I won't just let my brothers assume."

I break away from Maddox's mouth and lock my fingers around Rowan's neck. Pulling him to me, I kiss him desperately, brushing my tongue over his while silently guiding his hand from my thigh and to my tattered waistband, my clothes barely hanging on from being scorched.

"I want you to assume," I say, gasping against his lips. "I need all of you. It's all I can think about. The world feels as if it'll explode otherwise."

"Listen to our mate." Maddox hooks his fingers to the hem of my burned shirt and rips it open, exposing my breasts to the three of them. "Feel her."

Kash hums and kisses my bare shoulder, inhaling a breath of my hair. "Smell her. It's incredible. Like ecstasy."

Unbuttoning my pants, Rowan slides his fingers between my legs, feeling my excitement. I moan at the sensation of his finger rubbing my sensitive clit until he sinks it inside me. I try to rock my body to ride his hand, so desperately needing to increase the pressure, but Rowan pulls away and pops his finger into his mouth with a hum.

"Watch out brothers. I need to taste more of her," Rowan says, guiding me off Kash.

The three of them kneel around me, their bodies hard and rippling with their desire. I reach for Maddox's waistband, pulling him closer to me, so I can reach him. He bites his lip and adjusts his cock through his pants, waiting to see what I do.

I pop open the button and slide his zipper down, wanting to see the sexy excitement I arouse in him. "I need to see you," I say, moaning, my attention wandering to Rowan and Kash wasting no time to get my pants off by each blowing a smoldering breath to rip my clothes completely free.

Maddox strokes his cock, his body exposed, his eyelids heavy with lust. "You're so sexy. It's taking everything in me not to steal you from my brothers, restrain you, and fuck you how you love me to."

Damn it, do I love the sound of that.

"Only if I can taste you first," I tease, guiding him to my mouth.

Pleasure explodes between my legs at the same time I drag my tongue from Maddox's tip and to his balls to twirl my tongue over his soft skin. He moans and combs his fingers through my hair.

"That feels so amazing," Maddox says, meeting my gaze, fire lighting his golden irises.

I lick my lips and suck him as far as I can into my mouth. His pleasure radiates through our mind link, making my skin buzz.

"I'm going to flip you over, Nova," Rowan murmurs,

bracing my knees.

Kash kneels beside him, rubbing his hand over his erection while watching Rowan tease me with his fingers. I never in my wildest dreams expected such a life as this one, but I wouldn't change it. I'd even live through Max again as long as it meant that every experience led to this moment with my mates. With the four of us together, unashamed and open, wanting to just be together in a way that makes us happy.

"Get her nice and worked up," Maddox says, hooking his fingers under me to flip me onto my stomach. "I want to hear her scream."

My body tenses in excitement, the thrill of Rowan positioning my legs beneath me coursing through me. I brace my hands on Maddox's thighs, his hard-on flexing in anticipation for me to continue. Kash lies down next to me and shimmies his head into the small space between my stomach and the mattress and flicks his tongue over my tight, sensitive nipples.

My attention splits into three directions but somehow stays together as I feel my mates' bonds intertwine with mine. Our passion and pleasure merge together until I can't separate the all-consuming sensations that leave me moaning and gasping.

Maddox plays with my hair, rubbing his fingers between my shoulder blades as Rowan draws his tongue along the warm seam of my body, tasting and teasing every inch of me. I rest my head on Maddox's thigh and hold Kash's hand as he plays with my boobs. Rowan traces his slippery finger over my ass, his thoughts about what he wants to do whispering into my mind, waiting for my reactions.

"That feels good," I say, a dozen thoughts racing through my head. I'm not surprised by his desire to test me, to see what I'm willing to try, especially with all three of them vying to lose themselves in the intimacy and pleasure of our bond. "I'll try anything you want. I want to satisfy all of you anyway I can."

Maddox groans deep in his throat. "You're so perfect."

"Isn't she?" Kash murmurs, working his mouth up my clavicle. "You complete us, kitten. I knew that one day we'd have to share the woman of our dreams, but I had no idea that you'd bring us closer than I ever thought."

I smile at his words, squirming a bit at the sensation Rowan makes by drawing his finger over my ass again until he gently slips his finger in at the same time he sucks my clit, increasing my pleasure.

Arching my back, I moan so embarrassingly loud, my body buzzing with pleasure. The sensation is different yet exciting, and I lose myself to the lust clouding everyone's thoughts and excitement until my body craves for release. I gasp and dig my fingers into Maddox's thighs, on the verge of my body exploding.

But then Rowan stops and slaps my ass. He denies me my orgasm, leaving my body on the edge and aching in a way that makes me squirm for relief.

I groan, my chest heaving. "I'm so close."

Maddox chuckles, touching my chin until I tip my head back to look at him. "He knows, cookie, but you're going to have to wait."

"You shouldn't have been so naughty, kitten," Kash says, reaching around to spank my ass next. "Whatever agreement you made with the Darkonian guard has the asshole princes pissed."

"But we'll talk about that when we're through taking care of you." Maddox tucks my hair behind my ear to keep the wild strands from my face. "I'm not wasting another second thinking about anyone else."

"He's right," Rowan says, kneeling behind me. He teases me with his tip, making me moan. "Now flip her over, brother. I want to see her face as I give her what she wants."

Kash tosses me off him and onto my back on the mattress. "All right, Row. You better make her drip for us. Nice and slick. It's gotta feel good for her."

I pant in anticipation, nervous yet excited.

Leaning down, Rowan kisses me, aligning his body with mine. He doesn't try to do anal like I expect, but slips inside me with a moan. The pressure of his cock stretching me a bit to rub me in the best way possible leaves me spreading my legs wider. I want to feel his hips bump against my body.

Maddox adjusts me up, listening to my thoughts. Easing my legs into the splits, he lifts me higher and supports my body on his big palms, helping me be the right height so Rowan doesn't block his and Kash's view.

Talk about team work.

I stretch my neck and meet Maddox's mouth for a kiss, nipping his bottom lip with my teeth. Kash strokes his cock, jerking off as he watches his brother fuck me, his eyes lit with burning desire. I reach out and take over for him, rubbing and tugging him, watching his face scrunch in pleasure.

"Tell me how he feels, cookie," Maddox says, squeezing my ass cheeks harder, ensuring Rowan can thrust as deep as he can.

"So good." I gasp and moan, tipping my head back to rest it on Maddox's pec.

"Let's make it even better," Kash says, kissing me.

Kash plays with my nipple with one hand and traces his other hand lower to rub my clit. Tingles explode through me, and I wiggle in Maddox's hold, feeling the tip of his cock brushing against me. Pleasure cascades through me, my orgasm building, taking me to the edge of something mind-blowingly amazing.

"Keep her on the edge, brother. Wait for me," Rowan says, rocking his hips hard and fast against me, the softness of his balls slapping my ass.

I groan at his words, desperation twining around me as Kash slows down. I pant and wiggle and let go of Kash in an attempt to rub myself. Rowan grabs my hands and links his fingers through mine, stopping me.

"Please," I say, my body humming. "You're teasing me too much."

"Just another minute, kitten. It'll be worth it." Kash gently teases me with his finger, my body aching for release.

"You need to get me nice and wet if you want to pleasure us any way you can," Maddox murmurs, sneaking his finger between my ass cheeks, working me up for him. And fuck do the different sensations the three of them create feel amazing.

"What?" I ask through another breath, locking my gaze to Rowan's.

Rowan bites his lip, his face scrunching with ecstasy. Adding pressure once more to my clit, Kash rubs my body in a rhythmic motion to match Rowan's thrusts. A wave of hot pleasure tenses my body as I orgasm at the same time as him, my muscles spasming, tingles shooting through me as Rowan pulls out and Maddox slips between my legs without going in, moaning as I lock his cock in place with my toes curling. I've never had an orgasm last so long or feel so intense. And then Maddox slips free of my body's grip, his cock as wet as I am.

"Damn. She soaked you," Kash murmurs, talking to Maddox.

Heat flushes my face, their excitement a bit unexpected but so thrilling that I feel high on their emotions. Moving out of the way, Rowan flops on the bed beside us and kisses me, letting me savor the sweet softness of his lips.

"My beautiful mate," he whispers. "I can't get enough of you."

"None of us can." Kash takes the empty spot Rowan left behind to shower me with his affection, like he needs to stay close, even though he's finished and his brothers take over.

Maddox eases back until I'm flush against his body completely. His thrumming heart beats a rapid melody against my spine, and he adjusts his cock, creating pressure as he takes his time easing in. I gasp and bite my lip, the sensation strange and exhilarating as Maddox keeps his movements slow, letting my body get used to him.

Kash's eyes light with fire, his tattoos dancing across his skin as he flexes his muscles, his lust prominently displayed with his hard cock.

Maddox moans in my ear, a wave of his pleasure pushing away all my thoughts as he enjoys my body unlike anyone ever has. Kash strokes my clit, increasing the ecstasy, turning it back to my own as he tests me to see my reaction as he slides himself into my vagina.

And holy fuck. Them sharing my body, our pleasure mingling in an intense tangle of our essences feels like I was made for them and that they were made for me. Rowan kisses me again, stroking his tongue across mine, opening his mind completely, so I can hear his thoughts and the whisper of love swirling through his mind.

I lose myself completely to the pleasure and bond I have to these three men, all different yet who fall in sync to give me everything I need. Maddox kisses my throat and whispers a vow to always keep me safe into my ear. I've never heard him utter something so romantic in my life that my heart spills with a wave of warmth that sinks deep to my soul.

Kash bows forward, his knees between mine and Maddox's legs, and he sandwiches me to his brother to brush his lips to mine.

"I love you, Nova," Kash whispers against my mouth,

turning my thoughts to jelly. He's always been clear about the feelings he holds with our bond as mates, but something about his words feels so incredibly important in this moment. "No matter what. No matter who I share you with. You are my soul mate. Got that?"

I bob my head and smile, kissing him again.

Silence falls between the four of us, only our pants and moans of pleasure filling the air. I take turns kissing all of them, just enjoying each of their bodies entangling with mine like our sole purpose in life is to exist for one another as a clan, as mates, as if nothing else in the world matters.

Maddox moans and tightens his hands around my stomach, his body flexing with his oncoming orgasm. I clench with my own, my body reacting to his, and Kash soon follows like we trigger ecstasy with each other.

I pant, my chest heaving, my body zinging, and all I can think about is how lucky I feel in this moment despite everything. Kash eases off of me and heads to the attached bathroom, letting Maddox kiss and carry me to the enormous waterfall shower big enough for all of us. Hot water cascades from the rocky ceiling and onto the seat where I sit on Maddox's lap, kissing him as much as he wants, the two of us savoring each other's affection.

The four of us are so caught up with each other that we don't hear someone enter our room until a malicious laugh echoes through the shower.

"This looks like fun," Quillon says, standing in the open doorway. "If I didn't think you'd incinerate me, I'd join you for a bit."

Maddox growls, tossing me to Rowan to get to his feet. Scrambling back, Quillon holds his hands up in front of him, turning his nails into the talons poisonous to dragons. It's the only thing stopping Maddox from attacking at close range.

"Get out!" Kash yells, grabbing Maddox from behind and hugging him before he unleashes his dragon fire at the lycan. "You know you were supposed to fucking stay away."

"I have a message." Quillon glowers, his features twisting in annoyance. "And with the way things look and smell, you might never stop to allow me to deliver it. The warlock sent me a message, asking that Nova summon the Darkonians."

"What did he offer you?" Maddox asks with another rumble escaping his throat.

Quillon waves his hand over his body. "Can't you see for yourself? No chains, fuckers."

I blink a few times, my lust fading with the mention of Ambrose and how he basically gave Quillon a pass for his fuckups, which he doesn't deserve. Living should be enough. "Why does he want me to do that?"

"He thinks you're the only one who can convince the Darkonians to see reason," he says, staring only at me.

I squirm and hide my body more.

"Make him wait," Maddox says, answering for me, his words coming out hot with smoke. "He'd deserve it for the shit he pulled."

"You're always so fucking angry," he quips, lowering his arms to his side. Quillon turns back to me. "You'd think he'd be nicer after your bargain with the warlock. Helping you get me a cure to release Kash, though he has the hots for you. Poor guy. He should've just stayed out of it. He has far too much competition to even consider having a chance with you."

Rowan slams his fist into the rock wall. "What the fuck did you say?"

Uh-oh. I'm pretty sure my mates only heard half of what Quillon said. "It's not like that," I say, touching Rowan's arms. I glower at Quillon. "Dickless douche, stop exaggerating. It's not like that."

"Maybe for you," he says, grinning.

I groan. "Just get out and tell Ambrose I'll do what I can."

"What?" Maddox, Kash, and Rowan say at the same time.

Waving my hand at Quillon, I motion for him to leave.

I turn to my mates and try to hug their hulking forms at once. “Please try to stay calm. It’s not what you think,” I say, attempting to shower them with tranquility through our bond.

“Spit it out, cookie,” Maddox says, tightening his mouth. “No sugar-coating.”

I bob my head and meet his eyes. “Maybe we should sit down, because I have a lot to tell you. But promise me you won’t try to burn the world down or anything.”

“I can’t promise that.”

At least I tried.

Taking a deep breath, I close my eyes.

I tell them everything.

Intruder

"RED, PLEASE. DON'T LEAVE ME with them. I only want to talk to you, and I'll wait until you return." Quillon shoves himself into the corner of his tiny bedroom. "Don't you want to hear things firsthand?"

I bet the last thing he expected was to lose his power over us and end up basically in a cell once again. Ambrose might've released him from the chains he bound him with, but now my mates would prefer to keep an eye on him instead. His fear of retaliation is enough to stop him from demanding Kash remain in his dragon form, too.

Fuck. I feel so satisfied.

"I have other things to take care of, Quillon. You know that." I cross my arms over my chest. "If you had just been honest from the beginning with me, maybe you wouldn't have found yourself in this position, but you're a selfish asshole. Now, tell the Drekis everything you know about me and my family or I'll ask the warlock to neuter you permanently the second he gives you the cure."

Quillon scowls at me. "You're lying."

"Am I?" I ask, smirking. "You'll never find out if you dare try to use Kash again or lie to my mates about what you know."

"You're a real bitch, Red. We could've had a lot of fun together in the Mortal World," he mutters.

I raise an eyebrow. "With what exactly? Your resentful nub? I'd have to do the splits to barely feel your micro-cock. Even then, you don't have it half the time. Something could happen, turn you into a seriously overcompensating man-beast, and boom. Your dick falls off."

In normal circumstances, I wouldn't comment of the size of someone's junk. Hell, in the Mortal World, Quillon's average, and I wouldn't have given it a second thought. But this fucker had to go and make my handsome, romantic, too-good-for-this-bullshit mate bow. I'm bitter, and belittling his manhood really does help lighten my mood.

"You probably feel like tossing a hotdog down a hallway after being with the Drekis, anyway." Quillon flares his nostrils with his comment.

"What the fuck did you just say to Nova?" Kash fills the doorway to my room.

Quillon recoils but tries putting on a hard-ass expression.

"I think we should beat him until he understands that female dragons are made for giant cocks. She's flexible for a reason and just the scent of us triggers extra lubrication for her to increase the fun times." Maddox punches his palm with his fist. "So tell me again what you think you know of our mate?"

"Fuck, please don't," I snap, strutting away from Quillon so that he doesn't see my now flaming cheeks. Because I might not have known all of that either. "We don't have time."

Maddox huffs a breath. "Cookie, I don't know if I should allow you to go alone. What if—"

"Allow me, huh?" I smirk with my words. "How do you plan to stop me?"

His eyes narrow. "You want to test me?"

"We might be in Magaelorum again, but you're not my CO. You can't just throw me in the pit and have your way with me." I close the space to the doorway, where Kash leans quietly on the frame. I trace my finger over Kash's chest as I meet Maddox's eyes. "Though, you can, Kash. Just say the word, and I'm yours."

Maddox tightens his jaw, looking ready to grab me and spank me for teasing him.

Kash chuckles and snatches my wrist, pulling me to him before Maddox tries anything. "Careful, kitten. Maddy's in an extra asshole mood." Brushing his lips to mine, Kash kisses me softly, reaching down to pinch my ass. "And not the kind you like."

"That's what you think, brother," Maddox says.

Closing the space, Maddox sandwiches me to his brother. The heat of his skin warms me, his cinnamon breath coaxing me to twist my neck enough for him to kiss the side of my mouth. I practically melt between the two of them as my heart picks up pace.

"Isn't that right, Delphia? You love it when I tell you what to do. What you want. How you want it. I don't need a damn pit to cage you. I can do that anywhere." Spinning me away from Kash, Maddox shoves my back to the wall, locking his hands around my wrists to tug them up over my head. He nudges my hair from my throat and nips my skin before sucking it hard enough to leave his mark. "Now, accept that I'm going with you. You're mine, and I've decided only I will do in protecting you."

Damn him and his ability to make me want to submit to his need for power because I know how much it gets him off. But this isn't me doing it to use against him like at Max. I don't need to use his desire for me to get my way by beating him at his game. This is me loving his dominance and need to protect me. I also love that he is just openly himself, even with his brothers harassing him about our relationship. He unashamedly knows what I want from him and won't let anyone tell him otherwise.

"How will I seduce a Darkonian with you looming over me, *Maddy*?" I stretch and kiss his jaw. "I know you don't want to see it."

"The only thing I don't want to see is you do something you might not want to do," he mutters, meeting my gaze.

"And if I do want to?" I tease, knowing I'm pressing his buttons.

"Then that's up to you. And I will join." He remains expressionless with his words. "I will make sure things are done right and to your standards."

I blink a few times in surprise. "Wait, what? You'd be okay if I wanted to give the royal bling a ride?"

Kash laughs from behind Maddox and meets my gaze. "Come on, kitten. We'd only be a little bit jealous of those you think are worthy of you outside of us. Plus, we can feel your bond. It might be...unconventional and dubious, but as long as these fuckers know you're our mate too and you're okay with the situation like you say—"

"Fuck," I mutter, hanging my head to rest it on Maddox's chest. I can't tell if he says it only because he doesn't want me to feel badly about something out of our control, and it digs under my skin. Things were weird yet not as complicated when I accepted that the Drekis knew they'd share me with each other, but bringing others into things...shit. "I don't even know how to feel. I should be pissed the hell off. You shouldn't be okay with this. Right? It's...ugh."

"It's something we don't have to figure out and decide on this second." Rowan steps out of a room at the end of the hall, carrying a bag in his arms. "And you can feel however you want. Don't feel badly if you're not shooting fire at the world or angry that someone tampered with the fates. Maybe there is a reason the fates allowed such a thing."

I hadn't thought of it like that. "You think so?"

Setting the bag near my feet, Rowan kisses the top of my head. "The fates are fickle and unpredictable. Regardless, we're here no matter what. We'll get through this. Find our way to live together. I mean, you did agree to give the Darkonians a chance. We've accepted that."

I couldn't be more thankful for it, either. I just didn't know if I'd follow through. I'm not sure if I want to. I don't know what to think or feel or even how to act. Ambrose made me nervous, not wanting me to tell them about what we know of my aunt. But can I even trust a warlock who doesn't have a problem hooking a leash to the collar on my neck? Fuck. This. Shit. Why can't my life be easy?

Rowan closes their circle around me, and I realize I projected my thoughts for them all to hear. Engulfing me in a hug, the three of them attempt to squish the worry out of me. When Maddox would usually tell me to suck it up or some shit, he now floods me with loving affection, playing off the emotions from his brothers.

Something shifted even more between the four of us after I gave in to my deep-seated nature as a female dragon, and it's like my heart, mind, and soul align, confirming that what we have is real. Our mate bond connects us on an unimaginable level, and I can see past the mess of our lives in this moment and look forward to the future we will fight for. And hell, maybe I'll even have Maddox's babies like he desires. I could create a family, a clan, I never had the chance to have growing up in McKayla's care.

"I knew you'd want my children, cookie," Maddox

says, a cocky-bastard smile lighting his handsome face.

I pat his cheek, grazing my fingers over the scar. "Maybe after your brothers'."

He growls in my ear and links his fingers through my hair, holding me in place. Guiding me to him, he kisses me again until I have to gasp. "Don't tease me or I'll steal you away during mating season to ensure otherwise."

"He's not joking either," Rowan says, locking his hand around Maddox's wrist until he lets me go. "So get out of here. Save that pathetic warlock, so we can take care of the damn lycan curse and get on with our lives."

"You got this, kitten," Kash says, nudging me into the hallway. "And we'll take care of Quillon. He needs to be put in his place about what he can and can't say about you now that he's no longer in control despite my servitude."

I peek over Kash's shoulder and glare at Quillon, sweating in the corner I left him in. Before he made his stupid as hell comment, I had considered asking the Drekis to give him a break, but now I love seeing him regret his life choices.

Hugging my mates one last time, I exit the room and venture into the hallway. Now that I'm alone and undistracted, I drink in the details of this section of the palace. A red floor runner brings color to the dark rock walls arching into a high ceiling. Metallic light fixtures glow with magic, lighting every glittering facet of the mountain. The palace has obviously been here a long time, and I can't help wanting to explore.

"We can do that now, you know." The familiar feminine voice stops me in my tracks, and I spin around, expecting to see a ghost.

I summon dragon fire in my hands.

"Over here, Nova." Rose claps her hands together, drawing my attention to her. I freeze and open my mouth to shout, but she flutters closer, holding her finger to her lips. "I've learned my lesson about tricking you. There is no need to be frightened."

I scrunch my nose, trying to suppress my rising panic. "I thought you were dead. I watched you burn."

She smiles, her lips stretching into a devilish grin. "It takes more than a little fire to get rid of me, especially with my new protector. But, why don't we keep it this way? The Drekis will kill me otherwise. Plus, you owe me for getting me caught up in your bullshit. Next time someone nearly steals my ability to fly because of you, you have to promise to give me one of your wings, okay?"

A deep, guttural growl bounces around the corridor, shaking me to the core. "Don't respond to the murderous fae." Tiernan drops down from an opening in the rock ceiling and lands on his feet in front of us. "She will bind you to a contract without you realizing it. Now move, Delphia. She broke through the shield."

Shit. I flick my gaze at Rose, and she shrugs her shoulders with a smile. I should've known that she wouldn't go down so easily. Fairies are tricky. They have their own magic and will use it how they please.

"Well, someone owes me, Unlucky Twin. Will it be you? Will you be the dragon who will bow to Lazlo? He will get someone, but preferably you, Nova." Rose's wings flutter, sending my hair blowing in a breeze. "Don't you think you're better off elsewhere? We can find you a new plaything or ten."

Tiernan curls and uncurls his fingers, his green eyes smoldering with the intensity of his dragon fire. "Get back or I will kill you."

Rose flaps her wings, flying into the air a few feet to get at Tiernan's eye level. Raising her hand up, she points at Tiernan. "With wh—"

I snatch her hand and tug her back to the floor. I wouldn't put it past her to poke the beast man. "Stop, please." I grab Rose's shoulders. "Why are you doing this? I helped you. I was going to teach you about the Mortal World."

"You were taking too long," she snaps. "A better offer came up, so I went with it. You'd have done the same thing." A smirk crosses her lips. "You being here proves it."

I step away from her and cross my arms. "How so?"

"Don't bother arguing with a murderess fae." Spinning toward a wall, Tiernan slams his fist in a crevice, shooting a spark of power right at Rose. The fairy freezes, unable to move, her eyes widening. "She is no longer your concern."

Whoa. A part of me hates that there is no way the Darkonians will let her leave alive, but an angrier, more aggressive part of me wants her to pay for her betrayal. "What will you do to her?"

"It's best if you don't know. She will be handled appropriately. Now, let me get you out of here. I don't trust you to see reason, especially knowing this criminal hurt you and tried to give you to someone unworthy." He's speaking of Lazlo. Tiernan was there after all.

"Uh..." I flick my gaze to Rose, still trapped in a frozen cage of magic.

Tiernan straightens his shoulders and drops his gaze over my body, drinking me in. "Please, Delphia."

My skin prickles under the intensity of his stare. Taking a step closer, he captures my gaze, the fire in his eyes hot enough that if he were to check me out again, my clothes could very well burn off. His identical features to Theo make it easier to forget that Tiernan never got to magically bond with me, but my soul can sense it, and I want to tease his beast just a little.

Locking his fingers to my shoulders, he holds me in place, not allowing me to step back like sharing my personal space is his right. "I am capable of protecting you how you deserve, Delphia. It's nearly my time with you, so let me take you away while my brother comes for the intruder."

I twist my lips to the side, trying not to let his closeness distract me. A part of me wishes the Darkonians were unattractive to me, so my body would chill out. Another more vain part of me is so glad I do like them. Terrible? Maybe. Now if I can figure out how to manipulate this guy. I was supposed to distract him anyway, but...fucking Rose. What is she planning? "I think I'd prefer to watch you handle it. If you don't want to, I guess I could ask your brother."

Am I taking things too far? Definitely.

Tiernan flexes his muscles, his annoyance turning his features sharp. He slides his hand from my shoulder and to the back of my neck, tightening his grip on me. Leaning in, he gets in my face, the smoky sweetness of his breath caressing my mouth.

"You know, Delphia, I'm not one to play games. You say you want to see me do this, but you don't," he says. "You also might think you can manipulate me by using my brother's bond to you, but you're wrong. We're twins. Our souls are like one entity split apart between two bodies.

While it might help Theo connect with you faster, it won't make you want him more. I don't need a mate bond to get what I want. You will willingly give it to me. You're mine. Can't you feel it? We don't need the stars to align in our favor. I will rip them from the sky and put them together how I please."

Well, this took a turn in a strange direction. It's like he purposely distracts me from Rose. Her interruption might have been what I needed to do what I needed to. Is it the fates finally being kind to me? I'm afraid to find out.

The heat of Tiernan's body radiates against mine, our chests grazing together with each of our breaths. My nipples harden from the sensation, and I try not to react. Because damn. My rebel vagina clenches in excitement as I feel my willpower bending to his.

"I'll be waiting to see that." I lick my lips and swallow, drawing Tiernan's attention to my mouth. "Until then, do as I ask."

Tiernan tenses and roars, releasing me so quickly that I don't have a chance to catch myself as my legs give out. Spinning around, he snarls at Rose. She flaps her wings and glares, free from the magic trapping her. In between her hands glows a strange red light, like glowing red gel.

"She is not yours to claim! She belongs to Lazlo," Rose screams, her face contorting. "I will take her home as a present for him. Now don't try to get between us."

"You're dead, murderess!" Tiernan bends his knees to launch into the air to grab her.

Rose flings her hands out, sending the strange red gel pelting over us. "Now, get away from her. She's mine."

"Fuck," Tiernan mutters under his breath.

Rose's face transforms, her skin turning pale blue. "I said get away!"

I don't have time to react or move as Rose throws more of the red gel substance at Tiernan. Blobs of red melt through my shirt and plop against my breasts. Pain ignites over my skin, and I slap the strange gel away.

"Delphia, run!" Tiernan commands.

Rose flings her hands out again, but I can't dodge out of the way fast enough. My skin sears and burns.

I scream.

Seductive Games

TIERNAN CRASHES INTO ME, TACKLING me to the floor. He grunts and jerks on top of me as I see a splatter of the red gel spatter against the floor. My mouth falls open in surprise, my eyes widening. What the hell is that shit and where did Rose get it from? How did she escape the magic cage? Fuck.

"Don't move, Delphia," he says, shielding me protectively. "I got you."

Rose's shadow flits around us, but she remains out of my view. "You're not so powerful when faced with fae fire, Unlucky Twin, are you? Have you forgotten I am a princess born from the pyres of the Winter Court? You're lucky that the fire that warms me doesn't hurt like the ice in my veins. Now this is your last chance."

What the actual fuck?

"Rose, stop," I say, cringing as a glob of the red gel substance lands on Tiernan's shoulder and drips onto the floor above mine. "Stop!"

Her feet thump on the polished stone a foot away. The scent of roasted marshmallows wafts through the air. Tipping my head up, I peek at Rose, silhouetted in the light from overhead. Her shimmery wings sparkle, and the tattoos given to her by the Spring Court dance and twist on her arms.

"Stop? Why should I stop? He won't let you leave with me willingly." Rose's wings hum as she flutters them so fast that they look like pure rainbow light glowing on her back.

"He will if I agree to go." My words crack as I struggle to release them.

For the first time ever, I might be a teensy bit afraid of her. I had never seen her fae powers like this before. I knew she was powerful—so much so that she could remove a muter from my mouth in Max even under magical imprisonment—but now I wonder who the hell this fae princess really is and what she's capable of. No wonder Lazlo got to her. A winter princess that can send a dragon to his knees is quite surprising and a worthy ally.

"You think I'm going to believe you?" she asks, glaring. "It will take a bargain. If you don't, then I—"

Summoning fire into my hands, I surprise her and blast her with my power. She screeches and disappears into sparkling ash that vanishes before I get a chance to inspect it.

I touch the floor. "What the fuck?"

"She's not gone," Tiernan says from behind me. "She was wearing a protection amulet."

"We have to find her," I say, spinning around to meet his gaze. "She'll come back."

"My brother will handle it." Tiernan groans and falls to his side like now that Rose disappears, he can drop his guard. "Right now, I can't. I need to heal."

And fucking fuck. I can't believe he's not screaming his head off. I hadn't realized how much power Rose had used, but Tiernan's back glows with the gel residue like it embeds into every inch of his skin, melting the fabric of his shirt to his wounds.

Panic kicks my ass into action, and I swear under my breath and shake his arm. "Tiernan, Tiernan. What do I do?"

"Mud," he responds, trembling with his words.

I frown and grab his arm. "Come on. I need help getting you up. I can't carry you."

"Just give me a minute," he murmurs, blinking his green eyes.

"I'll get Maddox. He can—"

"No. Don't get anyone. It's a fucking little bit of fae fire." Tiernan grunts and tries to push himself from the floor but fails to hold his weight.

"Don't be a stubborn ass. You're hurt badly." I shove my hands under him, trying to hoist him off the floor. But it's no use. He's twice my size and built like a solid wall of muscle.

"I'll be fine. I just need to get to my room. It's on the second level through the opening on the ceiling." Gathering the fabric of my shirt, he tugs me closer. "I have everything we need. You're hurt too."

He's right, but I basically have papercuts compared to his bullet holes. Unfortunately, I'm not so sure the Drekis will see it that way. They might blow up and do something insane for my injuries caused by getting stuck in the crossfire between an enemy and someone they expect to protect me.

"Please, Delphia," Tiernan says, his voice lowering.

I purse my lips and bob my head. "Okay. Hang on. I'm

going to transform."

Closing my eyes, I summon my dragon, unleashing her faster than ever. Tiernan drinks in my dragon form like I'm an angel come to save him. Hot air puffs from my nostrils, and I stretch my neck to get at Tiernan's eye level. His now seemingly small hand, one that would usually swallow mine, touches my chin as he grazes his fingers over my scales.

"You're so beautiful," he murmurs, stretching his arms up to hook his hands around one of my big fangs. "I'm already in love. My clan arranged for such a stunning mate in you."

I growl, annoyed that he thinks he loves me because his beast probably wants to mate with mine. "I'm more than my looks," I think to him, opening my mind to let him in.

He hangs on as I stand at my full height, my head nearly grazing the vaulted ceiling near the entrance to the second level. "And you won't ever let me forget it. It's a good thing I like that."

Flapping my wings, I launch off the floor and manage to drag myself through the tight space in the ceiling. I feel awkward as hell in my dragon form, my body and mind slightly disconnected as my humanity clings tightly to me. It's hard to accept that I'm not a mortal, but especially in moments that I would prefer to be—like now. Something about being in my dragon form in the confinements of this mountain freaks me out a bit. All I can think about is either launching through the nearest exit leading outside or transforming back.

The world shifts with my thought, and I hug my arms over my body as I stand over Tiernan, completely naked, giving him the best view of my vagina. He remains utterly still as my feet remain locked in place at the sides of his head. I don't know what I was thinking just leaving my clothes with the mess Rose left behind.

And then the fucker pushes up, knocking me off my feet. I automatically catch his neck with my thighs, squeezing his head right into the heat of my body.

His hot breath tickles my skin, and I nearly curl around him, my body totally on board with sitting on his face, but Tiernan groans and tugs me off him and into his arms. He licks his lips like he can't resist, hoping to catch a taste of me. I suck my bottom lip between my teeth as his cock hardens under me, testing the fabric of his pants.

He exhales a sexy, hot breath. "Go fill the tub, Delphia. Help me, and I'll give you what you want."

I force myself to get up, my legs trembling at the strange, yet exhilarating, situation we've found ourselves in. Tiernan scrubs his hand over his face and heaves a breath. I watch him struggle to shift to his knees but try my best not to watch him in his moment of weakness. He obviously is trying to hide how much pain Rose caused him, and I should call him out, but a part of me wants him to know it's okay. He doesn't have to be a tough asshole all the time.

Entering the grand bathroom, I stare in awe at the rock-walled room. An overhead light blinks on with my movement, and I gawk at the massive tub inlaid within the shiny rocks. An overhang of glittery minerals makes the tub look as if it's nestled within a cave. Excitement swirls through me. I've never seen anything like this, and it takes everything in me not to slam the door closed to enjoy a moment of peace.

I would if Tiernan didn't release another groan, the low rumble of his voice relaying to me how much pain he's in.

"You said we need mud," I call, stepping into the tub to try to figure out the unfamiliar knobs. "How do I get it?"

"Turn all three knobs to the left. Our palace is equipped with everything we need in case of unexpected attacks. We're the ruling clan in this territory. Many try to test our power." Tiernan's rumbly voice echoes through the room as he uses the doorframe to balance on his feet.

"So will you ever tell me how to activate the magic traps?" I ask, turning the three knobs like he instructed.

"You will learn everything. This is your home now."

A gurgling noise erupts from the walls, and I jerk my head to look for some kind of spout. Chuckling, Tiernan points at the ceiling in time for me to spot a waterfall of thick brown mud cascading over a ledge to pour on top of me.

I screech at the icy sensation and scramble to get out of the way. My feet slip out from under me, and I land on my ass under the stream of mud. Swiping at my face, I clear my vision and glower, knowing well enough that Tiernan knew this would happen. His sparkling cock bling glints in the lighting a few feet away as he stands naked on the step to get in.

"Mind scooting over, Delphia? There's plenty of room for the both of us, and I'm not so sure I can wait much longer to cool the fae fire burns." Tiernan climbs into the big tub without waiting for my response.

I remain frozen, unable to really give him one.

"I only bite when I'm in the mood," he adds, gracing me with what might be his first genuine smile. And damn. He's gone from attractive to hot as hell. Even the cold mud filling the tub warms with his presence. "So keep your distance. You're the sexiest woman I've ever seen, even covered in this filth."

Stretching out, Tiernan floats on his back, doing nothing to hide his erection peeking from the mud bath. I inhale a few deep breaths, his closeness digging under my skin. This tub might be gigantic, but it feels tiny with his presence.

"Relax. It takes a couple minutes to absorb the toxins in the fae fire that burns us." Tiernan flicks his fingers, pelting me with mud. "You can't think sharing a tub with me is that awful."

Which is exactly why I need to get out. I don't find it awful at all. If anything, I want to float on the strange silky mud with him until it dries into dirt. But I have to find Ambrose. I know I shouldn't care what the Darkonians do to him. I should pretend that it doesn't bother me, because the dickhead warlock fucking leashed me. But that's not me. I do care. I don't want something to happen to the man who can help me...maybe. I can hope.

"I'm fine, really. Thank you for protecting me, but I need to get out. I need to tell the Drekis about Rose." I wade through the thick mud toward the steps to climb out of the tub.

Snatching my wrist, Tiernan pulls me hard enough that I fall into him. "Theo will inform them."

We sink under the mud together, my body flush against his. A shock of electricity zings from my groin and to the rest of me, setting my body abuzz. Tiernan snakes his arm around my waist and hoists me upright, wiping the mud from my face with his big hand. I gasp a breath and blink, trying to orient myself from going under with him.

Tiernan groans deep in his throat, the sound vibrating through me. "Fuck, Delphia. I'm sorry. I didn't mean to pull you down with me."

His chiseled chest presses against my boobs, drawing my attention to every place our bodies touch. I shiver at his closeness and how hard his cock feels trapped between my legs because he lifted me off my feet and it had nowhere else to go. Digging my fingers into his shoulders, I hold onto him, trying my best not to squirm. He realizes our position and accidentally—or maybe purposely—flexes his cock.

My. Traitor. Vagina. This bitch needs to chill. His cock is covered in mud for fuck's sake.

"Please forgive me," he adds, his voice softening. "I just didn't want you to go, Delphia."

"Call me Nova," I say, the words coming breathy from my lips. "I no longer go by my birth name. It carries a lot of negativity for me."

"Your father will be saddened to know that. He chose your name, you know," Tiernan says, loosening his hold on me.

I slip from his arms and to my feet, trying my best to ignore the sensation of his cock shifting with me. "Which is exactly why I don't give a shit about it. He wasn't there to teach me to appreciate it, and he obviously doesn't care now."

Tiernan's jaw tightens. "Because he's not here?"

"If he wanted to bring me to Magaelorum, he should've come for me himself instead of having sent Rhett. None of this—" I snap my mouth closed.

Can I truly be mad at a man I never met for something he couldn't predict happening? I'm not sure. I want to be. I want to be pissed and take it out on the world. But a more reasonable part of me knows that every bad thing that has come from this brought me to my mates, who are the best things to ever happen to me. I'd have never met Maddox, Rowan, and Kash otherwise. They had a contract with the High Council that was as long as a mortal life. Without being falsely accused, we'd have never crossed paths, and I'd have never known what finding the ones my soul calls to was like.

Tiernan reaches up and touches my cheek, combing the muddy tresses of my hair from my face. His green eyes spark with his dragon fire, and I find myself inching closer to him as I lose myself in his stare.

And then he leans in and kisses me, just grazing his lips to mine, gauging my reaction. I stand frozen and cling onto him. My mind whirls with a dozen thoughts. My heart beats out of control, banging around my chest hard enough that I'm sure Tiernan can hear the erratic thrums. I should push him away. I should slap him for not asking me if it was okay instead of stealing a kiss, but damn it. I crave more. My attraction to Tiernan surprises me. This moment alone with him and seeing him vulnerable shows me a side I didn't know he had.

He eases away from my mouth without getting carried away, leaving me yearning for more. I never expected such a sensual kiss from a hulking, tatted, dick-pierced, hot-headed, entitled man. I know he has a wild, aggressive side, but it's like he wants to prove to me he's capable of treating me like someone precious to him.

"I just wish things could've been different," I murmur, stretching on my tiptoes to rest my head on his shoulder.

"Me too. I'm sorry for everything that happened to you, Nova." He strokes his hand up my back to keep me close in a warm embrace like he knows this is what I need. "Our clan never gave up looking for you. I hope you know that. It was our duty as your intendeds to find you, so please don't blame your father for our shortcomings. I pray to the fates that you don't hold it against us, either."

"I'm trying not to," I respond, breathing in the wild scent of mud mixing with his skin. "You have to understand where I'm coming from. I had no idea that Magaelorum existed. I grew up believing I was mortal. In the Mortal World, things are different. I had no expectations for my love life nor had I even considered a serious relationship."

"You must've been shocked to find the Drekis." Tiernan guides me to sit down with him, and I let him, despite knowing what I'm supposed to be doing. My curiosity keeps me here, and I'm afraid if I leave now, Tiernan might not open up like this again.

I sit beside him in the tub, letting him hold my legs across his. "I think I was more surprised about discovering my whole life was a lie. Or that creatures were kidnapping mortals. How ruthlessly warlocks killed..."

"Mortals do the same." Tiernan's eyes search mine. "But even so, I still can't fathom what it was like or how hard it was. We should've been faster to find you. Tried harder over the years. We've given a lot to locate you just short of asking Ambrose to practice dark magic, which is why Rhett took over. He knew the Mortal World unlike us. But now I know why we couldn't. The fates didn't want us to find you first." Without having to ask, I know he thinks the reason is because of the Drekis, and maybe he's right. "If only things were clearer. I feel like you're my intended, Del—Nova. I know it might be wrong of me to demand you give me your time, but I've been waiting my whole life to meet the stolen Drakovich princess of the Litendrake Clan. I know you'll accept me. It's undeniable in my soul."

He slides his hand from my knee and up my leg, stopping at my thigh. His thumb grazes the sensitive skin where my leg meets my pubic bone, and I close my eyes in anticipation. But he doesn't move further, just testing me for my reaction. He is a charming asshole if anything, claiming that he knows I'll give in to him. And fuck, he might be right.

I swallow my nerves and open my eyes, meeting his cocky-bastard smile. He knows he's getting to me, wearing me down, and now I feel easy as fuck. It's been like a day, and I already think about kissing him again and experiencing what his cock would feel like inside me—if his and his brother's piercings are the magical gift Theo claims them to be.

"You know, your certainty makes me want to resist you," I say, finally managing to get my shit together to stop thinking about how close his finger is to stroking the spot that will make me scream in pleasure. "The fates chose the Drekis as my mates. How can you be so sure that I'm the one for you? That I'll be with you?"

"You were raised in the Mortal World," he says simply, finally shifting his hand back down my leg. "From what I know, it's not uncommon to mate and breed with those your soul doesn't call to. You were raised to bond with others, were you not? We don't need the fates to bind us to enjoy each other's company."

He's right about that. I've had plenty of one-night stands over the course of my travels with Galaxy Gold as one of his Sky Dancers. I bonded with him, Star, Orion, and Mars as if they were my true family.

"I'm not breeding with you or anyone. You're a bit mistaken over the concept. Mortals tend to have sex for fun and not for the sole purpose to procreate." The mud engulfing us rises in temperature, warming my core. I can't believe I'm having this conversation, naked in a tub, with a man who thinks he has a right to claim me and thinks I'll accept it.

"Is that what you'd like?" he asks, his face lighting with a smile. "I mean, to have sex for pure enjoyment? Because that's one of the reasons I've enhanced my cock for you."

"Are you sure it's not because you enjoy some pain in your dick? Don't think I've forgotten your erection over me roughing up your cock." I say it teasingly, trying to play his game of discovering my sexual enjoyment.

Grabbing his leg under the mud, I pinch his muscular thigh with enough pressure to make him shift. Tiernan snatches my wrist so fast that I don't have a chance to process him moving it to his cock. I automatically lace my fingers around his thick girth, my whole body humming in shock and surprise by his gesture.

Linking his other hand to the back of my neck, he jerks my head closer, stopping just short of my mouth. "Would you like to find out, Nova? Like I said earlier, I don't play these games. If you're not serious with your desires, don't taunt and tease me. I don't want to scare you. My dragon grows wild."

Scales prickle over his skin and he releases a small breath of fire. The heat dries the mud over my breasts, cracking the dirt coating. His cock throbs in my fingers, reminding me I still clutch his junk as my heart, body, and mind war with each other over what to do and how to think and feel.

Blowing another breath, Tiernan clears the cracked dirt from my skin to expose my breasts. I sit frozen, my chest heaving, my heart threatening to escape my ribs. Tiernan leans forward and drags his tongue over my excited nipple and up to my throat. I moan softly, the lust rising in me stealing away my good senses.

Our mouths meet, and Tiernan kisses me harder, deeper, more passionately than before. I grip his cock in my hand, slowly rubbing my fingers up its intimidating length. Slipping his tongue over mine, he explores my mouth, clutching my neck to keep me to him.

I shift more onto him, wanting to tease him with my body.

Tiernan yanks away from my mouth, his green eyes scorching with orange fire. Smoke puffs from his mouth, sending the sweet, burning scent of marshmallows through the air. His eyes flick back and forth, his gaze devouring my expression like he tries and fails to listen to my mind. I try to lean in to kiss him again, but he turns his head with a groan.

"Not like this," he mutters, sliding me off his lap. Standing up, he climbs out of the tub, spilling mud everywhere. "I'm sorry, Nova. I have to go."

What in the actual fuck?

I scramble to get to my feet.

Tiernan spins around and holds his hand up, stopping me from following after him. "You may stay here until I return. I just—I need to speak with my brother. I can't take you as I want until you know. I will not let an agreement ruin things for me."

I don't get a chance to respond and demand he tell me what the hell is going on. Grabbing a towel, he exits the bathroom, abandoning me in the mud bath, the heat of the moment still clinging to me, though it fades and chills as the seconds tick by.

"Nova..." The soft whisper of a voice trickles through my mind.

I blink a few times, trying to figure out if I imagined it or not.

"Nova, come to me," Ambrose says, his voice growing louder in my mind. "I need your help. Please."

I wasn't imagining things.

"Monosum ratitian vo de." The lights dim in the bathroom until one blinks in sync with my heartbeat. "Come to me. The lights will lead the way."

Confrontation

MY FEET SLAP THE COOL polished stone steps as I descend down a long, winding spiral staircase. It's creepy as hell, the only light trickling through the palace coming from flickering sconces below. In the Mortal World, I'd have hauled ass away from wherever I was if some whispering, haunting voice told me to follow some blinking lights, but I suppress my human rationale the best I can, reminding myself that I'm a fucking fire breathing dragon. I am the beast people should be afraid of, especially if they mess with me.

After what feels like twenty-million levels, I finally reach what I think might be the basement—or I guess, the dungeon—of this mountain palace. The quiet hum of magic in the air coaxes me to follow the blinking lights. I don't even bother looking around, knowing that no one will see me dressed in one of Tiernan's long shirts with dried mud plastered to my body. And if they do? Fuck them. They probably wouldn't recognize me anyway.

"Almost here, princess," Ambrose says, his voice humming through the air instead of in my mind. "Hurry. We're running out of time."

I pick up my pace, jogging across the expansive cave-like room, containing only a few crates stacked along the walls. I reach a dark hallway and hesitate, the icy air sending a chill shivering through me. I half-expect to hear the roar of a monster or maybe the cry of someone other than Ambrose chained to the wall of this dark dungeon, but it's just a stone corridor with dim lighting. There aren't dozens of cells hidden in this mountain. This isn't like the Maximum Magical Penitentiary. All it seems to be is an actual basement.

"My room's at the end of the hall. Only a Darkonian can open the door." Ambrose's shadow shifts along the light coming through a crack beneath the door, his silhouette moving as he disappears deeper into the room.

I frown and stare at the metal door without a door handle. "Okay, so how do I—"

It swings inward with a whoosh, the electric magic sparkling through the air. I hug my arms over my chest, the intensity of Ambrose's silver stare stopping me in place as it roves over me. His fingers curl into fists, and he narrows his eyes, looking at me as if now that I'm here, he wants me to go away.

"Your mate-bond to Prince Theo allows you access to anywhere in the palace," he says, answering my unfinished question. "Now come in and close the door."

I suddenly don't want to.

My instincts want me to spin on my feet and run away.

Something in Ambrose's eyes stabs into me, and I can't pinpoint what it is. My throat tightens as if he ignites my magical collar, but his hands remain clenched at his sides. He doesn't move or chant a spell, so I know it's in my head.

"Close the door, Nova," he repeats, striding closer.

I flinch and scramble back, a wave of panic washing over me. Ambrose catches me by the waist and spins me into the room, kicking the door behind him. I screech and summon dragon fire into my hands, preparing to fling it at him.

"Nova, what's wrong?" he asks, holding his hands up in

surrender. “What did I do? Why are you afraid?”

My throat burns, my words sticking to the tip of my tongue.

Shuffling closer, Ambrose closes the space to me. He tilts his head, searching my eyes for answers I’m not quick to give. Heat zings through my veins, my dragon threatening to burst free in the small space, the first room I’ve come into which can’t accommodate my massive size in my dragon form.

“Can I touch you?” Ambrose asks, shifting his weight between his feet. “I want to check something out.”

My head bobs without consulting with my mind, and I stiffen under Ambrose’s icy fingers. Pushing my dirty hair from my face, he gently presses the tips of his index and middle fingers to my temples. With the slight pressure, the fear coursing through me lessens until I can focus without needing to flee. It’s in this moment that I realize the fear was never mine to begin with. It belongs to Theo and came on so powerfully and intensely, I mistook it as my own.

I grimace, my heart throbbing, my soul feeling as if it weeps inside me. "I need to go. Something's wrong with Theo. It could be Rose.”

“I felt the intruder leave, and adjusted the shields. She can’t return.” Ambrose combs his fingers into my tangled hair, stopping me by holding my head. “Theo is fine, princess. The only thing he fears right now is you."

"Me?" The word comes out sharply with a gasp in confusion. That's fucking crazy. Why would Theo be afraid of me? Why would he panic?

"I don't have the answer as to why, but it's the truth. He's my familiar. We're connected mind and soul. While he and Tiernan purposefully block me out, I can still decipher that something is wrong involving you. Did he do something wrong? Please don't tell me you rejected him." Concern lines Ambrose's questions as he continues to lock me in his stare. "Is that what kept you away?"

I press my lips together, a dozen thoughts swirling through my head. "I haven't seen Theo since we returned."

"But you're wearing..." Stepping back, he gives me a once-over. "That's not Theo's shirt."

Warmth blooms in my cheeks under his scrutiny. And damn it, do I feel like I fucked up. Ambrose gawks at me, his thoughts clearly splashed across his face. My time with Tiernan was obviously unexpected, and now I feel like I have to defend myself.

"It's not what it looks like," I snap, grabbing onto his arms to get him to let go of my head. "And even if it was, it's none of your damn business."

"I—I'm sorry. I didn't mean to assume anything." Ambrose scratches his fingers against the back of his neck and tips his head back to stare at the glittering mineral-embedded ceiling.

I follow his gaze and finally take a moment to peer around the room. While the ceiling isn't vaulted, it's still spacious. A neatly made bed rests on top of a wooden platform with etchings all along the sides. Dozens of bookcases line the walls, full with all sorts of books, bottles, and trinkets. An open curtain reveals an altar separated from the rest of the room, and I want so badly to explore and look at everything.

"Nova?" Ambrose asks, drawing my attention back to him. "Is that okay?"

I was so distracted by the room that I missed what he had asked. "Um, what?"

"I asked if I could start my shower for you and get you something clean to wear. And then we can talk about the Darkonians...and what we know." He flicks his gaze to the door. "I have some concerns I'd like to discuss."

"But why?" I can't stop the question from escaping my mouth. "Why do you care? You serve the Darkonians. Shouldn't you confront them yourself?" Because damn it. With Rose managing to find me...I think we have worse problems.

Ambrose flares his nostrils and fidgets, messing with the hem of his shirt. "I—I have a moral obligation to ensure

I'm not dragging you into something that the fates will obliterate me for. As you imagine, this situation is...unusual. Dragons haven't been free to find their fated mates for probably a millennia. Every clan works with a particular coven and arranges unions for females and allying clans."

"I don't think I follow," I say. "The Drekis made it seem like they knew I was their mate. It wasn't random. They had my name. It was given to them by their clan leader before they were obligated to serve as COs at Max." At least, that's what they've told me. They had assumed Rhett had found me for them. They had no idea he was working with another clan.

Ambrose's eyebrows peak on his forehead. "That means their clan had arranged a union too. Maybe you're not actually their true mate. It would make better sense. The witch covens have been involved with re-arranging the fates for dragons because the claiming of a true mate led to many wars and was responsible for endangering your species. The clans sought help from the High Council to ensure only allied clans would bond. It helped the tension and allowed betrothed dragons to grow up knowing who their soul would claim."

Well, if that isn't some bullshit.

Ambrose purses his lips. "It's not as bad as it sounds. No one ever misses their true mates. The chance of actually finding your fated mates is nearly impossible. We create your perfect mate for you."

Like that makes it any better. "And you think I was promised to two different clans?"

He nods. "I have no other explanation."

"Except you used magic to bind my soul to Theo's," I say, narrowing my eyes. "There is no magic involved with my feelings toward Maddox, Kash, and Rowan."

He darts his attention to the door again. "You make a point, princess, but it doesn't hurt to ask. Now please, let me help you get cleaned up."

"Does my filth bother you that much?" I ask, crossing my arms.

He shrugs. "It's not that. I just..."

I dust off the caked on mud from my arms. "What?"

Palming his forehead, he releases a huff. "If you must know, seeing you like this fucks with my head. I can't stop picturing you with Tiernan in his mud bath."

"You don't like thinking about me and your familiar?" I tease, a smile playing on my lips. "Why? Because you wish it was you?"

Ambrose flicks a burst of electric magic at my feet, surprising me. I screech and leap out of the way. "The shower is that way. I'll summon you some clothes."

I gather a palm full of my dragon fire, tossing my power at him in retaliation. "You didn't answer my question."

Chanting something under his breath, he casts a spell that sends me flying across the room and into a small tiled bathroom. I shriek and laugh at the burst of water cascading over my head as he turns on the shower with his magic.

He appears in the doorway. "It doesn't matter, princess. Now hurry and get cleaned up. We don't have much time to figure out everything with your supposed mates."

Curling his fingers, he shuts the door with his power, leaving me in the small shower. The huge rain spout pours hot water over me, rinsing away the mud and dirt from my hair and skin. I shrug out of Tiernan's sopping shirt and hang it over the glass door just in case Ambrose doesn't follow through with summoning me clothing.

The scent of rose water and something fruity, maybe cherries, wafts through the air. Tingles bloom over my skin as suds of bubbles mix with the water without me even having to find a bottle of soap. Talk about a magical fucking shower. I scrub my fingers to my scalp until the water returns to normal, filling the bathroom with steam.

If a loud-ass roar didn't sound from Ambrose's room, startling the hell out of me, I'd have stayed in the shower forever.

"Where is she, Ambrose?" Theo asks, swinging the door open. He peers around the bathroom, his gaze flicking across the steamy bathroom but they never stop on me.

"I don't know. Ask Tiernan." Ambrose shoves past Theo, wearing only a towel. "If you want help tracking her, give me a couple minutes. I'm about to take a shower."

"Are you fucking kidding me? She could've been kidnapped." Theo smacks his hands against the doorframe. "She could've run away."

"I'd have known if another intruder came, and she wouldn't leave the Drekis, and you know that." Ambrose waves his hand toward the shower, opening the door. "Now leave me alone. You can't expect me to rush to help you after the shit you pulled. She probably wanted some space."

I stand frozen, soaking wet and naked, as Ambrose steps into the shower with me. He turns his back in my direction, nearly sandwiching me to the wall. And hell. I can't stop my eyes from sweeping down his broad, velvety dark muscles to his tight, round ass. Theo growls and slams the door shut, and something crashes in Ambrose's room. Ambrose must've spelled me from sight, because Theo couldn't see I was here.

"Why are you hiding me?" I whisper against his glistening shoulder blade. "How will I explain my absence?"

Ambrose twists on his feet, the small shower making it impossible for him to stand even a foot away. We both glance down at each other's bodies at the same time, sending blush crawling up my neck. I don't know what I was expecting—maybe for Ambrose to be built differently because he's a warlock—but what I didn't expect was for him to have several cock piercings along his long shaft.

I catch my damn hand attempting to stretch out, wanting to graze the row of piercings to see what they feel like and rush to cross my arms over my chest. Why in Magaelorum do cocks have to be so enthralling to me? I swear I wasn't like this in the Mortal World. Of course, I never had experience with dragon-sized batons and bejeweled warlock wands.

"You have to stop looking at me like that, princess," Ambrose says, drawing my focus to his hard expression. "It's difficult for me to think under your scrutiny. I've forgotten what you've asked."

Fuck. Me too. I can't even remember why I'm in this shower with Ambrose in the first place.

I chew on my bottom lip, stretching it between my teeth as I drop my gaze once more down his body. Because my eyes are damn rebels. Tell them not to do something and they want to look even more. It's like if I stare long enough, Ambrose's cock will grow to give me a real magic show.

"Why are you pierced?" I guess my brain admits defeat, my curiosity getting the best of me. "I know Theo said he did it for me, but what about you? Is that a normal warlock thing? Is it...for your mate?"

I hold my breath in anticipation. A part of me suddenly desperately wants to hear the answer. Another part of me thinks I'm crazy for even giving a fuck. I mean, why do I even care? What is it about Ambrose that draws me to him, especially after the shitty forced bond spell he pulled, linking me to Theo?

"I don't have a mate, nor will I for a long time. I serve the Darkonians and will remain celibate the rest of their lives. Joining a coven through a union of power that I can't fully commit to isn't fair for someone who should be my beloved." Ambrose's voice lowers, his face frowning with his admission.

"You know sex and relationships don't have to come together, right? If that were the case, I wouldn't have lost my virginity until I met the Drekis." I try to remain expressionless, the idea of losing my virginity to my mates...I'd have probably been terrified just from their sheer size.

He sighs and rubs his hand across his hair. "It's complicated. Warlocks live monogamous lives, so sex without the commitment—it's not something I desire."

"Are you a virgin?" I ask, surprised by his answer.

"You ask a lot of questions I'm not so sure I should answer, especially in our current state." He drops his gaze down my body again like he can't help himself.

"So you are." I wave my hand toward his cock, pointing out his piercings once more. "Which brings me back to my question of why do you have dick bling?"

"If you must know, it's to help with my celibacy. I..." He closes his eyes and scrubs his hands down his face. "I don't want to tell you. It sounds bad, and I've done enough to upset you."

What the hell? Why would his reasoning upset me?

Grabbing Ambrose's shoulders, I shake him. "Now you have to tell me."

"No," he says, turning away from me. Opening the shower door, he grabs a towel and hands it to me. "Now cover up. I'll be right back with your clothes."

Instead of taking the towel from him, I snatch his wrist to stop him from leaving. He startles and jerks back as if I burn him, throwing me off balance. I stumble into him, and together we slip on the wet floor. I screech as I land on top of him, our naked, wet bodies pressing together.

"Fuck," Ambrose says, his deep voice humming against my skin.

The door to the bathroom clatters open, and Tiernan growls deep in his chest. I tense, fear rising through me at his reaction. Fire erupts in his hands, and he looks ready to set the two of us ablaze like he has a right to be pissed by our closeness. Like me being in here somehow means I've betrayed him.

"Ambrose, are you fucking kidding me?" Theo shouts, stepping behind his brother. "You're—"

Rowan slaps his hand over Theo's mouth, cutting off his words. Dragging him back, he pulls him out of the way so that Maddox can tackle Tiernan before he lights Ambrose and I ablaze. Kash materializes in the doorway, standing tall like a wall of muscle, ensuring if his brothers lose control of the Darkonians, his body will keep them away.

I scramble off of Ambrose, my heart racing out of control. Snatching the towel from the floor, I quickly cover up. "Kash, I can explain."

"You don't have to explain anything, kitten," Kash says, turning his gaze to Ambrose. "But he does."

Ambrose pushes to his feet, his muscles rigid and flexing. "I—"

Snapping his mouth shut, he shakes his head.

Light flashes through the room, blinding me.

Ambrose disappears.

Mirrored Bond

"HE IS OUR GUARD!" THEO shouts, linking his fingers to the back of his head, tugging his black hair. We now stand in his suite and away from the magic of Ambrose's. "Delphia is ours! I trusted him, and look how he betrayed us. Trying to hide her. Seduce her. I—"

"Theo, calm down," I say, pushing up from my spot on the couch. The Darkonians' emotions run so hot and furious that it's a struggle to keep Theo's out of my mind. "He was not trying to seduce me."

"You don't know him like I do. We have a bond. I felt his rising desire for you." Theo growls and punches the rock wall.

Maddox gets between Theo's fist and the wall, blocking him before he can punch the hard stone again. "Have you not seen our mate? I'd be offended if he didn't desire her. She's the sexiest woman I've ever seen."

"He also proved he knows his place. Had it been any of us lying beneath her, we'd have had our way," Rowan says.

"Give the warlock credit. Our girl is irresistible, especially when she sets her sights on something she likes." Kash comes up behind me, hugging me. "Isn't that right, kitten?"

My mind whirls with a dozen thoughts. How am I supposed to respond to that? The Drekis are a lot calmer than I expected them to be, considering the position they found me in with Ambrose.

Leaning in, he rests his chin on my shoulder. "It's okay. You can't help who you find attractive."

"But why is that? She shouldn't. Her bond is exclusive to us," Theo retorts.

"Except I don't share the same bond." Tiernan speaks up from his spot sitting on the armrest of the loveseat in the sitting area of my bedroom.

Theo glowers. "Yeah, but—"

"But nothing. We're twins but we're also Ambrose's familiars. Perhaps the bond encompasses all three of us." Tiernan gets to his feet and closes the space to me. He offers me a small smirk and grazes his fingers along my cheek. "Now shut the fuck up before you make Nova feel guilty for something we caused in the first place."

"You need to also call your warlock back." Maddox straightens his shoulders. "We have some things we need to discuss."

"About what? The fairy?" Theo asks, crossing his arms over his broad chest. "She won't be a problem."

A bright flash of light explodes through the air, blinding me for a few seconds. "You," Ambrose says, his deep voice wrapping around me in its delicious melody.

My heart jumps in my chest at the sight of Ambrose, shielding himself behind a protective wall of magic. Maybe Tiernan was right about the bond. It would make sense that I could feel such a connection, and so quickly. What that means for all of us? I wish I knew. I have so many questions and not enough answers.

"About the union arrangement," Ambrose adds. Green light flickers in his silver irises.

I frown and look between the Darkonians and Ambrose. "What are you talking about, Ambrose?"

"You have to understand." Theo blocks my view of

Ambrose, cutting me off from their conversation. He ignores my question, falling silent. Without having to ask, I can tell they have a quiet conversation that none of us can hear.

It pisses me the hell off.

Striding away from Kash, I lock my fingers to Theo's shoulder and spin him away from Ambrose. He releases a growl with fire lighting his eyes. I take an automatic step back, my body recognizing his threat.

Maddox, Kash, and Rowan all close the space to me, looming behind me. Raising his hands, Theo breathes a heated breath and puts space between us. He flicks his attention to Tiernan, who remains quiet, allowing his brother to handle the situation.

"If you don't tell Delphia, I will," Ambrose says, his low voice stabbing into me as deeply as his stare. "She deserves to know."

"But it could ruin everything!" Theo's voice blares through the room as he releases a breath of his dragon fire.

"Tell her, Theo," Tiernan says. "It will ruin everything, and you know it can't be me. You're intended to lead."

Theo roars with his transformation into a dragon, knocking everyone away. My back hits the cool floor, and I skid a dozen feet toward the balcony. Fire engulfs me in a circle of orange light, separating me from the others.

No one has a chance to move or intervene.

Snatching me with his dagger talons, Theo flings me from my room and off the balcony. My stomach rises into my throat as I freefall a dozen feet, heading straight toward the jagged mountainside below. I squeeze my eyes shut, trying to summon my dragon, but I'm too slow. Theo roars a breath of fire and launches from the palace, diving down toward me. My hair blows everywhere, my body stiff and bracing for impact to the ground.

But I don't smash into it.

Theo catches me with his claws and throws me up and onto his back. I curl my body around his massive dragon form and squeeze my eyes shut. There is nothing I can do except hold on and wait.

Flapping his wings, Theo ascends toward the sky.

We leave the Darkonian territory behind.

Fog clouds the expanse of jagged mountains below as night descends on the world. The ice blue frozen ground sparkles with the white glow of Theo's dragon fire. I shiver, colder than I expected to be. All I wear is a tank top and shorts with my feet bare. It's not like I knew Theo would basically kidnap me and hide the two of us on a wintery mountain.

"Come sit down, Delphia," Theo says, standing naked in front of his make-shift fire. "I want to talk."

"We could've talked back at the palace." I rub my hands up and down my arms.

"Delphia—"

"My name is Nova!" I throw my hands, blasting him with my dragon fire. "How many fucking times do I have to tell you that? Now take me back. I don't want to be here with you."

Theo strides closer to me. "Not until we talk."

I shake my head, scrambling back. "No."

Closing my eyes, I transform into my dragon form. If he's not going to take me back, I'll figure the hell out how myself. I'll call for my mates. I know they'll be looking for me. Ambrose can use a locating spell.

An enormous body crashes into me, and teeth sink into the back of my neck. I screech, my dragon scream echoing through the still night. Theo flips me over. The world shakes as I slam into the ground. Smashing his front feet into my chest, he pins me down and bites me again in the throat.

"Stop fighting, Nova." Theo's thoughts explode through my head. "Just stop! Stop and look at me."

Smoke billows from my nostrils, and Theo locks his front foot to my throat, keeping my head still. Bowing down, he meets my gaze, his jade eyes shining like stones against his metallic black scales. His desperation courses through me, silently pleading with his soul to hear him out.

So I give up.

I submit to his power and let my humanity cage the wild beast within me. My naked body presses against the frozen ground, hard like ice but not slippery like in the Mortal World. The rough, sparkling texture prickles over my skin. I shiver and curl my knees to my chest, waiting for Theo to lift me into his arms like he thinks about.

Another few thoughts cross through our bond, his mind open and raw, fully at my disposal to hear what's on his thoughts. He thinks I'm beautiful and hypnotic, powerful yet in need of protecting. He wants to do right by me in a world he thinks will continue to do me wrong unless he takes control.

"Nova," he whispers, his voice a smooth melodic breath that caresses my soul. "May I hold you?"

I slowly nod my head but don't meet his gaze. I should be angry. I should fight and shout at him that his idea of controlling the situation and my life isn't the answer. I've already been stripped of my freedom and my life as I knew it. I don't need him to be my prince or knight. What I need is for him to tell me what the fuck is going on and how he has come to think of me as his and his brother's intended. I need to know the secret Tiernan thinks will ruin his chances with me.

Theo slides his muscular arm under my knees and around my back, lifting me from the icy ground. Heat radiates from his skin, his dragon fire emanating from him as if he gathers it just below the surface to melt the cold clinging to my very soul.

Strolling to the dancing flames of his bonfire, he grabs what's left of my tattered clothes and piles them on the ground. Theo sits on the fabric and cradles me in his arms, holding me in silence until I finally look at him. I should feel weird about letting him embrace me while we're both naked, but I don't. My deep-seated nature as a dragon, or maybe it's the forced bonding of our souls, feels completely natural. Familiar. This isn't about sex. It's something far more important.

A dozen emotions run wild between us, and all I can do is search his eyes for the answers he struggles to share with me. His hesitation, his sudden vulnerability, screams how he fears this could be the possible undoing of everything he had hoped to claim with me.

And who knows? It just might.

"I've fucked up," he finally says, his eyes lining in the corners with his grimace. "My clan has fucked up, and I'm afraid that nothing I do can fix this. I know I shouldn't have stolen you away, but I needed you to hear me out in a place untouched by the clans, by covens, and protected from the rest of the universe. No one will ever find us here."

"But why do this? What is so bad that you're afraid to tell me in front of my mates? In front of Ambrose? I don't know exactly what you two are to each other with the whole familiar bond, but I know you care about him. I can feel it." I keep my hands linked together across my chest, the warmth of his body and the blazing fire only doing so much to melt the cold dread clinging to every fiber of my being.

"Because a part of our union agreement was that you were never to know the truth about what your parents went through. If I tell you and the Litendrake Clan discovers it, we will face a war. Alliances are fragile, and as the eldest of our line, we're entrusted to secure our power. Our half-brothers and their future intended mate depend on us. As well as many other lesser clans. We rule and protect an entire territory. Our position gives us a voice with the High Council, but our alliance with the Litendrake Clan guarantees it." The info-bomb Theo shares only leaves me with more questions.

I frown, trying to process his words. "But why can't I know? Why hasn't my father even reached out to me? Does he even know I'm here now? It just all seems so...strange. How can you expect me—how can the Litendrakes expect me—to be a Darkonian mate if I can't know the truth? How am I supposed to trust you?"

"Nova, please. You can trust me. Just feel our bond. Everything I do is for you," he says, shifting me to face him straight on.

I'm so annoyed by his comment that even the fact that our bodies are only an inch apart does nothing to distract me. "Everything you do is for me? For *me*? Are you fucking serious, Theo? You considered having Ambrose sever my bond to my mates. You wanted to steal me away and be done with them. Hell, you didn't even introduce yourself before you tied our souls together!" My voice echoes through the chilly night. "None of this bullshit is for me. I should deny you as my mate and go to my father and tell him to fuck off. I mean, how could he have been alive all this time and not have tried to come for me? I should have the honor of punching him in his face for thinking he could just give me away without ever even seeing me."

Raising his hands from my sides, Theo surprises me and cups my face. He leans in ultra-close, our lips a mere inch apart, but he doesn't try to kiss me. Instead, he locks me in his stare. "I wish I could help you fulfill that desire."

"Why can't you?" I ask, huffing a breath.

"I told you—"

"Just stop. I don't give a shit about whatever the fuck stipulation is involved in this fucked up union between us. Tell me why I'm not supposed to know anything. Tell me,

Theo. Now." I shake his shoulders. "I deserve to know. If you ever want me to give you a chance—a real chance—we can't start things off with secrets. I need to know the truth."

"Nova, I'm—I'm afraid," Theo says, his voice coming out as a whisper. "I'm afraid I'll lose you either way before I ever even have the chance to have you in the first place. Tiernan thinks our bond will save me and screw him over, but I think he's wrong. I'm going to lose."

I want so badly to shake him again, to slap him, to do something to get him to realize this isn't even about him. It takes everything in me not to. "This isn't a game. There isn't winning or losing. There is just the truth."

"And you deserve it." He squeezes his eyes shut like he can't bear to look at me another second longer.

"So tell me." I slide my hands from his shoulders to cup his cheeks in my hands.

Closing the space, I rest my forehead to his. Our breath mingles as the silence drags out between us. I can't hear his thoughts now, but every single one of his emotions floods through me. Fear, anger, defeat, heartache—these cruel feelings battle against my will to stay strong in my desire for answers. As each quiet second passes, I lose myself to everything Theo is in this moment, struggling to keep myself free.

I've never had such an overwhelming urge to kiss and

murder someone at the same time. How can I want so badly to tell him things will be okay while also threatening to destroy any chance of giving this fucked up situation a chance? How much can I actually blame him? We grew up in two completely different worlds. And perhaps, and this is a big fucking maybe, I'd think differently if I wasn't raised by a witch posing as my aunt in the Mortal World.

"Please, Theo," I add, my voice caressing his lips.

He sighs. "Can I kiss you first?"

I crinkle my nose. "Kiss me?"

"I know it's fucked up to ask you, but I need to know what it's like. It might be the only time I ever get to." He combs his fingers into my hair. "Please."

Fuck it.

Crashing my lips to his, I kiss him with the anger and annoyance coursing through me, setting off my wild side. Tingles explode through me, my emotions stealing all my senses, and I deepen our kiss, slipping my tongue against his, kissing him as if my kiss is lethal and deadly, savoring that he's willing to risk it anyway.

"You could very well be the death of me," Theo murmurs against my mouth, responding to my thought. He kisses me again. "The end of the Darkonian reign."

I don't respond, clinging to him like we stand on the edge of a cliff, waiting to plummet over to find out if our dragons will save us in the end.

"But to kiss you, to feel you, to fight for even another moment with you—it'll be worth it," he adds. "I hope you know that. You're my mate despite everything. Mine."

Why do I love the sound of that?

"Theo, you can't distract me. Tell me now," I say.

Inhaling a deep breath, he meets my gaze. "You were not to know about the circumstances because your father doesn't want to ever lay eyes on you. Your mother—she betrayed not only the Drakovich Clan but also the Litendrakes. My clan allied with the Litendrakes to help them with the threat your mother posed. You see, she killed the crown prince of the Litendrake Clan and betrayed your father."

The edges of my vision shadow as my heart slides into my stomach. "I don't understand. Are you telling me my father gave me to your clan because of my mom? He's holding her shit against me?" What the actual fuck? My eyes burn at the thought. "Aunt McKayla told me I reminded her a lot of my mom."

"I'm sorry," Theo says. "This is why you weren't supposed to know. Being able to choose your mates and use you to increase the Litendrake Clan's power was part of your mother's restitution for her crimes."

I clench my fingers into fists. "And you just agreed?

Fuck!"

"Nova, I—"

"Take me back to the palace, Theo." I've never felt so angry and sick in my life. I need to talk to the Drekis. I need to find my aunt now, no matter what it takes.

"Please, just give me a few more minutes. We can talk this through," he says, tightening his hold on me.

I breathe fire in his face. "I said take me back. Now!"

Hate Passion

"I'M BEGGING YOU FOR THE sake of our futures, don't tell the others. The fewer who know, the better." Theo clutches my hand on the balcony, refusing to release me.

"If you want me to even consider basically anything with you ever, you will take that back." I try to tug away, but he only tightens his fingers even more. "You will never ask me to keep anything like this from the Drekis."

"I don't want them to try to do something in your honor. I'm protecting them." His nostrils flare with his annoyance. "Why can't you see that?"

"Because you have no reason to. You only even tolerate them around because you don't have a choice." This time, I stomp his foot, trying to get him to let me go. Still, it doesn't work.

Theo shifts on his feet and pulls me flush against him, not allowing any space between our naked bodies. His cock flexes against my stomach, my closeness setting him off with a raging boner, and I can't stop thinking about the angry kiss on the cold mountain.

"You know what? You're fucking right. If I had things my way, I'd keep you to myself. I wouldn't even allow Tiernan to get an ounce of you either. I've tried being nice. I've tried letting your emotions influence me into giving you what you want, but what you feel you want and what you actually desire are far different, and it confuses and infuriates me." His hand slides to the small of my back. Spreading his fingers, he teases my ass cheek, digging his nails in just enough to excite me.

"You know nothing, Theo," I snap, glaring into his eyes.

"I know that it pisses you off how much you want me, despite everything. If you didn't, you would've rejected me.

You would've put up more of a fight," he mutters, leaning down, getting into my face.

"Fuck off. You're delusional. If anything, I haven't because I thought you could use your power and status to help me, but I was clearly wrong. You're a coward. You hide behind supposed weak alliances so you don't have to do anything for me." Our warm breaths mingle, the space between us hot and angry, our wills battling to make the other see what we believe to be the truth.

"I should just hand you over to the High Council," he mutters, his eyes lighting with fire.

"Then do it. See what happens." My breasts caress his hard pecs with my deep breathing. "Like I said, I'm not afraid of going back to Max."

He moves his other hand to clutch me harder. "You're lying, Delphia. You're counting on my brother to intervene. You expect Ambrose and the Drekis to help him. I can feel it."

I swallow my nerves, my whole body hot with my rising fury. "I thought Tiernan was the bigger asshole of you two, but I was wrong. You're the monster. You nearly had me fooled with your fake nicety."

"And you nearly got away with making me think I had a chance with you without just taking what's mine." His eyes brighten with his dragon fire, his lust raging hard and hot, his cock throbbing between us.

"You're crazy if you think you can even try." Tingles burst between my legs, the intense need of my dragon to show him that if anything, he belongs to me, running wild. "I'm not a possession. I'm not your damn mate."

He growls, clenching his jaw. "You're fucking mine. Mine!"

Closing the space between our mouths, he kisses me with all his hot intensity, his raw, commanding emotions shattering my resistance to him. Grabbing his head, I kiss him back, yanking his hair to stop him from even trying to pull away from me. Because he's wrong. I'm not his, but damn it, he is mine. He's mine and I'll use him as he wants. I'll take what I need.

I don't have to like him. I don't have to agree to be his complacent little female dragon. He will learn that once he gets even a piece of me that he will be the one on his knees, bowing down. I'll ensure it. He's going to hate how much he wants me, and I'll savor the power I have over him.

Biting his bottom lip between my teeth, I nip him hard enough to make him grunt. My back crashes to the stone wall as he cages me to it, lifting me off my feet, so I have to curl my body around his. He flicks his tongue over mine, kissing me deeper, exploring my mouth, setting my body off. I gasp a moan, my back scratching on the cold rocks.

I can't believe how much I want him in this moment. I'm so angry and annoyed with him and this entire situation, but damn it. I want to fuck the asshole attitude out of him.

"You're mine," he mutters against my mouth. "Do you understand?"

"Fuck you," I respond, reaching between us to lace my fingers around his hard cock. "This doesn't mean shit."

"Is that so?" he says, breaking from my mouth. "You're going to feel stupid when I'm through with you. You'll see."

Lifting me up higher, Theo balances me on his shoulders, using the wall to keep my body in place. He drags his tongue across my sensitive skin, moving his head from side to side as he shifts my body to expose my clit to him.

And oh fuck.

An intense vibration bursts from the barbell in his tongue, the magically enhanced piercing making me scream in pleasure. I clutch onto his head, pulling his hair, squirming at the intensity of his mouth sucking and licking me that I swear I see stars in my vision. If no one knew we were back, they do now.

"You're fucking mine, Delphia." Theo's words swirl through my mind, his thoughts open to me in this crazy-ass, hate-filled moment of passion. "Tell me."

"Fuck you," I say, tipping my head back through the

wave of ecstasy already bringing me to my peak.

He growls and sucks my clit with more fury while sliding one of his fingers into me from behind. I arch and wiggle, my body desperate for release. I want nothing but to explode and take him with me, to teach him that I'll decide his place in my life, even if it's just to be here for my damn enjoyment.

"I will enjoy you more," he thinks, sending me over the edge.

I gasp and scream out, my whole body tensing and convulsing with my orgasm. Clinging onto Theo's head, I squeeze him between my thighs, rocking my hips. I plan to ride his face for the rest of the night if this is how it's going to be.

"Not happening, you little firecracker. It's my fucking turn if this is how you want to play." Theo pushes me off him, dropping me two feet, only to catch me by my ass. "You're not going to be the only one ever getting off."

"You say that like this will happen again," I say, my chest heaving, my back aching in the best way from being man-handled.

He glowers and aligns our bodies. "That's a promise."

Swinging his hips hard, he thrusts into me with a sexy moan. Pleasure steals my breath, my body reacting to the motions of him, his passionate rhythm pounding every thought from my mind. How can I relish in the ecstasy created by someone who enrages me? Fuck. I guess I have to work out my frustration somehow. Might as well be with the man desperate to have me. One who will seemingly do anything to ensure it.

Theo's mouth meets mine, and he plunges his tongue practically down my throat to silence the noise escaping my mouth.

I fight back and sink my nails into his shoulders, kissing him deeper, gliding my tongue across his like I can unscrew his tongue ring so he doesn't have the advantage of magical sex jewelry over me. Because I don't want this to stop. I want him to pin me down and rough me up so that I think about the pleasure he awakens in me for days.

"Forever," he thinks, breaking from my mouth to suck my neck hard enough to leave his mark. "I want you wet just thinking about me. I want you to have to beg me to carry you because you can't find the strength to walk when I'm through."

Oh, fuck. Who knew I'd want that too.

He moves to the other side of my neck and sucks the supple skin of my throat. "You're mine. I will not let anyone take you from me. Fuck the damn alliance with the Litendrakes. Fuck the High Council—"

I press my hand to his mouth, squeezing his scruffy

cheeks. "Just shut up and fuck me harder. Make me scream."

Growling, he bares his teeth, and the world spins again. I heave as my belly hits the railing of the balcony, and Theo locks one hand into my hair while reaching around to play with my clit. He thrusts into me from behind, and I tighten my torso and stretch my legs into the splits to feel every inch of him. He moans and arches my head back, kissing me upside down.

My muscles ache in the best way, the new position exciting and hot, the cool air caressing me with a thrilling sensation where his body sets mine ablaze.

"Tell me who you belong to, Nova," Theo says, his deep voice reverberating through my soul.

I bite my tongue and don't respond.

Rubbing my clit with more pressure, he huffs and picks up pace, bringing me to the verge of another wave of ecstasy. "Tell me."

"Make me," I gasp, losing myself to Theo.

Tightening his hand around my hair, he restrains me in place. His hand works faster over my body, his thrusts penetrating me so deeply I swear I can feel him in my stomach on a mission to fuck my brains out.

And then something shocks my insides, the strange pulse hitting me right in my g-spot, freezing every muscle on my body. The pleasure consumes me in a wave so intense that I scream out Theo's name. It's like I can feel my orgasm in even the follicles of my hair, blowing my damn mind.

"Who do you belong to, Nova?" he demands, his hot motions banging starbursts in my vision as if the night sky falls to the mountainside.

"You," I gasp, the word sounding like a whimpering plea. "I belong to you."

With my admission, Theo flips me over and kisses me, fucking me fast and furious, so full of pride, satisfaction, raw need, and something else. Something hot and dangerous and completely intoxicating until he moans with his release.

He eases his mouth from mine but doesn't let go of my chin. "Remember that next time you even consider rejecting me. You're my mate, and I'll do what I have to. You will see that even with rewriting the fates, this was always meant to be."

I heave a breath, his words swirling through my mind.

Theo doesn't give me a chance to respond and transforms into his beautiful metallic black beast. Leaning his head down, he meets my gaze with his jade eyes. I brush my fingers along his snout without a word.

Flapping his wings, he launches into the air, abandoning me on my balcony. Ice fills the absence he leaves behind, and I hug myself.

I've never been so confused in my life.

What happens now?

Finding Answers

I BARELY MAKE IT TO the ginormous bed before the door cracks open and Maddox strolls in alone, carrying a plate of something I can tell he expects me to eat. If only my stomach didn't twist in knots. I'm so emotionally out of control that I can't stop the tears from filling my eyes as I break down sobbing in front of him.

Where his brothers would rush to me, scoop me into their arms, and try to hug the trembles away, Maddox doesn't treat me like I'm in need of comfort. He doesn't treat me as if all he wants is for my crying to stop. He's not the one to try to guarantee it won't happen again.

"Are you injured?" Maddox asks, standing at the edge of the bed, running his gaze over my body to ensure I don't lie.

I sniffle and groan. "Where are your brothers?" I ask instead, using the blankets to scrub away my angry tears.

He tilts his head, narrowing his eyes. "With Quillon and Ambrose. Tiernan went after Theo. So, tough luck, cookie. You're stuck with me."

Maddox sits on the bed behind me and touches my back. I cringe at the blip of pain his fingers create as they glide across the scrapes and scratches from what I can only describe as my hate-sex with Theo. I'm pissed at myself just thinking about it—how he got under my skin and into my soul. How I liked it. How I'm upset he just took off and left me.

"And it's probably a good thing, seeing your condition. My brothers don't understand that you enjoy getting roughed up and pushed into submission. They think you always want to feel strong and powerful, but I know you get tired of always having to be. It's okay, Nova. You don't have to feel guilty."

"I don't," I snap, gathering the blankets in my hands.

"You don't have to be angry at yourself for giving into Theo, either. It's not a weakness to desire such things. Look at us. We disagree all the time." Maddox combs his hands through my hair, untangling the knots with his fingers.

"That's different." I lean back against his body, silently asking him to just hold me. "I sometimes like you. I just hate him."

Chuckling, he shifts me in his arms and picks me up. "Is that how you really feel or how you think you're supposed to feel?"

Damn him. "What kind of question is that, Maddox?"

"Come on, Nova. Answer me. You know I won't judge you. You're my mate. You're mine." He leans in and kisses my forehead.

"I seem to be everyone's," I mutter, pursing my lips.

"And it's okay if you want to be. I am never leaving you no matter what you do, what you think, or how you feel," he says. "Just don't go murdering bars full of people. I do have some morals, and it confused the hell out of me thinking you did that shit when I took you to Max."

I glare. "Maybe if you believed me in the first place."

"No one is perfect, and we're all doing the best we can. Fuck, I know I fail you half the time. I thought I had this shit all worked out, thinking we could use these assholes and then drop them. But now here I am, trying to get you to calm your tits and realize shit's going to work out no matter what you want, even those bastards." Maddox carries me toward the bathroom, careful not to touch me anywhere I'm hurt. "But don't think I won't remind them for the rest of time who had you first."

"Kash will appreciate that," I tease, his words helping to ease the hurricane of emotions colliding through me.

Maddox growls against my mouth and adjusts me in his arms to spank my ass. "You love asking for punishment from me."

"Maybe." I smile and ruffle his hair. "Maybe I want you to help me forget tonight as to not give Theo that kind of satisfaction until he earns it."

Humming, he meets my mouth with another kiss. "Or maybe you're just insatiable. Either way, I'll give you what you want tonight."

"Or not. I need to speak with the princess, Dreki. You were supposed to feed her and give her the exam you demanded." Ambrose materializes in front of us with a flash of his neon light. "We have priorities, and you know Theo already took care of the least important one."

Uh-oh.

The world spins as Maddox swings me out, using my legs to throw Ambrose off his feet. Skidding across the polished rock floor, Ambrose chants a spell and stops himself from crashing into the wall.

"Delphia's needs are the most important thing in our clan. If you cannot accept that, then you will never stand a chance in finding a place among us despite your mirrored feelings for her." Maddox clenches his jaw, practically spitting fire with his words. When he uses my name in such a way, I know he's utterly serious. I can't even blame him. Strangely enough, it doesn't bother me coming from him like it does from anyone else. It's like he earned his right to use it.

"My place isn't among you," Ambrose snaps, his eyes flickering with his power. "I am here to serve the Darkonians, and that's it. Nova cannot and will not ever be mine. It is not my place."

I blink a few times, the sudden rejection bothering me way more than it should. But I can't help taking it personally with the way he says it.

"You're going to deny her bond?" Maddox asks, anger lining his words.

Ambrose groans. "It's misplaced."

"It's there regardless. Your denial hurts her." Maddox shocks the hell out of me by spinning me toward Ambrose, forcing him to stare at me directly. "I know you can feel it."

Ambrose's silver eyes rove over me, drinking in the sight of my naked body as I stand vulnerable in front of him. My knees tremble, my body weakening under his scrutiny. He doesn't look anything like Theo, but yet, he still reminds me of him. And I still hate how confused I am by all of this.

"Maddox, stop," I say, my voice coming out a whisper. "I know you want to assure I know that you and I are okay, but it's too much for you to demand someone else feel the same. I just met Ambrose...and the Darkonians for that matter. You shouldn't be okay with all of this. It's weirding me out."

Maddox growls, the scar on his face lighting with his dragon fire. "What do you want from me, cookie? I can't keep up. I know you're worried about how I feel, and I want you to know it doesn't matter. We've claimed each other. I don't fear for my standing within our clan. I don't fear your rejection."

I squeeze my eyes shut. "I just—I want you to stop doing what you think I want. That goes for everyone. It's not about me. It's about us and how the hell we're going to survive this mess. It's about getting answers, especially now that I know I'm only here because my own fucking father hates my mother so much that he was willing to basically sell me for power just to spite her."

"What?" Maddox and Ambrose say at the same time.

I shrug. "You heard me. The Litendrakes wanted to

punish my mother by giving me away in exchange for power. I'm the child they got for restitution because she killed one of the princes. I wasn't supposed to find out because—"

"I'll kill them," Maddox says, snarling, his rage crashing into me. This was what Theo feared would happen, and now, I'm afraid too.

Ambrose braves stepping closer to Maddox to meet his gaze. "You can't."

"By messing with Nova's fate, they messed with the Dreki Clan's." Maddox flexes his muscles, his dragon form yearning to break free. "You heard Quillon. Delilah ran and entrusted Nova in McKayla's hands to protect the Dragon Lands. Our union was to stop the covens from trying to gain control over the skies."

I blink a few times, hearing this information for the first time. "My aunt was the reason my mom escaped Max." This, I know. Her twin McKenzie told me as much.

"The first time," Ambrose says.

"What is that supposed to mean?" I ask, crossing my arms over my chest.

"She was captured again after your birth, convicted of treason against the High Council. Her and her mates." Maddox grabs my hand and clasps it gently, quietly trying to fill me with his strength. "They were working with a rebel clan, trying to rise against Magaelorum. Quillon doesn't know all the details, but he's helped them portal between the Mortal World and Magaelorum."

"And somehow, the Litendrakes knew this," Ambrose adds. "They made a deal with him for his help on the inside when we were arranging to get you. I wish I had known. I just thought he was some asshole with connections."

Anger rushes through me, and I yank Maddox with me toward the wardrobe.

He watches me in silence as I rush to throw on the first thing I see—a dress—and stomp my way to the door. Appearing in front of us, Ambrose blocks our way, not allowing me into the hall.

"Wait, princess. Before you beat up the lycan, we have something else we have to do," Ambrose says.

"What?" I ask, staring past him like I could possibly shove him and make a run for it to do as I want.

"We need to visit the Lioht Coven. The only way we can piece this all together is to find McKayla, and I know how, but I need something from them." Ambrose turns his attention to Maddox. "Are you sure you can handle the task? I need as much time as I possibly can get."

Maddox jerks his head once in agreement. "They'll never see you coming."

Ambrose holds out his hands. "Good. Now take my hands. It's time to go."

I touch my throat, the burning sensation of the magical collar igniting fear inside me. McKenzie tried to kill me in this house and the memory hits me hard as I stare around the guest house. She said the Drekis would be better off without me, considering the mess their lives turned into to save me from prison. But now, knowing everything I do, I'm certain it was never for their sake but hers and the Lioht Coven.

"I shouldn't be here," I whisper, my breathing turning into quick pants. "They'll know."

Ambrose grabs my shoulders and gets in my face. "You're panicking. Take a breath. In and out. Come on, do it with me."

Following his lead, I inhale and exhale, keeping my stare locked to the flicker of magic lighting his eyes. "What if this doesn't work?"

"It will. The reason she tried to kill you before was because you will prove her treachery toward the High Council, especially if you prove McKayla's alive. Why do you think they didn't capture you all and turn you in?" Ambrose brushes the strands of my wild red hair off my forehead. "This will work out."

I struggle to believe him. It never seems to be the case. "And you're sure your magic is strong enough?"

"Positive. No one but Maddox can see or hear you.

You are safe. As long as he keeps the Liohts distracted, none of them will feel my magical interference." Ambrose lightly caresses his fingers to mine, still messing with my neck. "And if they do, they won't be able to do anything. We'll already be gone."

"Just be quick, okay," I say, continuing to rub my throat, wishing his words were enough to ease the anxiety blooming in my chest. "I don't like this."

"Which might be a good thing. You're powerful when you're on edge. You could burn this place down before McKenzie has a chance to react." Tugging my hands from my neck, he gently gets me to drop them to my sides. "Now go get close to Maddox. McKenzie's coming. He's going to need you to help him answer certain questions she might have in regards to McKayla."

With his nudge, I shuffle my way from the hallway to join Maddox standing near the sitting area. He offers me a tight smile but keeps his eyes trained on the door as McKenzie enters with a familiar man behind her. I try not to react to Baker and his similarities to his brother Rhett. One more woman saunters up the sidewalk, her blond hair dancing in the wind. She remains outside, not joining her coven mates.

"CO Dreki, I would be lying if I said it was nice to see you," McKenzie says, her eyes flashing with purple light.

"Give me one good reason I shouldn't summon the High Council to arrest you?"

Maddox gathers dragon fire in his palms, straightening his broad shoulders. With a glower, he turns his complete attention to McKenzie. "We both know you won't do it, so lay off the empty threats, High Priestess."

Her expression falters, and the scent of white florals permeates the air. She's nervous. "Don't test me."

Maddox growls, causing McKenzie to back up. She summons lavender electricity between her hands. I tense at her power, just the sight of it making my throat dry. The edges of my vision shadow with anger. How dare she threaten my mate like this. It takes everything in my very being to control the urge to release my inner beast and tear her in half. The idea is far more satisfying than it should be.

"Why don't we all calm down for Rhett's sake?" Baker says, stepping between Maddox and McKenzie. He motions toward the sitting area. "He wouldn't want any of us to fight. He was like a brother to the both of us."

Maddox presses his lips into a frown. "He's not to me. Not after everything. But that doesn't matter. I'm here because I have something you want, and you can help me with something I want."

McKenzie follows Baker's lead and saunters toward the loveseat. Crossing her legs at her ankles, she remains stiff and on guard, never taking her eyes away from Maddox. The three of them glare at each other, allowing the silence to grow uncomfortable. I know Maddox does it on purpose, but damn it. It bothers the hell out of me.

"Is this about the Drakovich descendant's collar?" McKenzie asks, finally breaking the silence. "It will take something quite valuable for me to even consider paying the price to remove that...though, I can collect a favor from the warlock responsible. It was his fault for Rhett's death, after all."

Dread washes over me at her revelation. She mentions it so casually that I can't help wondering what the actual fuck is going on.

"But you already know that, don't you CO?" McKenzie adds.

Maddox's arm muscles flex, his dragon peeking from beneath his skin. "We're not interested in involving Lazlo or the removal of his wretched collar. We have higher things on our list of priorities."

Tucking her hair behind her ears, McKenzie shows off her glittering earrings. "Such as?"

"The Darkonians. They've stolen our mate, and I need information I know you possess to null their contract for a union. Delphia doesn't belong to them. The fates fell in our favor, and I cannot stand by and accept anything else. She's a Dreki." Maddox growls with his words, sounding utterly convincing in his fury over the thought.

And maybe he is. Maybe he keeps his cool about everything for my sake. The thought alone makes me worry about what the hell I did fucking Theo. What if—no. I can't think like this. I knew the plan. I knew he was going to use this opportunity to find out more about my mother and her wrongdoings while also helping Ambrose get what he needs to find McKayla.

"What makes you think I have those answers or that there could possibly be any information in the world you'd have that I'd want in exchange?" McKenzie purses her lips narrowing her eyes. "You've wasted our time."

Stretching his arms over his head, Maddox groans and turns away. "I guess I'll take the information I have to the High Council and see what it's worth to them. I didn't want to, considering how much I hate the fuckers, but Delphia is mine. I'll not let anyone have her."

Maddox strides across the room to the door.

"Ezeerf et rod," McKenzie chants, waving her hand. "Wait."

Locking his fingers to the knob, Maddox tries to open it, but it doesn't budge. He summons his dragon fire and swivels on his feet. Our eyes meet for a brief second, his lip curling slightly in the corner. This is what we wanted—to make the Liohts nervous. Desperate. We need them to think we're a better ally than threat but also know that we're powerful enough to destroy them if we have to.

"Now you're wasting my time, High Priestess." Maddox releases a guttural noise from his throat. "Do you plan to test my power? You will regret it. My brothers stand guard. We will destroy this house and your coven before you can utter another spell."

Baker grabs McKenzie's hand. "That won't be necessary, Maddox. We seem to have the same interests. I'm sure you're unaware of this, but we too, are tired of the control of the High Council."

"You work as a gatekeeper," Maddox snaps, his fire growing more intently. "You're lying."

Holding his hand up, Baker says, "We can prove it."

"Baker, shut up. We don't know if the information he has is of any use to us. This could be a setup," McKenzie hisses.

"We've found McKayla's location." Maddox remains expressionless with his words. "Delphia discovered the truth of another coven's false conviction. It would be a shame to our chances at a future alliance if we had to resort to bringing this news to the High Council. It would mean—"

McKenzie's face morphs into the hideous beast version of herself meant to intimidate others. Throwing her arms out, she shoots electricity from her hands. Maddox dodges out of the way and chucks a huge fireball at her, knocking her off her feet.

The ground shakes.

The lights turn off.

Power shocks me to my soul.

Battle of Wills

A DEEP ROAR REVERBERATES THROUGH my bones as I hear Rowan's dragon call over the buzzing of the Liohts' magic. Fire blazes past the window, lighting the dark room in an orange glow. A lavender burst of light ignites outside the glass door where the other witch stands guard, and she encompasses herself with her magical shield.

Maddox strides across the room, barely flinching at the blast of power McKenzie throws at him. "Do you really think we'd come unprepared?" Grabbing the collar of his shirt, he yanks it down, revealing an amulet embedded above his heart. "You're not the only coven who had owed us a favor."

The room quivers again, and my heart nearly explodes upon the sight of Rowan in his dragon form landing outside. Smoke billows from his nostrils, and he bares his sharp fangs with his deadly snarl. My gaze travels over his gigantic body, and I balk at the sight of Quillon clutching onto his back for dear life. I had no idea they were here in the Mortal World, but I'm relieved to see Rowan, even with a damn pest on his back.

Maddox grins, his wicked smile hot enough to melt my panties off. I fucking love seeing him all powerful and demanding. "Now, get on the ground and keep your mouth shut. On behalf of the High Council—"

"Wait," McKenzie says, keeping her hands toward the floor. "Wait. I'll give you what you want. I was only testing you, Maddox. I needed to be sure you weren't lying. But if you're willing to summon the High Council, then I know you speak the truth. You know where my traitor sister is, and I need to know."

Maddox snuffs out his flaming hands, rubbing his palms together. Glancing at the window, he nods his head at Rowan, giving him the cue to take off. I nearly run to the window to watch him go, but my brain screams at my body to keep it together. Rowan isn't abandoning me to the night sky. He's only taking flight to better protect us.

"That's right, my doe-eyed woman. I'm always here," Rowan says, thinking his words through our mental link. "Quillon's our bitch now. The fucker didn't even complain about coming through the portal with me."

I hum in satisfaction, already imagining the day Ambrose helps pay Kash's debt by giving Quillon a cure. The little shit better run like hell when he does, because my dragon wants to gobble his hairy beast up, even if it means dealing with a damn hairball in my throat.

"Give me her location, and I will answer any questions," McKenzie says, clapping her hands, using her power to turn the lights on.

Maddox barks a laugh and shakes his head. "You think I'm stupid, witch? I've been dealing with different covens all my life. I've learned my lesson with the Dreki contract to the High Council. I will not risk having one to you. Now, tell me. Who arranged the union contract between Delphia and the Darkonian Clan? Was it you?"

McKenzie flicks her gaze to Baker, standing silently and on guard next to her. "It was Rhett. Rhett arranged everything after McKayla betrayed us and nearly fractured our good standing with the High Council. Her betrayal, abandoning us and leaving our coven with the mess, nearly ruined everything. All because of her bleeding heart and devotion to the very fates that try to control us."

Stepping closer toward me, Maddox gets in front of me like he thinks I might do something to jeopardize the spell hiding me from view. "Where do the Litendrakes come in? Why them?"

"Delilah Drakovich's offspring belong to them for nearly destroying their bloodline. She was intended to be their mate but betrayed them—" Purple power blinks in her eyes. "With the very clan your bloodline replaced. The Litendrake Clan was lucky that Delilah happened to have a female heir bred from their bloodline before things occurred. It was lucky that one Litendrake prince managed to seduce her."

My father.

Fury ripples through me at her words, and I clutch onto the back of Maddox's shirt to steady myself. A dozen thoughts swirl through my mind. I used to hold the memories of my parents at a distance. I was too angry with the criminal path my mom chose that kept her from me. But now, I can't help but think there is more to this. It almost sounds as if she could've been in the same situation as I am—betrothed to one clan when my true mates are in another.

Everything about this situation is so utterly and terribly wrong. How can the dragon clans do this? How can the witches agree and think it's okay to control every aspect of our lives as if they don't truly belong to us?

"And what of Delilah?" Maddox asks, shifting more to block me completely. "Delphia's arrival was expected by my clan. It was foreseen by a fate-teller. The Drakovich heir would bring power, prosperity, and fertility to the Dreki Clan. It was written in the stars and sealed by powerful magic, a gift, from the Drogony leader."

"The Drogonys were the ones to steal Delilah's fate," McKenzie snaps, baring her teeth. "They corrupted my sister and turned her against her own coven."

Maddox curls his hands into fists, falling silent at her words. Without having to ask, I know he didn't know. All along, he believed fate brought me to him. But what if that's not the case? What if the Drogonys influenced it? What if the idea of a true mate doesn't exist?

I shake my head, pushing the thoughts away.

I refused to believe it when Ambrose mentioned something similar, and I still refuse to believe it now. We weren't bonded by magic. Our lives weren't arranged by others to come together in a union of power. I know deep in my heart, my mom wanted to ensure I didn't end up with the clan brutal enough to steal me from her, and the best way she knew how was to alert the Dreki Clan of my future arrival. Fate did the rest. Fate dropped me kicking and screaming at their feet and dragged me right into their lives.

"Now tell me where McKayla is." McKenzie rubs her hands together, sending sparks glittering toward the floor. "I've given you the answers you seek."

"Except for one. What did the Litendrake Clan give Rhett to make such a bargain?" Maddox asks, despite us knowing the answer. He's buying more time for Ambrose. I know it. "That kind of contract...I know the stipulations involved. It's abnormal."

"You can thank McKayla for that. We needed someone to place blame on and hide evidence of our plans to break away from the High Council." McKenzie smirks. "It actually worked out quite well. Despite McKayla's failures, we managed to obtain the power we needed to be seen worthy enough to control a gateway. It makes things much easier for what we have planned."

Maddox takes a step back, bumping into me. His demeanor changes, and he summons dragon fire in his hand. "Don't try anything stupid, McKenzie. You'll never find the location of your sister if you do. My brothers—"

"Vieta le aspara ti og et!" McKenzie shouts, igniting the room aglow with lavender light.

Throwing his hands out, Maddox shoots his dragon

fire at her, attempting to break through the wall of magic surrounding her and Baker.

"I told you all you needed to know, and now you will give me what I want. You think you're powerful, Dreki, but you have no idea." McKenzie's power eats across the carpet encircling us.

Static sends my hair blowing on magical currents, and I hug Maddox from behind, afraid that if I let him go, something will separate us. I need to do everything I can to stay with him. We're stronger together.

"Tell me where McKayla is. If you tell me and act as an obedient dragon and bow before me, I'll accept your allegiance. We can work together for a better future. It's what Rhett would want. He was preparing you to join our side. It's why he ensured you bonded with him. It's why he demeaned himself to act as a loyal friend to you." McKenzie raises her hands, her face hardening as her teeth elongate into fangs.

And this bitch.

I'm going to kill her.

She will regret even thinking she was better, stronger, and more powerful than us.

Maddox roars, unleashing part of his dragon, his scales breaking through his skin. His veins glow with his dragon fire, and heat fills the small room, combatting the electric magic sizzling through the air.

"Ambrose!" I yell, letting Maddox's hulking form herd me farther from the Liohts. "Ambrose, hurry!"

McKenzie tips her head toward the ceiling. "Lazlo, I summon you! Nommus eht ew lali vekki High Priest of Infinity!"

The floor trembles under my feet, and I screech, the force of the earthquake knocking me off balance. I trip and grab the wall, trying my best to brace myself against the powerful magic threatening to send the roof caving in on us.

"Take this gift, dear fates. A life cursed and soiled. Vi lev tion eht lok!" McKenzie shoots power from her hands, sending a huge chunk of the ceiling blasting into the night.

Rowan's dragon screech rings through the air, and I clutch my stomach as pain rips through me, leaving me breathless. Maddox shouts and blasts more of his dragon fire at the Liohts, but it doesn't stop them. Baker keeps the shield intact.

Nothing prepares me for the hairy body that drops from the sky and lands on the hard tiles in front of us.

I scream, my heart shattering into a million pieces. The force of Quillon's fall cracks the floor. Blood pours from several places on his broken body, his legs bent in the wrong direction. Without having to rush to him and flip him over, I know he's dead. There is no way he'd have survived a fall from the sky. Too much blood seeps across the floor. It's as if the force liquefied his insides, and now they're pouring out.

And if Quillon's dead—

"Lazlo, I summon you! Nommus eth ew lali vekki High Priest of Infinity!" McKenzie shouts again, her high-pitched voice ringing through the air in desperation.

Rage blinds me, turning the world dark. Every fiber of my being shreds to pieces, and all I can feel is Quillon's death in my soul. Because with his death, so comes Kash's.

"Nova, no!" Maddox shouts, spinning around to grab onto me.

But it's too late.

My beast ignites her dragon fire inside me, and I give in, giving her complete control. The world shifts as I smash through the roof, sending debris raining upon the Liohts. I will not allow them to make it out of here alive. They have done nothing but ruin my existence. They were responsible for ruining my mother's as well. I cannot stand another moment knowing that they live and breathe and control the world with their dark power. I will no longer allow another person to fall victim to their evil desire for power and conquest.

Inhaling a deep breath, I unleash my dragon fire at McKenzie. She screams another spell while Baker continues to protect her.

"Nova, expand your wings," Rowan calls through our mind-link, his fire igniting the sky above me.

"Ambrose, get us the fuck out of here," Maddox yells, hooking his arms around my leg.

"Lazlo, I summon you! Nommus eth ew lali vekki High Priest of Infinity!" McKenzie shouts once again.

Green light bursts through the world around me as Ambrose casts a spell, fissuring the Liohts protective shield.

"Sister, the beast! He's not dead!" Baker's deep voice shocks my senses, and I bow my head to peer at Quillon.

A high-pitched wail of relief escapes my mouth at the sight of the lycan rolling over onto his side. Blood coats his front side, and he can't get to his feet, but Quillon is still alive. The fall didn't kill him, but in this moment, it looks like he wishes it did.

Bending my neck, I jerk my head down, blocking the Liohts from Quillon. I snatch his broken body between my teeth and drag him away from the witch before she can try to finish him off. There's no way in hell I'm allowing her to sacrifice this piece of shit, no matter how much I hate him. He's the luckiest cursed bastard in existence right now. He better remember this.

"Nova!" Rowan shouts in my mind again. "Now!"

My body reacts to his command, and I stretch my

wings out. Sharp claws dig into my sides as Rowan lifts me into the air. Lavender and green light spark through the air like fireworks exploding too close to the ground. Maddox blasts his dragon fire, creating a barrier between the Liohts and Ambrose.

The world shrinks as Rowan ascends into the sky so fast that all I can do is let him carry my dragon body as if I weigh nothing.

"Shael eht nogard!" McKenzie's voice rings in my head. "Ti vit alla cas totita voz! You're mine, Delphia. Bow to me!"

A chain of purple magic whips through the air, the shock of power tightening my muscles. My dragon screech cuts off as it latches to the magical collar on my throat, stealing my breath. Pain explodes through me. I jerk and thrash, my mind whirling, my body panicking. Rowan loses his hold with my movements, and I fall from the sky and toward the earth.

"Use your wings!" Rowan and Maddox shout at the same time.

But my body refuses to react. It refuses to do anything apart from clutch onto Quillon and brace for impact.

"Delphia ti vit osmod!" The world stills, and I hover frozen midair a dozen feet above the house. Glowing with power, Ambrose stops me from colliding into the ground.

Maddox growls and continues to shoot fire at McKenzie and Baker. Bursts of orange and white flames light the sky above as Rowan blocks the other witch. I close my eyes and will my humanity to tame my dragon. I beg the universe to grant me this one favor, to lower me into Maddox's outstretched arms, where I know I'll find safety.

"That's it, cookie. Come to me," Maddox says, blowing another breath of fire at the Liohts, engulfing me in his hot flames that never burn me. If anything, they warm my soul.

My thrashing heartbeat mellows as Ambrose lowers me in his magic. I manage to clutch Quillon to me, his soft groan humming between my breasts. Rowan lands beside us and transforms, his naked muscles rippling with the ferocity lighting his eyes. He reaches to grab Quillon from me before I even touch my feet to the floor.

"No!" McKenzie screams, her voice ringing in both my ears and in my mind. "Ti vit alla cas totita voz."

Jerking her hands, she yanks the chain attached to the collar around my neck. I drop Quillon and fly through the flaming barrier Maddox tries to grow. Ambrose shouts something I can't understand, my head spinning with my body. Static sizzles in the air, and a bright blue light ignites in my vision blinding me.

"The High Council!" Ambrose yells. "We have to go!"

"We can't leave her," Rowan and Maddox say at the

same time.

"She has a better chance alone. We don't. We'll get her back. Don't worry." Ambrose's words stab me through my soul.

Maddox growls. "I'm not leaving."

"You don't have a choice!" Green electricity fills the air, and agony coils around my very being.

The Drekis and Ambrose sudden absence leaves me reeling.

I don't get a chance to move or react.

"Freeze!" a woman shouts. "Release the dragon's chain."

McKenzie releases the magic chain from the collar on my throat. "It's okay. We were handling things. I just caught her and this filthy lycan crossing the barrier. I was about to—"

Anger rips through me, a dozen thoughts colliding through my mind. I can't believe I'm here, facing the High Council's authority. I can't believe I'm doing it alone. The Liohts will turn this all against me. She'll lie and tell them the Drekis set them up.

I can't let this go on.

I'm not going down silent and alone.

I'm taking this bitch with me.

Raising my hands into the air, I drop to my knees,

blinking through the blinding light in my face. A strange, calming emotion trickles through me. I can feel Kash through our mate bond, and it's as if he knows exactly what I need in this moment to get through this.

"Wait, please. McKenzie Lioht is lying. She used her influence and magic to steal me from Magaelorum. They used this lycan to break open a portal not far from here, trying to set up the Drekis. She wanted to frame them for a crime like her brother did with me. You have to believe me." I pant, my chest heaving with my breath. I could scream that Lazlo Infinity was behind all this, but he's not here. McKenzie is second best. Maybe it'll help McKayla in the end. Who knows.

"You cannot possibly believe a deadly fugitive, can you?" McKenzie asks, her voice rising.

"Then explain my collar! I never wanted to be here. I didn't kill anyone, and you know it." Every fiber of my being begs that whoever stands behind the magical white light gives me a chance. I know if they don't bring the Liohts in, they'll be gone forever.

"This is preposterous," Baker snaps, his deep voice cutting over the hum of magic.

A loud clap of lightning strikes the floor a few feet away from me. My muscles seize, and I fall over, unable to move.

McKenzie screams.

"Guards, arrest them all. This is a matter to be resolved in front of the High Council," a woman says.

Oh, fuck. It worked. I almost don't believe it.

If only I didn't feel like everything will crash down on me at any second.

I wish I didn't feel so unlucky.

Captured

"WAIT, IS THERE NOT GOING to be a trial? I know I wasn't allowed to be present during mine, but don't you need me? I'm a witness." Nerves bunch inside my stomach as a beast of a man with biceps as big as my legs throws the familiar jumpsuit in my face.

"No talking, Inmate D64901. Now get dressed and wait for High Council Woman Laveau." The buff CO pushes me toward an open door to an interrogation room.

My palms sweat, my mind dragging the memory of Maddox's interrogation upon my arrival as he screamed and belittled me, making our start rough.

I clutch the jumpsuit, resisting his shove. "Please, CO. I've been through so much. You have to help me. I have no one left to turn to. Your fellow COs—"

A flash of light startles me as a familiar woman with red eyes materializes in front of me. "Let's make this quick, Delphia Drakovich. Tell me where the Drekis are."

Oh, shit. She knows my name.

I stiffen under the weight of her stare, the woman far more intimidating than I recall. Perhaps Maddox's fierce authority outshined hers, but now that the CO marches away, leaving me with High Council Woman Laveau, I suddenly realize how powerful she really is. She is a leader of this damn world, and she has the ability to save or ruin my life, depending on her mood.

"They—they—" I suck in a deep breath, praying she doesn't kill me for my response. I have no idea what the Liohts could've said, but I'll do whatever it takes to protect my mates. "They disappeared. The Liohts didn't like that they couldn't collar them. They were fighting on behalf of the High Council."

"And do you have proof of this?" High Council Woman Laveau says, keeping her red eyes locked on mine. Power flickers across her fingers, raining glowing sparks across the tiled floor.

I swallow. "I—"

"Because as far as I know, the Liohts are in good standing with the High Council. They've served us greatly for many decades, and I can't see why they would jeopardize this now, for the daughter of a well-known criminal, to say the least." Pursing her lips, she waits for me to argue.

What am I supposed to say? I was guilty the moment I was dragged to Magaelorum the first time. Nothing can change that now.

I meet her glare with my own. "Because Rhett had a deal with—"

Waving her hand, High Council Woman Laveau shoots a burst of magic at me, sealing my mouth shut with a muter. She cocks her head, jerking her attention toward the hallway like she hears something I can't. My chest tightens the longer she stands there, looking creepy as hell. If she doesn't plan to hear me out and disregards everything I have to say because of my mom, then what's the point of trying to argue with her anyway? I'm tired, afraid, and in need of time to process. I wish she would hurry up and send me on my way to my damn cell already.

"High Council Woman Laveau, please," I mumble, sounding like I'm just humming in frustration, but I have to try.

Her red eyes flicker and she finally darts her gaze to me. "Hmm. It seems things have grown a bit complicated. Get dressed and wait for CO Rover to return."

"Wait, what? Please! You can't do this!" I yell, my breath stretching the muter against my mouth. Damn it. I wish she'd let me speak.

With a flourish of her hand, High Council Woman Laveau smashes my back to the wall of the interrogation room. Her red magic sizzles across my skin as she pins me in place. I wiggle and thrash, trying to break her spell, but nothing works. I'm utterly helpless.

"Until we confirm the confession of Baker Lioht and can find the Drekis whereabouts for confirmation, you will remain imprisoned in this facility. We will need time to verify your story, but it does not mean you won't be held accountable for your previous crimes." The witch chants something under her breath, summoning a glowing red block into her hands. I cringe and try harder to fight at the sight of the magic iron that'll brand the marks onto my skin to permanently cage my dragon.

A part of me dies inside. It feels as if she's stealing the best part of me. Now that I know who I am and of what I'm capable, what I will lose due to these injustices, it hurts worse than ever.

I scream as High Council Woman Laveau brands the top of each of my hands, sealing my fate as Inmate D64901 once again. With a burst of bright light, she disappears and I fall to the floor, my whole body giving up.

"Fuck my life," I whisper, pulling my knees to my chest. "Fuck this all."

Something bangs on the doorframe. "Get up and dressed, inmate," CO Rover says, returning into view.

I ignore him and try to force the world away.

He clomps forward. "Get the hell up or your ass will start off the night in the pits."

"I don't care," I snap, not turning to look at him.

"Last chance, Inmate D64901." He kicks my back with his boot, pushing me over.

I grind my teeth. "Fuck you."

Pain explodes through me, stealing my vision.

The world disappears.

My head throbs, and blood drips down my forehead. Biting my bottom lip, I suppress my groan. If I make a sound, the bastard CO might hurt me again. I don't know what I was expecting besides this power-tripping beast man to force me into compliance with violence.

And it feels a million times worse than my arrival with the Drekis as my guards. I can't explain it, but I wasn't afraid of them as much as I should've been. Maybe it was my mate bond twisting my head and heart, knowing that we belonged together. My sexual attraction to them made things easier.

But with CO Rover? Fuck that shit. From the look of him, all he's capable of is saying 'yes, ma'am' to High Council Woman Laveau. Guys like him are only made of muscles and shit for brains.

The best I can hope for is that he stays true to his threat and tosses me in an isolation pit. At least then I can mentally prepare myself for this bullshit. With the Drekis, they were confused and angry. They wanted revenge for the death of their friend, but our mate bond muddled everything. I don't have that kind of protection now. This asshole can decide to teach me a lesson and throw me to the—

Sirens ring through the air, sending shooting pain behind my eyes. CO Rover grunts and spins around, slamming his hands to a metal door. My hazy vision makes it nearly impossible to see, and I heave, my insides threatening to come out. The alarm continues to blare. Static crackles across my skin, and the chains around my wrists warm, growing hotter and hotter by the second.

"Shit," CO Rover says, tossing me to the ground.

Wind whips through my hair, stirring up the scent of dirt and something subtly tangy, like lemons or oranges, definitely citrus.

"Inmate D64901, don't move while I take off your restraints. I'm going to need you to cross the prison yard and wait by the door to Cellblock S. Can you manage that, or do I have to lock you to the damn fence?" Something rattles, and CO Rover proceeds to unlock the magic restraints around my wrists.

I try to respond, but my dry tongue sticks to the roof of my mouth.

Locking his hands under my arms, CO Rover hoists me to my feet. I wobble on my shaking legs, trying to orient myself to what the hell is happening. CO Rover gets in my face and meets my gaze, his strange, diamond shaped pupils growing in size under his intensity.

"Did you hear me, inmate? Straight across the yard and to the entrance to Cellblock S. A guard will let you in. Now go!" His hot breath slaps my face, and he spins me around and shoves his hand into my back.

My legs fall out from under me, and I hit my knees to the dirt, my body begging me to give up and lie down. Pain radiates from my heart and to the rest of me, my caged dragon wailing in grief. CO Rover charges away from me, not waiting to see if I get up or not, and I can't stop the blip of fear from tightening my chest.

"Get up. Get up. Get the fuck up," I command myself,

trying to pep-talk my body into obeying. There is no one on my side out here. I can't expect a guard to save my ass if something happens...and the growing fear inside me, my human rationale, senses something dark and dangerous lurking nearby. It's the same feeling of being followed in a dark parking lot. The same feeling of dread that screams I might die any second.

A shadow moves in the corner of my vision, and I dig my fingers into the dirt, clawing as much as I can into the palm of my hand. My thoughts war with each other on what to do. A part of me wants to let the asshole now stalking me know that I see him and won't go down without a fight. Another part of me says that kind of shit doesn't work, and I should pretend I don't notice the fucker creeping toward me from the wall. Surprise might be the only thing on my side.

Groaning, I roll to my side, acting as if I'm struggling to get to my feet. I don't know if it's my sheer will to survive or my angry need to kick some asshole in the balls, but my body listens to my mind, doing what I beg of it. The soft shuffle of footsteps calms my heart instead of sending it plummeting out of me. I half expect the shadow to turn into someone familiar, someone who can protect me, but I realize I react the way I do because my mates must feel me. They must know that I could really use their strength right now, so they give me everything they can. It's what pushes me to get to my knees. To prepare to fight.

One footstep. Two. Three. The inmate moving through the shadows closes the space, sneaking up on me.

Something bangs from behind me, and I cringe at my body startling. I jerk my attention to the closed door CO Rover abandoned me to run through. A single bulb illuminates soft light along the wall. My shadow looks impossibly long, tall, and broad, and I don't have to turn back toward the prison yard to know the bastard made the noise to distract me.

I wiggle my fingers, feeling the roughness of the dirt rubbing against my palm. It's not exactly the best weapon, but it's the only one I have.

Fingers lock into my hair and jerk me around. Screeching in pain, I throw the dirt in the inmate's face. The shock of seeing the vampire baring his capped teeth freezes my moves. I can't ever fucking get over what they do to criminal blood suckers.

"Looks like the cat left me a lizard snack," the vampire says, jerking my head back, forcing me to look at him. "I'm not usually one for spicy, but they don't let the fae out with us."

Is he for real?

"You're sexy enough to overlook the smokiness, even

with that black eye." Swiping his thumb across my forehead, he smears the blood from getting clobbered with a magical baton from my skin. Popping his finger into his mouth, he licks the coagulating sticky liquid. "So what do you say? Let me feed on you and you can live. Fight me, and I'll—"

Jerking my fist forward, I attempt to punch him in his cock. The fucker hops back and yanks my hair. He slams his palm between my shoulder blades, winding me, and I gag and cough, the only air managing to fill my lungs being contaminated with dirt.

The vampire pins me down, yanking my arms behind my back. His strangely citrusy breath consumes my senses. This douchebag probably watched CO Rover throw me down.

"I wasn't supposed to kill you, but you've pissed me off, Drakovich. They said you'd be compliant. Scared of your own damn shadow." Shifting my hair, he pushes his chest into my back.

I should've known. Fuck.

Lazlo probably set me up, knowing that I could use the information of him trying to break open the gateway to the Mortal World against him.

"Aren't you going to plead with me? Ask me who put the bounty on you?" he asks, shaking me in annoyance.

"Why should I? I already fucking know," I snap. I should threaten him that my mates will come for him if he tries anything. I should beg for my life. But damn this all to hell. I just want to knock this guy off me and extract his fangs for even considering threatening me.

"Because—"

Bashing my head back, I manage to smash into his face because of his closeness. Pain erupts from my scalp as his teeth sink into me from the force. The sensation of my blood dripping to my neck kicks my ass in gear, and I alligator roll, knocking him off me. My stunt surprises the vampire so much so that all he can do is lick my blood from his lips. I scramble in his direction, scooping up another fistful of dirt.

Climbing on top of him, I shove the soil into his eyes. A deep, guttural noise escapes his throat, and he gnashes his jaws like he can reach me and tear my throat out. I swing my fist and sucker punch him in the nose and then the throat, using the moves Maddox helped fine-tune over the last few weeks.

My anger gives me the strength to fight. I fight with everything inside me—with the power of two dragon clans swelling in my very soul, yearning to break free—and show this bitey bastard that I'm not some little defenseless animal for him to prey on. I'm a wild, untamable dragon, and I will devour him whole.

"Daed eb tiv shum nus!" a velvety, husky voice shouts into the night.

Bright power engulfs me and the vampire, setting the world around us aglow as if the sun rises from the horizon only to fall to the ground. I expect to explode. I expect agony to leave me defenseless.

The vampire shrieks, the noise at such a high pitch, I'm sure all of Magaelorum can hear him. Wavy light zigzags across his body, turning his skin red.

His head explodes, sending guts spraying in my face.

I blink and freeze, not expecting this nastiness, and now I'm afraid I'm next.

"My dear pet." Lazlo's familiar voice trickles through my mind as my throat tightens. "It seems you owe me a debt for saving your life."

I throw myself off of the dead vampire and swipe the guts from my face. Rage sizzles through me, threatening to ignite the fire of a thousand dragon clans to incinerate this asshole. The tops of my hands burn, the brands glowing red, fighting to suppress my inner beast. I've never wanted to murder anyone so much in my life.

"Like hell I do. I didn't ask for your help, especially because you're the asshole who convinced this guy to hurt me." I shove my hands to the dirt, pushing to my feet.

Running won't get me anywhere, but I damn well will try to get away from Lazlo. If he kidnaps me, my mates may never find me again. At least if I manage to stay here, I have a fighting chance.

"Calm down, my beautiful beast. I'd never hurt the one bound to serve me, but you have put us in a terrible position. I mean, this wretched place again? Haven't you had enough? Your service to me will be far better than this," Lazlo says, waving his hand around.

He steps closer, the blue light of his power flickering in his eyes. I shuffle backward, keeping space between us. I wish I wasn't so afraid to take my eyes off him, because I can't see if any threats come from behind me. But right now? Lazlo is my biggest threat. Another vampire is like a tiny dog compared to the monster lurking beneath his elegant, tailored suit façade.

"Stay back. I'm not serving you or anyone," I say.

"You would rather stay locked up rather than learn to fight the power that put you here in the first place? Smarten up, my beautiful dragon. You cannot want to see your life go to waste, and for what? Moral standards? Fear of consequence? You murdered my coven brother, yet here I am, ready to forgive you, so save the bullshit. Give me your hands." Gathering light in his palms, he stalks me, picking up his pace. "This will only hurt a bit, but you've left me no choice."

Something inside me snaps, and burning heat floods through me, washing away the cold dread. Fire ignites in my hands, and I throw it at Lazlo, catching him off guard. I have no idea how the hell I manage to summon my power, but I don't think about it long.

Gathering my bravery, I blast more dragon fire at Lazlo and then spin and run.

Lazlo shouts a spell, and blue light flashes over the prison yard. A few dozen vampires shield their eyes, confused by the glow. Other inmates shout, ones I can't tell what species they are, but I ignore them and rush toward Cellblock S.

Cold electricity zaps my feet out from under me, and I skid across the ground and collide into the brick wall of the building.

I didn't make it. I can't believe this shit.

Power blinds me, and pain follows.

I scream until someone slaps a muter on me. Thrashing my body, I fight with everything in me, setting the world ablaze. I'll fight until I have nothing left. Until I am nothing.

"Emat eht teab yi ki ta!" a feminine voice shouts.

My fire consumes the world around me.

It consumes me.

Hope

"FUCK, KITTEN. SHIT." WARM HANDS slide under me as Kash lifts my cold body from the dirt. He shifts my hair from my face and releases a deep growl. "Who did this? I'm going to kill the bastard."

"Let me see her. I can help." Ambrose's voice whispers through the air of the dark pit.

Blinking, I try to clear my vision. Ambrose's green magic stings my eyes. I have no idea how long I've been in here, maybe days, but the time no longer matters with the closeness of these three and their familiarity.

"Careful, Ambrose. We can't disturb the magical shield any more than we have. Nova's tough. She'll be okay." Tiernan completes their circle around me, gently touching his warm finger to my cheek, drawing a soft line under my eye. "Isn't that right? My brother doesn't call you firecracker for nothing."

I lick my sore lips, trying to moisten my mouth. "H-Hey," I manage to say, the word barely a puff of breath. It's all my brain allows.

Kash's eyebrows lower over his gorgeous hazel eyes, but he holds his smile like he's afraid frowning might hurt me worse than I am. "Hey, kitten. You thirsty? Can I help you drink something and then kiss the hell out of you?"

I smirk and bob my head, the sweetness of Kash's voice filling me up with the hope stolen from me by this situation. I could kiss Ambrose for his stellar magical abilities and for bringing him here. Hell, I'm about to kiss all three of them. I'm so happy.

Kash raises an eyebrow. "I can't hear your thoughts, so I need you to tell me what you're thinking. That warmth you filled me with—fuck I need more."

Blush crawls up my cheeks, my body going haywire. Tugging a flask from his jacket, Kash offers me a sip of water. I snatch the container from him and chug it, the cool liquid ridding my mouth of the never-ending dirt from sleeping in this hole.

Tiernan caresses my arm, testing my reaction. I slow down and lick my lips. His green eyes search mine and travel to my mouth. He wants to kiss me as badly as Kash does. If only my stomach didn't roar like the beast caged inside me. All three of them narrow their eyes on my belly, and I clutch my stomach in embarrassment. I can't remember the last time I've eaten. During my last stay here, I was served raw meat that I wouldn't eat. But this time, I've been offered nothing. I've seen no one since...fuck. My head throbs with thoughts of Lazlo.

Ambrose rubs his hands together and whispers something under his breath. My stomach clenches at the sight of the banana materializing between his palms. No one has a chance to react as I lunge at Ambrose from Kash's arms, tackling him to the ground. Tearing the peel away, I shove the banana into my mouth, barely even chewing the thing. It's like my wild nature possesses me, turning me into a beast. And fuck.

Ambrose's eyes widen. "Princess, my fates."

Tiernan releases a strange, deep, sexy noise from his throat like the cross between a moan and a hum. "Did she just deep throat that thing?" he asks Kash, his voice a mixture of awe and amusement.

Kash chuckles and drops to his knees next to me. "Our mate has many incomparable talents."

My damn face. I'm never going to recover.

Tiernan follows Kash's lead and kneels on my other side, smirking at Ambrose as I continue to straddle the warlock like I'm afraid to let him up.

I hang my head, veiling Ambrose with my hair as I suck in a few deep breaths, trying to settle the feral beast consuming my actions. A warm hand presses between my shoulder blades, and Kash kneads his fingers into my tight muscles. I relax under his touch and turn my head to gaze at his smiling face. Combing his fingers through my hair, he pushes the dirty strands behind my ear.

"I need to kiss you, kitten," he murmurs, leaning in closer. "I can't wait any longer. I need to make sure you're okay on every level, and right now, I suffer from the sadness in your heart. I need you to know and feel what I do—that we're going to get through this. We will handle everything."

I want to ask him how, but he brushes his lips to mine, proving that he can't wait another second to give me his affection. His closeness sets me off in an unexpected way, igniting a burning desire inside me. I want nothing more than to distract myself from the fact that I've been hurt and thrown in a hole. I need to fill myself with everything Kash can give me and more.

Tiernan's gentle touch glides over my other shoulder, playing with my hair. His affection sends tingles through me, reminding me of our moment in the mud bath. And now, I yearn to kiss him too.

Breaking away from Kash's mouth, I bend my neck to kiss Tiernan next. Soft lips travel across my throat as Kash takes the moment to explore my skin, kissing my neck inch by inch. Ambrose's hands grab my knees, reminding me that I still pin him down. Sliding my hand over his, I squeeze his fingers. His body hardens with desire under me, and I gasp and pull away from Tiernan. I lock my eyes to Ambrose and watch the magic dance across his irises. He licks his lips, drawing my attention to his mouth, and now all I can think about is how much I want to kiss him too. Could I? Should I?

I mean, everything's a damn mess.

But when isn't it?

"I want to kiss him," I say, panting, and squirming, my body reacting to the desire I awaken in him by just straddling his waist. "I want to keep kissing all of you. I need—fuck. Is this wrong?"

Kash hums his disagreement under his breath and caresses his lips to mine again. "You get whatever you want right now."

"We don't need to waste time talking," Tiernan adds, leaning in. He surprises me by joining in my kiss with Kash, not waiting for his turn. "Ambrose will enjoy her regardless. Our jewelry ensures it."

Whoa. That's what Ambrose didn't want to tell me about his dick piercing. That's—really fucking thrilling.

My vagina clenches in anticipation and lust, feeling Kash and Tiernan's tongues gliding across mine in a sensual race to leave me breathless. I rock my hips in excitement, grinding my body to Ambrose's. He moans at the sensation and arches up, joining this strangely exciting tangle of our tongues and lips as I give attention to each of them.

I take initiative and rub my hands over both Kash and Tiernan's pants, feeling the massive desire I elicit from them in this moment. It's like they both can sense what I want next, because I don't even have to fumble to pull their cocks free as they do so for me. I stroke them in the same rhythm, smiling and kissing them, enjoying the wave of desire zinging through me.

Flicking his fingers, Ambrose uses magic to open the front of my jumpsuit. I try not to think about the ugly undergarments, but it only lasts a second because Kash unhooks my bra, baring my breasts to them. Like they know exactly what to do, Kash and Tiernan each suck on one of my nipples, sending pleasure spilling down my body and between my legs. My mind whirls with a dozen thoughts and desires. My need to lose myself in the ecstasy of being with three men who adore me lifts my spirit, filling my heart and soul.

Ambrose draws his tongue down my stomach, following the tight line of my body. He lies flat on his back, and Tiernan lifts my body up while Kash strips my jumpsuit off completely. I gasp at the sensation of my underwear ripping off a second before Kash lowers me right onto Ambrose's face. I should be weirded out how easy this is, how accepting and calm Kash is, knowing he's my true mate while Tiernan and Ambrose—fuck, I have no idea who they are to me. I'm not even sure it matters. I just crave being touched. Being drowned in everyone's hot intensity. It eases the anxiety and nerves revolving around the uncertainty of what happens next.

An intense vibration buzzes across my clit as Ambrose kisses me between my legs, sending goosebumps over my body. I gasp and squirm, grabbing onto Kash and Tiernan's shoulders, digging my nails into their skin. My mind turns to mush, and I bow my head and lock my eyes to Ambrose's, watching as magic sparks across my body. His power induced pleasure stiffens my muscles, and Tiernan silences my mouth with a passionate kiss. I drop my hand and lace it around Kash's cock, stroking him again, determined to get him off as fast I get off under all of their attention.

Grabbing my wrist, Kash slows me down. "You're cumming first, my sexy mate. Now I'm going to hold you still and let the warlock take good care of you."

Oh. My. Fuck.

Kash kisses me, squeezing my ass cheeks to stop me from squirming so much. I gasp and pant, savoring the thrilling sensations of my magically induced pleasure. Pinching my nipple, Tiernan rolls it between his fingers, playing with my breast. I tip my head back, wanting more from him, and he kisses and nips my sensitive skin between his teeth. I can barely handle any more ecstasy, my body reaching its peak. Kash slides his tongue into my mouth, muffling my scream. I clench Ambrose's head between my thighs and ride the wave of sizzling tingles bursting through every cell on my body.

Snatching me by the waist, Kash moans and sets me on my knees. His broad form covers my back as he leans over and kisses my shoulder. "I need to make love to you. I'm desperate and need to feel your closeness because the magic suppressors not only cage you, but it cages you from me. I never knew how much I could miss the sound of your soul serenading mine with the thoughts you let me always hear."

I nod my head, digging my fingers into the dirt. "I need it too. I feel so...incomplete."

"Let me make you whole again. At least for a while. I'm afraid for you. I want you to hold on for me," he whispers, stealing a private word as Ambrose and Tiernan wait with panting breaths.

"Then give me something to hold on to," I tease, twisting my head to kiss him. "Something to feel for days. All of you."

Tiernan gathers my hair and uses his free hand to tip my chin up. Fire lights his eyes, his rippling body as excited as I am as he watches my expression, waiting to see my reaction.

"You are damn lucky to have her bond completely," Tiernan murmurs, stretching my bottom lip while talking to Kash. "Isn't that right, Ambrose? Don't you want to know what it's really like. To feel her enjoyment. To know her on a level of the soul? Just look at her breathtaking face. A woman so perfect needs many men to take care of her."

Ambrose touches my jaw. "She can take care of herself. Right, Nova? I mean, look at her handling all of you."

"Always. I call her kitten because she's not afraid to use her claws." Kash hums and grazes his teeth to my shoulder as he positions himself behind me, his raging boner throbbing to sink between my legs. He moans, rubbing his shaft against me without going in. A whimper escapes my mouth at the aching need the gesture creates. I wiggle and shift, my body begging for more.

"I can't wait to see you use them more." Tiernan tightens his fingers in my hair and keeps my face tilted up to him. "Now prove them right. I need to see how exquisite you truly are."

"Then come here...unless you're afraid I'll bite." I link one hand around Tiernan's hip and pull him closer, licking the tip of his cock, flicking his ring.

Kash chuckles, his husky voice turning me on. "Looks like we'll find out if you're the one who can handle her."

I suck the tip of Tiernan's hard-on in my mouth and pull back. "I hope so. I've been thinking a lot about everything you can do."

Leaning down, he kisses the top of my head. "Me too."

Silence falls between us as I take the lead and drag my tongue along Tiernan's shaft. Ambrose strokes himself, gliding his fingers over my back like touching me anywhere is all he needs. I savor the different sensations exploding across my body, from Ambrose's gentle fingers to Tiernan pulling my hair to guide my mouth in a way he enjoys.

Kash continues to test and tease me a moment longer, watching me suck off Tiernan from over my shoulder. He groans and nips my ear and works his way to the back of my neck. Caressing my shoulders and mapping his hands down my spine, Kash straightens his back and massages my ass cheeks, teasing me with his tip, sliding it against my slick excitement. My body craves for him to hurry already. I can't stand another moment more. I want this so badly that my body clenches with anticipation.

Kash thrusts into me, making me moan so embarrassingly loud with Tiernan in my mouth that my voice vibrates across him. A sexy gasp of breath escapes his mouth, and I bob my head faster, letting him rock his body to my mouth as hard and as deep as he can. Shifting my weight onto one hand, I blindly reach for Ambrose and join him in rubbing his throbbing body. He moans and covers my hand with his, guiding me along, showing me what he likes.

The pit fills with the soft sounds of our pleasure, how perfect this moment is as we bond and enjoy the kind of intimacy only found within a clan with their mate. But this isn't about clans or power or breeding for a future for that matter. It's about trust and knowing that in this moment, these men will do anything for me, even if it means blending their clans unexpectedly. They do it for me and for a chance to have an amazing future by my side...if I ever get out.

"I'm going to cum, Nova," Tiernan warns, drawing my attention from my spiraling thoughts.

Instead of slowing down, I ignore his warning until he grunts and tugs my hair, jerking my head enough to watch me swallow his release. A burst of tangy flavor explodes across my tongue at the same time Ambrose cums across the dirt beside me. Kash tightens his hands to my hips and thrusts into me harder from behind until I scream with another orgasm. He moans with me, his muscles tight and flexing. His weight presses into me as he leans forward to hug me close from behind, keeping me off the dirt because of my weak legs.

"Damn it, I love you so much," Kash murmurs, kissing my shoulder as he lifts me up. "I can't leave you here." Puffing out a breath, Kash lets a tendril of smoke waft toward the grate above. "Ambrose, figure it out. Now. We're not leaving without her."

"He's right. Another day in here—no. It's unacceptable. She could be hurt worse." Tiernan stands close to Kash, the two of them turning into a wall of muscles ready to fight off the entire world. "This is your fault. Had you not acted rash and carelessly, we would be in the comfort of our palace."

Ambrose scrubs his face with his hand. "You know we can't hide forever. We need to figure this—"

"We need to break her out and take her home. What if something happens to her? Next time it could be an inmate and not a CO," Tiernan argues, whacking Ambrose in the back.

"It could be Lazlo," Kash adds. "He's who broke her out before. He killed her to cross the barrier. She could've never come back."

"I don't have that kind of capability unless I use dark magic, and the price for that—" Ambrose shakes his head. "No."

Tiernan straightens his shoulders, towering over Ambrose. "What do you mean *no*?"

Slapping my hand against Tiernan's chest, I block him from trying something stupid like lifting Ambrose off his feet. I jerk my attention to Kash, stopping him from doing what Tiernan tries with one look. Because despite these awful circumstances, I don't want Ambrose to pay the price. If it's anything like what Quillon has on Kash, it's not worth it.

"I'll be fine, okay? Give Ambrose time to work things out that won't cost sacrifices or whatever bullshit. You can't expect him to do something like that for me. He...he might not even want to be in this position. It could all be influenced by your brother's bond." I keep my gaze trained on the dirt.

My hair falls in my face, veiling my view of the three of them. I don't want them to see that it bothers me a bit, the idea of that being the case with Ambrose tightening my chest. I was starting to like him and accept his constant presence, and now? Letting myself be open and vulnerable? Fuck. This was a mistake.

"I—I survived a vampire attack and Lazlo coming already," I add, sucking my top lip into my mouth. "Why do you think I'm in here? My dragon fire broke through the spell."

Kash intakes a breath. "Fuck, you're not helping his case, kitten." Grabbing my hand, he pulls it to his chest like he needs to feel my palm against his racing heart. "Why didn't you say all this immediately? We—"

"I wanted to forget, even if it was for only a bit, Kash. I've missed you. I just—I didn't want you to start burning the place down. This is the last place I want you to be. Any of you. So please, just find a way. I'll hold on the best I can," I say, sliding my arm around Kash. "Especially if you can keep coming back."

"I'll collect on some favors," Tiernan says, taking my other hand. "I'll make sure you're safe."

"We will work together to ensure it," Kash adds.

"And I won't leave until I know no one will leash your collar. I thought for certain that the High Council would've removed it." Ambrose traces his finger across my throat.

"Because they want the option to control me," I mutter, staring at the brands on my hands. "Even though they know that Rhett had something to do with the murders at his bar. They're holding my mom's criminal history against me."

Ambrose clasps the same hand Tiernan quietly holds. "I swear on the fates, we will figure this out."

"What about the collar?" I ask, lowering my chin to my chest as if I might glimpse the magic peeking from my skin. "You'd have to stay with me to make sure no one binds me."

"That's not true, Delphia," Tiernan says, my birth name sounding so natural on his lips. "There is a way."

"How?" Kash and I ask in unison. He offers a small smirk and squeezes my hand.

Ambrose looks at him, then Tiernan, and lastly he holds my stare with his flickering silver gaze, sparkling with his electric magic. "She can bow to me."

My heart slides into my stomach.

"No," Kash and Tiernan say, the heat of their rising protectiveness sizzling across my skin.

Fuck. The idea goes against everything inside me, but what else am I supposed to do? I can't risk getting leashed by Lazlo or the High Council.

I swallow the burning in my throat. "Will you promise to release me when this is done?"

"I swear on my life," Ambrose says, touching his chest.

Nodding, I squeeze Kash and Tiernan's hands. "I don't

see any other way."

"You don't have to do this, kitten." Kash clenches his jaw.

My whole body trembles with my thought, with knowing he's wrong. "But I do."

Reunion

I TURN OVER ON THE dirt and feel the empty space where Kash was cuddling me when I fell asleep. Tiernan and Ambrose are gone too. I knew they had to go, and I asked them to leave after I drifted off to sleep so that I didn't have to see them leave, but waking up alone feels much more worse now that I experience it.

Maybe it's because their presences—all of my mates—lingers with me. I want so badly to hug them, tease them, hell, even fight with them. But now? All I have is this strange green energy flickering between my breasts and down my torso from Ambrose's magical leash controlling my collar. Only the two of us can see it, but every one of the guys can feel it, even Tiernan, because of his twin bond to Theo.

Metal bangs against metal, and I roll, squinting up at the silhouette blocking the pale rays of dusk. "Get up and show me your hands, Inmate D64901. I'm dropping the ladder. You have ten minutes in the yard. If you can prove that you can handle it, you might get ten more tomorrow. But no fights. Got it?"

I thrash my head up and down. "Yes, sir."

The idea of leaving this hole, even only for a few minutes, fills me with relief.

I'm willing to risk facing the dangers of the inmates for a breath of clean air and sun on my skin. Being locked in a hole, isolated from the world, constricts a part of my soul, making it hard to carry the warmth of hope that I'll get out of here.

"Good. I'm jeopardizing my good standing to pay a debt. Don't make me regret it. You're not supposed to be out at all, considering the High Council thinks Rhett had spelled you to resist the magic suppressing your murderous beast." Lifting the grate on the pit, the CO sets it aside as if it weighs nothing and drops down a rope ladder.

A dozen questions flit through my mind. McKenzie must've really pushed all of Lazlo's wrongdoings onto Rhett, and I can't help but wonder why. Why stain her good standing? Why sacrifice her coven brother?

"They think Rhett spelled me?" I ask, gripping onto the rope.

The CO hoists me up so quickly that I nearly release the rung of the ladder. If he didn't snatch my wrist and drag me out, I'd have fallen back down into the pit. "They will figure it out. Once they do, we might be able to move you into gen. pop. if you're obedient and stay out of trouble."

Fluttering my eyelashes to adjust to the light of the setting sun, I clear the shadows from my vision. I finally gather my bravado to meet the cold stare of the CO and spot brilliant iridescent wings on his back. "That's kind of hard with a target on my back."

"What do you mean?" His brows furrow with his question.

I clear the dirt from my face the best I can and lick my lips. "What do you think set me off? An inmate attacked me. Was supposed to rough me up."

He peers past me. "So you turned him to ash?"

"He was already dead..." Damn it. It sounds like I just admitted to guilt.

The CO flaps his wings and curls his hands into fists. "Keep that shit to yourself. I'll keep an eye out as a courtesy to the Drekis, and you can tell the Darkonians my debts are paid in full. Now stay out of trouble for ten minutes. I want to be able to give a good behavior report when the High Council reconsiders your isolation sentence. I'm sure you don't want to spend more time in the pits than you have to."

I'm not sure how I feel about that. I hate the idea of spending day after day in the pit, but with it comes secret visits with my mates.

I know from Maddox that the High Council focuses and pours their power into keeping inmates caged in rather than keeping people out, so sneaking in isn't as difficult.

"I will try my best," I say, taking the sweet approach.

The CO flares his nostrils and purses his lips. "If you don't, it'll be the Darkonians who owe me."

Grabbing my hands, he locks a magical chain around my wrists, restraining my arms. Annoyance washes through me. How the hell can he do this knowing that someone is after me and seeking revenge? He says he'll keep an eye out for me, but how can I trust him?

I shake my hands, feeling a small shock of power. "Is this necessary?"

He crosses his arms. "It's protocol. Now go walk or

some shit. I can't have you hanging out with me."

"Bad for your reputation?" I retort, shuffling my feet instead of testing my luck.

"Something like that, princess." With his words, he launches into the sky and flies toward a platform overlooking the prison yard.

He motions for me to scram, but I don't even know where I should go. I guess I'll just walk the perimeter and hope no one notices me until I'm forced back into the pit for another night.

Energy hums above me as green electricity crackles atop the high, barbed wire protected walls. Another barrier, made of chain-link and more razor wire separates me from an open walkway for the guards to move from building to building in this mega prison.

I spot a couple of fae with clipped wings hanging out in a few different clusters. I wonder if they knew Rose. With the thought of the murderous fairy princess, my chest clenches. I can't even think about her without fear and anger. So I shove thoughts of her into the dark recesses of my mind and stroll faster toward a patch of grass to sit on. Maybe I can use it to rub away some of the grossness from the pits.

A quiet whistle cuts through the hum of magic zinging across the barriers. "Hey, Red. You look like shit. They been keeping you in the pits this whole time?"

Quillon stands a dozen feet away near some empty stone bleachers, used as a sitting area of sorts during yard time.

I stop in my tracks and hold my chained wrists close to my chest. I knew Quillon was with me when the High Council arrived and arrested us, but somehow his appearance still surprises and unnerves me. I should be worried that he's here and unprotected. Baker knows Kash bowed to Quillon and if he dies, so does Kash. The thought flips my stomach. My sudden need to protect this asshole really messes with my head.

"What? Can't talk?" Quillon asks, twisting his lips to the side.

Inhaling a deep breath, I straighten my shoulders and stride toward him. His cocky-ass smile disappears with my approach, and he takes an automatic step back and raises his palms to me.

"Easy, Red. I've been hurt enough because of you," he quips, shuffling back another foot. "I only want to talk."

Fury explodes through me. "*You've* been hurt because of *me*? Are you fucking kidding me, Quillon? You're insane! You tricked me! You've been manipulating us all this whole time. Be thankful I can't kill you."

He releases a growl, his features hardening. If his hands

didn't glow with the same magic suppressing brands that mine do, I know he'd try to intimidate me with his lycan form. Like that could even work after everything I've been through.

"Be thankful I don't bite your head off, you bitch," he mutters, glowering. "All of this could've been avoided had you just been smart enough to know your damn place. You act as if you're fucking better than me, but you're not. I have power far greater than you can imagine. Enough that Lazlo will be getting me out soon. He knows I'm useful. He'll even let me keep your mate as my little pet. I might allow you some occasional alone time in exchange for a show every now and then. Hell, you can earn more than that if you give in and let me fuck you. It could be a good life. Lazlo offered you a deal to ensure your freedom from this hell. I bet he would—"

Launching forward, I surprise the hell out of him by tackling him to the ground. I slam the magical chain into his face, and he bucks his body, managing to knock me off him. My back hits the ground with a thud. I somersault, throwing my legs over my head and scramble to my feet. Quillon swipes blood from his face, sending it spattering across the ground. Fuck, I've never seen something so satisfying. I know Kash will forgive me if he felt the pain. I'm damn certain he'd tell me to do it again.

Quillon charges toward me, his eyes flickering with green as his lycan tries to break through. I brace to fight him, showing him his true place. Because I am better than him, and he's beneath me. If he even thinks for another second that I'll ever resort to doing what he wants out of desperation, he'll be sorely disappointed.

"Inmates, down!" a deep, sharp voice yells before pain bursts in my hands. "Get down and don't fucking move!"

I glare at Quillon, my anger snuffing out my good senses. He just gets under my skin and in my head. I can't help myself. I've never wanted to see someone punished more in my life than I do with him. He deserves it. I want to beat karma and take matters into my own hands. All I know is that even if he doesn't want the cure, I will force it down his throat and murder him with my dragon fire. He will regret ever messing with my life, the fucking selfish bastard.

"Last warning!" The familiar voice of the fae CO, who brought me out of the pit calls, touching his feet to the ground to assist—damn. I recognize the other CO, CO Lowe, from my time here before.

The second our eyes meet, I know something is wrong. Fuck. Fuck. Fuck.

A hand locks into my hair and forces me onto my stomach, trapping my hands between my body and the compacted dirt. Pain swells through me, and uncontrollable tears blur my eyes. The fae CO straddles me, roughing me up on purpose, like he doesn't want CO Lowe to know he's supposed to watch out for me.

"You both are going to the pits," the fae CO says, growling in my ear. "Two nights."

I clench my jaw as the fae CO hoists me to my feet. He sets me beside him, gathering the back of my jumpsuit in his hand like I might rush Quillon again. I try my best to keep my cool, knowing that going back to the pits is for the best. Ambrose promised he'd sneak Maddox and Rowan in to see me tonight. As for Theo? Who the hell knows. I don't particularly want to see his asshole face, but I'd choose to see it over having to deal with Quillon ever again.

"Make it three nights," CO Lowe snaps, dragging Quillon to his feet. "And after your visitation hours. Inmate D64901 and Inmate D64876 have been summoned by the High Council for questioning in regards to the Liohts."

The fae CO cocks his head. "I didn't get the—"

A loud buzzer blares, announcing yard time is up for the inmates, cutting him off. Icy dread trickles through me. A whisper of a smirk crosses Quillon's face, though CO Lowe remains expressionless.

"I'll escort them, all right? Your shift's about up anyways," CO Lowe says, shoving Quillon in the back. He doesn't hook chains to him or anything, and I know my instincts were right. Something is wrong. Terribly wrong.

I try to back up, but the fae CO holds me in place. "Don't let him," I plead, jerking my head to meet his gaze. "I want you to escort me. Please."

CO Lowe gives me a once-over and shakes his head. "Don't be scared, Inmate D64901. The Drekis are my friends. I'll make sure you make it safely."

Nope. Not happening. There is no fucking way I'm going with CO Lowe and Quillon, especially because I realize he was the CO to take me to the Visitation Center where Lazlo tried to kill me.

And fuck. With the memory, a dozen emotions rush through me. This isn't even regarding the High Council. I know it. I can feel it deep in my bones.

"Are you sure? I don't mind," the fae CO says, turning his attention back to CO Lowe.

His eyes flicker with blue light for a split second, but I know I didn't just imagine it. "I got them. Don't worry."

Heat rushes from my core and into my hands, triggering pain as the brands and restraints shock me with power. I stiffen, my body going crazy. There is no way in hell that I'm going with CO Lowe.

"Delphia," CO Lowe says, using my birth name. "Don't fight—"

My dragon fire breaks through the magic suppressing spell once again and explodes between my palms. I chuck it at CO Lowe and Quillon, blasting them off their feet. Jerking away from the fae CO, I make a run for it.

Something zaps me in my back, stealing my breath. I fall forward and hit the dirt, crushing my arms in the process. Strong hands grip my waist and dangle me facing out. Silence falls over the prison yard.

With a shock of blue light, Lazlo appears in front of me. "Delphia, my pet. Must you always make things so hard?" He closes the space and grabs my chin. "I'm giving you one more chance, so let's talk."

I spit in his face.

Coward

"TRICKY, TRICKY, MY BEAUTIFUL BEAST," Lazlo says, drawing his finger along the magical collar around my neck. "Who did this? I'll devour their whole coven's power line and feed them to you when I take control back."

I flare my nostrils, trying to jerk away, but I'm frozen in his magic. The Visitation Center remains as I remembered it, dark and empty. A table rests in the middle of the room, yet Lazlo forces me to sit in a chair in the corner.

"It had to have been Ambrose," Quillon says, leaning on the wall of the small visiting cell.

"A dragon clan would never allow such a thing. Which coven did you say he was a part of?" Lazlo asks, straightening his back and rubbing his hands together, sending sparks of blue magic through the air.

"He is alone as far as I know." Quillon keeps his eyes trained on the ceiling, refusing to look at me. Fucking coward. "Rose said he was far more powerful than expected. She nearly didn't get out alive." What the fuck? He knew she was going to attack. His pleas, begging me not to leave him alone with the Drekis were fake. I can't help but wonder if the two of them had been working together all along. I mean, he never even mentioned or reacted to her supposed death by my hands...fuck.

"Impossible. No one can have this kind of magic alone." Clapping his hands, Lazlo disappears, only to reappear in front of Quillon. Lazlo points his finger at the lycan and lifts him off his feet with magic, hanging him like a ragdoll by the neck without even touching him. "Now tell me who. You've been with them for weeks. Don't make me regret including you in my bargain with the fae princess." Shit, I was right.

Quillon growls, his face turning red. "I don't fucking know."

"Then you are no use to me!" Lazlo gathers power in his palm, preparing to throw it at Quillon.

I scream, the noise muffled and low, but it's enough to get Lazlo to freeze and turn his attention to me. Dropping Quillon, he claps his hands again and materializes in front of me. He traces the seam of my mouth, tilting his head with a leer.

"Do you have something to tell me, my beast?" Lazlo asks, getting into my face close enough to catch the strange powdery scent of his skin. "Go on, speak up."

I gasp, my mouth finally opening, though the rest of my body remains frozen. "He's telling the truth. Please, don't kill him."

Lazlo narrows his eyes. "After everything he's done, you plead for his life?"

"As long as her mate is my guardian," Quillon mutters.

I cringe and slowly nod. "Please."

Sighing, Lazlo grabs my hair and pulls my stiff body closer, the chair squeaking on the tiled floor with his magic. Pressing his lips to my earlobe, he says, "Then tell me—quietly—how the warlock managed. If you don't, I'll kill the lycan."

Shit. I don't really know. If I say the wrong thing, this could be it for my sweet, romantic mate. And then me. Because I will kill Lazlo if he tries.

I puff a breath between my lips. "I—I don't know exactly but—"

Flicking his fingers, Lazlo sends Quillon crashing into the wall. Quillon hollers and thrashes, the shock of Lazlo's power hurting him.

"Wait!" I screech. "Wait. It might have to do with—"

Lazlo slaps his hand over my mouth. "Whisper it, my pet."

It takes everything in me to control the pitch of my voice. "The Darkonians. Ambrose told me they're his familiars." I pray to the universe that my answer is enough to get him to spare Quillon. I have no fucking clue if their bond to each other could possibly be the reason.

"Are you sure?" Lazlo asks, his eyes flickering with blue bolts of power.

I nod. "That's what he said."

"Well, that makes this a bit interesting." Waving his hand over me, he releases me from his magical hold. "I have a deal, my pet. I know you will continue to put up a fight until I break you, but I see that might not be necessary."

"So what? Are you going to leave me alone? Go after Ambrose?" I ask, hating that I must know the answers. He shouldn't have this kind of power over me.

"Perhaps. Perhaps not. That will depend on you," he says, his face contorting into the strange monster he truly is.

His teeth elongate into fangs, and he grows in height, towering over me like his size could even intimidate me.

"Of course it does," I mutter, shifting in my seat, preparing to get up to attack if I have to.

"I want you as my pet, Delphia. I want you to serve me and help me dismantle the High Council. But you can't do that if you serve another." His voice deepens with his words. "I'm also aware of his power and know better than to test the Darkonian guard without knowing everything, so I want you to kill him. Kill him and break his hold on you."

He's crazy.

"Or you could get the Darkonians to bow to me. With their loyalty will come Ambrose's." Lazlo grins at his ultimatum, looking ready to high-five himself. The fucker.

I consider screaming at him that I choose neither, but I know better than to lose my chance at using Lazlo. There is only one way I can accomplish what he asks, and it isn't possible being locked away in Max.

"I will get the Darkonian's to bow," I say, remaining expressionless. "They'd deserve it for forcing a union bond on me." If I just agree, Lazlo might know I have other plans. He might not give me the chance to try and instead use me to get to Ambrose. I can't let that happen. I need Ambrose. I like him and don't want to be the reason for his undoing.

"Is that so?" Lazlo asks, turning his attention to Quillon.

Quillon gives a sharp nod in confirmation.

"Interesting." Turning his back on me, Lazlo closes the space to Quillon and extends his hand. "I'll be in touch, my pet. Tell no one of our visit."

I open my mouth to tell him to wait, but he grabs Quillon and the two of them disappear, leaving me alone.

Grabbing the chair, I throw it at the wall and scream in frustration. The fucker should've told me what his plan was. He should've just broken me out of here. But now? Fuck. I can't stay here, waiting around for him. I need time to plan what to do. I don't even know how bargains like this work. What cost will I pay if I fail?

A buzzer sounds through the room, and the door swings open to the hallway. I expect CO Lowe to be waiting for me, but an unfamiliar guard takes his place. The familiar flicker of magic dances across the man's eyes, the lavender color setting off my fear instincts. He looks nothing like McKenzie, but I don't think coven members have to be related.

"Hands up, Inmate D64901," the man snaps, yanking the magical chain from his belt. "Time to return to the pits."

"Those won't be necessary. I'm not going anywhere," I say, wringing my hands together.

The CO steps closer, a scowl marring his face. I spot the word Bright sewn on his uniform and wonder if he might have an alliance with the Liohts. "Hands up," he commands.

"What? Are you afraid of me?" I ask, stepping around the chair, using it as a barrier. "If you want to restrain me, you're going to have to use your magic."

He growls and tries to dodge around the chair to grab me. "Inmate, get on the floor. Now!"

"Make me! Use your magic to make me!" I yell, anger rushing through me. "Or are you afraid someone will know?"

Snagging the chair, I swing it, clocking him in the head. He yowls but doesn't use his magic like I expect. In this moment, I know I'm right. He is afraid someone will know. Magic leaves a residue behind and a powerful witch might discover it.

"Ambrose, help me! Please, where are you?" I call, rushing toward the open door.

My heart sinks into my stomach at his lack of response. He probably isn't arriving until later. By then, it might be too late.

"Lazlo!" I shout next, racing down the long hallway in the direction we came in from. "Lazlo, help!"

I hate—and I mean, fucking hate with a passion—the

fact that I call out for the dickwad who wants to control the rest of my life. But I don't know who else to call. I don't know what to do. I expected an enemy being an inmate, and not a warlock guard. I should've known better than to think that the vampire attack was the worst of it.

Reaching the exit, I try to push the door open, but it doesn't budge. I slam my shoulder into the heavy metal, praying that I can somehow manage the strength of all my dragon mates. Still, it doesn't open. It doesn't even quiver.

"You fucking bitch," CO Bright growls, locking his fingers to the back of my neck.

I scream and thrash, trying to swing my body up in an attempt to knock him over. He slams me into the metal door, smacking my forehead hard enough for starbursts to pepper my vision. Blood trickles down my forehead, sending panic through me.

The door whooshes open, engulfing me with cool night air. I gasp and heave, my whole body rippling with agony. Marching forward, CO Bright rams his hand into the chain-link gate, separating the Visitation Center from the prison yard. He hops over a body lying face down in the dirt, and I thrash as hard as I can, trying to break free. Because this traitor killed CO Lowe. He murdered him and will blame his death on me. No one will believe me otherwise. If I can't get out of here before the other COs find out, I'm dead.

"Hold fucking still, Drakovich," CO Bright snaps, swinging my body to smash me into the chain-link fence. "The Liohts request you pay them restitution with your life."

Oh. My. Fuck.

Dragging my hands over my head, CO Bright locks me to the chain-link fence. He whistles through his fingers, the loud sound piercing my ears and making me flinch. I yell and swing my body, trying to break the damn plastic tie. He couldn't get the chain out quick enough, which is my only saving grace. I know I can break free. I have to.

CO Bright locks his fingers around my throat and holds me in place, jabbing his fist into my stomach. I can't even scream at the force of his punch. My eyes water, my whole body feeling the agony that swells in my core. And like a coward, CO Bright turns on his heels and runs away. He abandons me, leaving me vulnerable and restrained to the fence.

A catcall whistles through the night, and I jerk my attention to the vast, dimly lit prison yard. Panic tightens my chest, and I push past the pain and twist and yank my arms, trying to contort my hands to slide free of the ties.

"Baker, my man, I can't believe your brother actually came through," a guy says, his voice light and full of excitement. "Just look at her. A filthy slut. I can't wait to taste her."

Shit. Shit. Shit.

"Not until she begs to end her life." Baker's husky voice constricts my muscles, threatening to freeze me in fear. "I want to enjoy this—for Rhett."

Grinding my teeth, I link my fingers into the chain-link. I turn my attention to Baker and another inmate, strolling in my direction. It's like they want their slow approach to torture me, but all it does is give me a moment to think.

I might be stuck to this fence, but I'm not defenseless.

Forcing a small whimper through my lips, I play on these assholes' need to frighten me. They crave seeing me weak and defenseless. But what they don't realize is that I'm stronger than ever before.

Heat burns through my veins as my dragon fire sizzles under the surface of my skin. A calm wave of tranquility slows my racing heart, giving me better focus. The two men grin at each other, their sadistic smiles nothing compared to anything I've faced.

"Grab her arms, Malone. Make sure she won't break the ties. Dragons are strongest when threatened," Baker says, rubbing his hands together. Something sparkles as it slips from his sleeve and into his hand. "I'll start by giving her my mark."

My muscles scream, my mind whirling. The strength of my mates falters as my fear shoves it away, warning me that I'm in trouble. The vampire, Malone, shows off his capped fangs, the sight the only thing stopping me from screaming in panic. He holds up his hands, getting closer, expecting me to fight.

But I wait. I will not give him the chance to figure out how to hold me still by seeing any of my skilled kicks.

"Hurry up," Baker snaps. "We only have minutes before yard time."

Minutes? I can fight for a few minutes...right?

Malone jerks his hand out and grabs one of my arms. I guess I'm about to find out.

Swinging my leg up, I perform a high kick and hook my foot to the chain-link instead of trying to kick the vampire. I hold on tightly with my fingers and manage to swing my other leg up into a modified bridge pose. My muscles burn at the move, but I only hold it long enough to flip back down, kicking Malone's shoulder and buckling his legs with the force.

Baker lunges at me, crushing me with his weight. The fence bounces from his strength. It's not enough for me to shove Baker off, and he jerks his hand down and stabs me with his makeshift shank in the leg.

I scream, pain bursting through me, weakening my legs. The weight of my body giving out from the pain stretches my arms, pulling them in an awkward position. Stepping on my shin, Baker ensures I won't kick him and unzips the front of my jumpsuit. I thrash and scream again, my body running on adrenaline, pushing the pain away.

"Hold her still!" Baker commands Malone, and the vampire gets his shit together and locks his fingers through my hair.

Sparks pop in Baker's eyes, his magic vying to break free. Tugging my jumpsuit off my shoulder, he exposes part of my breast. Malone hums and shifts, his body hardening with desire. My stomach twists, and I buck and fight, trying everything to get the two sickos away from me.

"This is for my coven," Baker says, his fragrant, florally breath blowing in my face.

Swiping his shank over the top of my breast, he starts to carve something into my skin. Agony consumes me, and I screech and shriek, the pain unbearable as he draws something with his blade. My vision shadows and light bursts around us, setting the prison yard aglow with orange flames. My hands drop from the fence, my dragon fire melting away the plastic ties.

A buzzer cuts over the sound of my screams, and I expect Baker and Malone to flee, but Malone drags me to the ground and smacks out the flames flickering in my palms. He twists my hair again, yanking my head up. Hissing a breath, he growls into my ear.

"Burn me and I'll break your hands," he says, bending my fingers back hard enough to make me scream.

Voices hum through the night, and I scream again, praying for someone, anyone to help me. Baker slaps me, cutting off my voice with his hand. Climbing on top of me, he straddles my waist, bringing the blade to the other side of my chest.

I convulse, my body breaking, my mind screaming for reprieve.

I black out, icy darkness swallowing me whole. Savoring the nothingness, I think about my mates. I wish with everything in me to speak to them one last time. To tell them how much they mean to me, even after only these few short weeks.

"Nova, fight!"

I jerk upright at the sound of the Drekis and Darkonians voices erupting in my mind at once. A wave of heat burns the chill from my body, and fire explodes from my mouth. Baker's eyes widen, and he holds his palms up, chanting a spell that does nothing. My dragon fire consumes him so quickly that all that remains is a pile of ash in his place, scattering and disappearing on the breeze.

Someone hollers. I whip my attention to a group of inmates grabbing loose rocks and whatever they can find on the ground.

"She's mine," Malone says, his voice echoing through the night. "Stay back!"

"The Lioht Coven has a reward for her head," an inmate says. "Get her!"

A hulking man tackles Malone and punches him in the face. Yells and hollers, twisted noises of excitement sound out as more inmates race to capture me. Vampires fight warlocks and witches, each trying to outmatch the other to kill me.

McKenzie will get what she wants after all.

I can't see any way out.

Someone throws a rock, pelting me in the forehead, knocking me back. I blink through my hazy vision and can't do anything but stare at the night sky. My body trembles, my fire dying with the all-consuming pain. There's no way I can face all of these inmates. I'll never make it out alive.

I never thought I'd ever beg the universe for a swift death.

I never thought I'd end up in a magical prison either or fated as the mate of dragons.

A shadow looms on the ground and a man peers down at me, a frown crossing his face. "I won't hurt you. I'll get you somewhere safe."

I don't respond. I'm not even sure if I can.

Reaching down, he lifts me into his arms, his minty scent somehow manages to calm the fear cooling my blood. Another inmate growls and charges at us, and the world spins. I heave as the man tosses me on his shoulder only long enough to watch the body of another warlock drop dead to the ground with a broken neck.

Taking off into a sprint, the guy runs in the direction of the pits, keeping close to the fence to better watch his back. A siren finally rings, blaring through the night, and several spotlights roam over the prison yard to light a few guards' ways.

"Almost there," the man murmurs. "You're lucky your keeper contacted me in time. It was quite the surprise. I haven't had the pleasure of receiving a telepathic message in a long, long time."

I lick my swollen lips, my mind barely able to concentrate. "Hmm?" It's the best I can do to ask what the hell he's talking about.

"Ambrose," he says, navigating the area with the pits. "He asked me to help you."

Stopping near the last row of grates, the man sets me down and surprises the hell out of me by prying one open. He winks at me and scoops me back into his arms only to dangle me over the hole.

"At what cost? What do you get out of it?" My muscles tense, my mind thinking the worst. I will murder him if it's something like making another one of my mates bow.

"Brace yourself, Delphia. It's a long drop," he says instead of answering my question, like he knows what swirls through my mind.

"Wait, I—" My voice cuts off as my stomach rises into my throat at the sudden plummet into the pit.

I land in a crouch and fall back, landing on my ass. I tilt my head back and watch the man place the grate back over the opening.

"Wait! Come back here!" I yell, trying and failing to get up. "Tell me at what cost!"

The man's silhouette disappears as he abandons me.

I smack the ground in frustration. "Damn it, asshole! At what cost!"

The soft thuds of footsteps thump across the compacted dirt behind me. I was too busy yelling at the man who saved me to realize I'm not alone. Swiveling my torso, I prepare to once again fight, but a familiar woman stops in her tracks a few feet away, closing the small amount of space from her place in shadows against the dirt wall.

"Your warlock vowed to take down the Liohts if my brother helped you," Tasha Tenebris says, dropping to her knees to get on my level. "It won't do much for our life sentences, but at least we'll get some of the justice we deserve."

I open my mouth to respond, but a strange sensation crawls up my feet and spreads through the rest of me.

Tasha reaches out and grazes my hand. "You're being summoned by the High Council."

And I thought my night couldn't get any worse.

"I expect you'll ensure Ambrose keeps his word," she adds with a hint of her lavender power sparking in her eyes. "Now don't resist. If you do, it'll only hurt."

I disappear.

The Litendrake Heir

“YOU HAVE ONE HOUR TO bring me proof or Delphia Drakovich will return to where she belongs,” High Council Woman Laveau says, standing a foot in front of me. “Until then, you may wait with the princess.”

“My brother is already on his way.” Tiernan kneels beside me, releasing a growl under his breath. “And when he does, you will be held accountable for her condition.”

“We’ll see.” Clapping her hands, High Council Woman Laveau disappears, leaving the two of us alone.

Sliding his hands under me, Tiernan picks me up off the floor and cradles me in his arms. My head lolls, my mind reeling. Everything from tonight catches up to me, and I can't stop the cry from escaping my mouth. Tears burn my vision. I sob, my whole body aching and hurting, my soul feeling as if the night cracked me open to never be healed again.

"Ambrose, hurry," Tiernan says, carrying me across the room and to a small cot. "She needs Maddox."

Light flashes in the small room, and the familiarity of Maddox's growl fills me up with everything I need to open my eyes. I extend my arms out, silently begging for him to close the torturous space between us. Fire lights his eyes, his handsome features hard as he drinks in the sight of me, beat up and bleeding, on the verge of losing consciousness again. It's only his presence that keeps me holding on.

"I need space," Maddox says, his deep voice reverberating through my bones. "Return to your brother and ensure everything is in order. I will heal her and guarantee she is prepared if things don't go as planned."

Tiernan kisses the top of my head and slides me onto the cot. "Hold on, Nova. You're getting out. Tonight."

"We promise," Ambrose says, taking Tiernan's hand. The two of them disappear in another flash of light.

Maddox groans deep in his throat, examining my body without touching me. He doesn't have to tell me to know how bad I look. I swear I can even feel pain in my hair follicles.

Reaching into a bag, Maddox pulls out a glass bottle with strange ruby liquid. It sparkles under the bright lights above, stealing my attention. Popping the cork off with his thumb, Maddox swirls the elixir a few times, mixing it enough to send the rancid smell into the air.

"I swear, cookie. If you give me a hard time and don't do as I ask—"

"You'll spank me?" My words come out as a heaving breath, and I wince, my body wanting to laugh at his glowering reaction but the pain stops me.

Sitting me up, Maddox positions me in his arms. He cradles me in the crook of his elbow to support my head and presses the bottle to my lips. My stomach clenches, and I nearly whack him, but he pins my arm to his hard abs and uses his free hand to plug my nose.

"Just chug it. The faster you drink it, the faster you'll heal. Then I can have my way with you," he murmurs, keeping his voice even. "I fucking missed you. If Rowan and Kash didn't fight me and get me to think with my brain and not my beast, I'd have destroyed Max and everyone there."

I quietly swallow the liquid, gulping the disgusting flavor as quickly as I can. I shake my head and shudder, trying to will the grossness away.

"Here, drink this next," Maddox commands, offering me another bottle filled with black liquid this time.

I nearly gag at the thought, but he tips it and fills my mouth with a thick, sugary liquid that sends tingles blossoming over my skin. The pain fades with each passing second, and Maddox strokes his hand over my cheek, just staring at me without saying a word. Silence fills the air, and I shift in his arms, resting my head to his chest to listen to his heartbeat.

"Can I clean you up to make sure you're healing okay?" Maddox asks after another couple minutes of comforting quiet. "It looks like you've had one helluva good time in the pits without me."

I crack a smile and bob my head, teasing him. "Kash was listening all of those times you bragged about screwing me in the pits."

"Mmmhmm," he says, humming the words. "Sure, cookie. Kash refuses to accept that part of you loves it rough and wild. He is confident that you prefer making love."

I narrow my eyes and purse my lips. "Maybe I do."

"I'm fully ready to prove otherwise." Kicking the bathroom door closed, he sets me on the small counter and turns on the shower. "I have to make sure you're back to normal, and I can't think of a better way."

"You really go all out, Dr. Dreki," I say, shifting on the sink. "But you should know. I still ache."

Fire dances in his golden irises. "Where?"

Sliding off the counter, I swallow vanity over my filth and shrug out of the singed and torn jumpsuit. It drops to the floor with Maddox's gaze, and I stand bare in front of him, showing the fact that I don't wear any undergarments.

I draw my hands over my breasts. "I hurt here," I say, sucking my bottom lip into my mouth.

His muscles ripple and flex. "Where else?"

Working my way down, I caress my fingers between my legs. "Here. I think only your kisses can help ease the ache inside me."

Maddox rushes to me and crashes his lips to mine, lifting me off my feet. I scramble to tug his shirt over his head as he kicks out of his pants and carries me into the steaming shower. Hot water cascades over me, rinsing away the filth and dirt of the night while Maddox's soft tongue pushes away the pain and turmoil I suffered at the hands of Magaelorum's vilest criminals.

My back hits the cool tiled wall, and Maddox breaks from my mouth to kiss my neck. I rub my hands over his broad shoulders and savor the sensation of his mouth caressing over my skin, kissing away the remaining pain from my body.

His hard cock flexes at the apex of my thighs, his desire as prominent and desperate as mine. I can barely handle the anticipation of feeling him slide into me that I reach between us to align our bodies.

"I need you now," I say, running my fingers into his long hair, grabbing it in my hands to pull his mouth back to mine. "Fuck me how you like. I just want to forget the world exists outside of us."

With a moan, Maddox props me on the wall and thrusts into me hard and deep enough to feel his balls slap my ass. I gasp and cling onto him with my arms around his neck while stretching my legs open to brace myself in place and feel every thick inch he has to offer. The gesture frees his hands, and he digs his fingers into one of my hips while rubbing fast circles over my exposed clit.

Bursts of moans escape my mouth with each of his fast thrusts, and I lose myself to the pleasure he awakens inside me. Maddox knows exactly what I want and need from him and gives it to me with sexy passion that makes me crave more.

He licks my throat up to my jaw and finally meets my mouth. His cinnamon kiss curls my toes, and I cup his face, not allowing him to stop. Moaning, he hums at my desperation, gliding his tongue over mine managing to be sensual yet rough, bringing me to my peak. My muscles clench as I scream a moan, bliss rolling through me in wave after wave. My legs weaken and Maddox grabs onto my thighs, swinging his body hard and fast until he groans in satisfaction, holding me in place, his cock throbbing inside me as he cums.

"I will never be without you by my own freewill, Delphia," he whispers through his panting breath. "You're my infuriating, fierce, sexy, and most spectacular mate in the universe. I know we don't always agree on things. I know I act like an asshole sometimes, but I just can't help myself. You push my buttons unlike anyone else, and I love you for it. I love that you test my strength and my desire. I want to always do right by you."

I smile and hug him with my whole body, loving this tender moment with the man that pisses me off half the time. "Who are you and what have you done with my sexy, broody, demanding asshole?" I tease, kissing his throat.

He growls and pinches my ass cheeks. "Don't make me spank you until you admit you feel the same, cookie. I can already feel it through our bond. You love me and want to have my children. You know we will bear a powerful future by expanding and blending our clan."

I laugh and look him in the eyes, his face utterly serious as he returns to the cocky bastard he is. "You're partially right. I do love you, but as for your babies? No. Not happening."

"Now you're lying." He narrows his eyes. "Which makes me want to punish you until you admit the truth in your soul."

I stick out my tongue. "You can—"

Ambrose materializes outside the shower, his eyes automatically devouring the sight of me in Maddox's arms. Releasing a growl, Maddox grabs a towel, annoyance rushing through him at the interruption. Ambrose swivels and turns his back on us as Maddox carries me out of the shower and wraps the towel around me.

"We're supposed to have an hour," Maddox says, vigorously drying me off inch by inch, examining my body as he does. "It's only been fifty minutes. There is still a lot I want to do for Delphia in the remaining ten."

I grab Maddox's shoulders and turn him to me. "It's okay. We'll have time later..." Flicking my attention to Ambrose, I add, "Right? You're getting me out?"

Slowly nodding his head, Ambrose turns to meet my gaze. "I have to warn you. There is a stipulation. I don't want you to freak out from any surprises."

Ah, hell. Of course it can't be easy.

"Because you're still considered a threat, the High Council is only allowing you to be transferred temporarily and under strict house arrest with an assigned CO of their choosing." Ambrose lowers his voice with his words like I might explode if he says them any louder.

I grimace. "I don't understand. Why only temporary?"

"They're releasing you for the upcoming mating season. Theo managed to pull some strings with a few members of the High Council. Because of Baker's confession about him working with Rhett against Magaelorum, the supreme judge ruled you as a willing accomplice."

"But—"

Maddox grabs my chin, getting me to look at him. "Take a breath. There is no point in arguing with Ambrose for being the messenger. All we need is extra time to turn things in our favor. Trust me when I say you will never, and I mean never, return to Max."

I puff a small breath between my lips and nod my head. "I do trust you." I reach out and grab Ambrose's hand. "All of you."

"Good. Now listen to me. You need to act like an obedient mate. Don't talk to anyone and keep your head bowed. Act shy and nervous in front of the Darkonians, and don't let on that you've already bonded with Theo. It's important." Maddox turns me toward Ambrose. "If anything happens to her in your care, I'll eat you alive, warlock. My brother might be warming up to you, but I still need you to prove yourself. This is your chance."

Waving his hand, Ambrose magically dresses me in an emerald green gown that sparkles with glittering stones woven through the lace. I blink a few times in surprise, wondering why the fuck am I wearing this.

Ambrose smirks and takes me by the hand before grabbing Maddox's arm. The world disappears in a burst of light, and my legs wobble as I try to orient myself. A firm hand locks onto my arm and tugs me away from Ambrose. The CO snaps chains around my wrists, startling me. It takes everything in me not to react. Maddox is no longer with us, but Tiernan and Theo fill his now empty space.

"Breathtaking, isn't she, brother?" Tiernan says, reaching up to touch my cheek. I step away, confused and thrown off, my mind taking a couple seconds to catch up with what's happening.

"She will do." Theo cocks his head and gives me a once over.

I frown at his words. Fucker.

Opening my mouth, I start to ask what the hell is going on, but the CO slaps a muter over my lips, not allowing me to speak. Fire ignites in both Theo and Tiernan's eyes, their anger hot enough to feel sizzling from their skin.

"Misters Darkonian, please give me the Litendrake contract for approval. I know this all must be frustrating on your part, and I'd like to ensure you get what belongs to you despite everything." High Council Woman Laveau's voice snaps my attention to her. "I will perform the union ceremony myself to hopefully ease any tension, fight, or disobedience from the Drakovich heir."

Oh my fuck. Fury explodes through me. I know I'm not supposed to fight but this is sick. The High Council plans to bind me to men who are supposed to be strangers. She granted them this to procreate. What the actual fuck? I might be a dragon, but I'm not an animal. I hate to think how often this happens, and it has to be stopped.

"That sounds perfect. Thank you, High Council Woman Laveau." Theo motions to Ambrose. "Please show her the contact."

Rubbing his hands together, Ambrose summons a scroll within a bejeweled cylinder. He offers me a whisper of a smile and strolls toward the Darkonians. High Council Woman Laveau extends her hand, taking the contract from him.

Nerves twist my stomach. This is finally it. The Darkonians will stake their claim on me and get me out of this hellhole. We'll figure out how to prove my innocence with the Drekis by our side—and then...I swear I'll change things. I cannot stand the thought of other people facing the same fate I do.

The guard pushes me forward, and Theo and Tiernan both reach for my arms. I can't take my eyes away from the cylinder as High Council Woman Laveau twists open the glittering cap and tugs out a scroll of yellowed paper.

It bursts into flames, shocking High Council Woman Laveau.

Dropping the container, High Council Woman Laveau shakes out her fingers and watches the paper turn to ash on the floor. My heart beats wildly, and the Darkonians glance at each other before turning to Ambrose.

Shit.

Theo closes his eyes and scrubs his hand over his face. "We've been set up. Someone must've tampered with our contract."

"No, it seems you've breached your end of the deal, Misters Darkonian, nulling your union. Without the contract, you have no claim on the Drakovich heir," High Council Woman Laveau says, tightening her mouth. "I'm sorry. I cannot release her into your care, and honestly, it might be for the best."

Panic steals my breath. "No!" I scream, my voice muffled by the muter. "No. No. No."

Yanking away from Theo and Tiernan, I spin and rush toward Ambrose. He's the only one who can get me out of here.

"Seize her!" High Council Woman Laveau shouts.

Spinning on the ball of my bare foot, I sweep kick the CO, knocking his feet out from under him. He latches his fingers onto the hem of my gown, catching me, and drags me toward him. I expect Ambrose to intervene. I expect Theo and Tiernan to ignite the room ablaze.

But they don't move.

They don't stop the CO from shoving his hands between my shoulder blades and forcing me into submission.

Angry tears burn my eyes. "I thought you were my mates," I yell, trying to scream the words.

"Timbus steab won!" High Council Woman Laveau shouts, shooting cracking power at me.

My muscles tense and freeze, trapping me in place. Everyone's emotions run hot and wild, but nothing compares to the hurricane of fear and hopelessness swelling through me. I can't go back to the Maximum Magical Penitentiary. I don't think I'll survive if I do. If the Darkonians can't get me out of this mess, I'm afraid I won't have a choice. I might have to call upon Lazlo after all. Because I can't do this. I hate that he might've been right all along about the High Council. If they do this to me, I will burn this world down. I will not be their prisoner.

My dragon won't be caged.

Heat swells in my middle, my body reacting to the

threat High Council Woman Laveau poses. I gather strength from my mates and prepare to do what I have to. I'm not going back. I won't. I'll accept High Council Woman Laveau's ashes on my hands. I'll—

A bright flash of lavender light erupts through the air. I tense at the sight of McKenzie and a strange, hulking man stepping in my line of fire, blocking High Council Woman Laveau from my attack.

Curling her fingers, McKenzie chants a spell, engulfing me in a cage zinging with her purple magic. Theo and Tiernan glower, looking ready to set her ablaze.

The man clears his throat. "Hello, High Council Woman Laveau. It's nice to see you again."

"Mr. Litendrake, what a pleasure to see you." Her gaze flicks to McKenzie, but she doesn't acknowledge the witch. "I'm assuming you're here for you heir?"

He nods. "I was quite surprised to discover these terrible circumstances, but I'd like to offer you my service to take Delphia off your hands. As you know, I'm entitled to take her as restitution for the turmoil the Drakovich Clan put my clan through."

High Council Woman Laveau nods. "Yes, but—"

"I will take her. Today. Do you understand?" the man says, fire lighting in his eyes.

High Council Woman Laveau once again nods. "There

will be stipulations. She's a convicted criminal."

He waves his hand. "We'll work it out later. But for now, we'll be on our way."

"Wait, Franco. We can work this out," Tiernan says, blocking his way.

Twisting on his feet, Franco ignores Tiernan and motions for McKenzie to follow him as he strides to where I'm caged in her magic. Tilting his head, he drinks in my features. His serious eyes sharpen a second before he smiles. He sticks his hand through the magical currents, not even flinching as they crackle and pop.

"You may arrange a meeting later," McKenzie says, smirking. "I'm sure you might have something we want."

Franco pulls me toward him and meets my gaze. "You are your mother's daughter, aren't you, Delphia?" he asks, pinching my wrist hard enough to make me wince. "Perhaps we can break you from following her dreaded path. Now hold on tight. I'm taking you home."

Palace Prison

A SHADOW FLITS ACROSS MY floor, blocking out the glow of the pale moonlight illuminating my bedroom. The Litendrake palace might not be built of bars and magic, but it isn't any less of a prison than the Maximum Magical Penitentiary.

A chain clamps around my ankle, ensuring I don't escape. Only one person—an ever-silent, old woman—is allowed to enter my quarters to bring me food, but I've left the last three plates untouched. I plan to leave a dozen more until Franco comes to face me. These last two days have felt like eternity without seeing or speaking to my mates, and I'm afraid there will be many more ahead of me.

"Nova, come here," a soft voice whispers. A gust of wind blows my wild hair, engulfing me in a smoky, toasted marshmallow scent. "Please, I can't go in."

Tiernan's voice trickles to me from the balcony, and I drag the heavy chain across the floor. I can step three feet outside to watch the world pass me by, but I haven't cared to look until now. My nightie sways around my thighs. Tiernan transforms from his magnificent beast and to the tall, ruggedly handsome man I've been trying to push from my mind.

"Where are the Drekis?" I ask, stopping short of stepping onto the cold stone of the terrace. "I need to see them."

His brows lower on his forehead with my words. "Ambrose is working on a spell as we speak to break through the magical shields undetected. He'll bring them when it's finished."

"Okay, thanks," I say, turning on my feet, my heart hanging heavy in my chest. I can't stop replaying the moment High Council Woman Laveau announced she was sending me back to Max and how he, Theo, and Ambrose stood there without putting up a fight.

"Nova, wait. Please. Don't leave." Tiernan stops short of the doorway and holds himself back by bracing on the wall.

I close my eyes shut, refusing to look at him as I face him. "I thought you wanted to be my mate, Tiernan. I thought you liked me and wanted to try to build something together, even without the mate bond."

"I do," he says, his voice rising in desperation. "Why would you think otherwise?"

I snap my eyes open, my anger getting the best of me. How can he not see his mistake? Locking my fingers to the chain, I hoist it with me, striding toward him. I jab my finger into his chest and glower. "Because you wouldn't have stood there and done nothing when they were trying to take me from you. The Drekis would burn the world for me. They—"

Snatching my hand, Tiernan yanks me to him and restrains me against his bare chest. "They live recklessly! The Drekis have nothing but you to lose. I have everything that can help build a future fit for you as my princess at stake."

Fire lights his eyes, dancing down a bulging vein in his neck. His tattoos move with his flexing muscles, his rough hold forcing me flush against him. My closeness sets off his desire, and his body awakens against me.

I grab his hard girth and squeeze, clenching my teeth. "I don't need a lavish life. Now let me go or you'll need ice for days."

"Do it, Nova. Punish me like you want to. Yell at me. Scream and hit me. Get out your anger so you can see that you might not need everything I have to offer, but you damn well fucking deserve it." He growls and leans closer, the scent of his sweet breath drawing me closer.

"I think only that will make you feel better." I let go of him and shove my hand to his chest, pushing him away. Shuffling back, I put space between us, returning to my room. "Now, don't come back without the Drekis, Tiernan. I'm not your princess. I'm not you—"

A bolt of lightning strikes Tiernan on the balcony, shooting him off his feet. He hollers and goes over the edge, flailing his arms and legs in surprise. I gasp and rush toward the terrace, but a low chanting voice sounds from behind me. I whip my head and look, catching sight of a woman in a flowing dress. Magic dances across her palms, and lavender light sparkles in her blue irises.

"You have a debt to pay, Delphia," the woman says, sauntering closer.

I try to run toward the balcony, but she uses her magic and yanks my chain. My back hits the floor, knocking the breath from my lungs. I can't move or fight or scream, staring at the sizzling magic dancing on invisible currents through the air.

"Hold her still. We must be quick," McKenzie says, materializes above me. I hadn't heard or seen her coming.

"Please," I whisper, forcing air through my lips.

"You have a debt, daughter of Delilah," the other witch repeats, unsheathing an athame.

McKenzie rips the front of my nightgown open and presses her hands to my chest, pinning me down.

"Please, I'll do anything. What do you want?" I try to move, but my body remains frozen.

"You have a debt to pay," the other witch repeats again, a strange glassy look flickering across her eyes.

McKenzie smiles down at me. "There's only one thing I want, Delphia. Only one thing worth the price I've had to pay."

"Please, there must be something else." Tears burn my eyes as she glides the dagger between my breasts.

She shakes her head. "No, I'm sorry. Only a dragon's heart will do."

To be continued...

Thank you so much for reading *Freed by Her Dragons*! Don't forget to check out the thrilling conclusion *Saved by Her Dragons!*

Other Reverse Harem Novels by Ginna Moran

THE VAMPIRE HEIRS WORLD

La Vega Vampire Showstoppers
Vampire Nights

The Divine Vampire Heirs
Blood Match
Blood Rebel
Blood Debt
Blood Feud
Blood Loss
Blood Vows

The Royale Vampire Heirs Series:
Rebel Vampires
Rebel Dhampir
Rebel Match
Rebel Heir
Rebel Fight

Academy of Vampire Heirs Series:
Dhampirs 101
Blood Sources 102
Coven Bonds 103
Personal Donors 104
Blood Wars 105

THE MATES OF MAGAELORUM WORLD

The Pack Mates of Lunar Crest:

The She-Wolf Games

The Wolf-Mate Trials

The Omega Hunt

The Witch Chase

Winter Wolf Games

Fated Mate of the Dragon Clans

Caged by Her Dragons

Freed by Her Dragons

Saved by Her Dragons

SEVEN SINNERS WORLD

The Seven Sinners of Hell's Kingdom

Her Personal Demons

Her Deadly Angels

Her Darkest Devils

Her Sinful Saints

GINNA MORAN IS the author of over seventy novels including the popular La Vega Vampire Showstoppers, The Pack Mates of Lunar Crest, The Seven Sinners of Hell's Kingdom Academy of Vampire Heirs, The Divine Vampire Heirs, and The Royale Vampire Heirs WhyChoose novels.

She always carried a fascination for all things paranormal and wrote her first unpublished manuscript at age eighteen. Her love of the supernatural grew stronger through her adult life, and she now spends her days with different creatures of the night. Whether it's vampires, werewolves, dragons, fae, angels, demons, or mermaids, Ginna loves creating and living in worlds from her dreams.

Aside from Ginna's professional life, she enjoys binge watching TV, crafting and design, playing pretend with her daughter, and cuddling with her dogs. Some of her favorite things include chocolate, mermaids, anything that glitters, learning new things, cheesy jokes, and organizing her book-shelf.

Ginna is currently hard at work on her next novel and the one after, and the one after that.

www.ingramcontent.com/pod-product-compliance
Lightning Source LLC
Chambersburg PA
CBHW030524310726
48979CB00010B/1793/J
9781951314576